Love Changes Life

by
Katie E. Laine

PublishAmerica
Baltimore

First printing

ISBN: 1-4137-2193-1
PUBLISHED BY PUBLISHAMERICA, LLLP
www.publishamerica.com
Baltimore

Printed in the United States of America

ACKNOWLEDGMENTS

I wish to extend a special thanks to my husband and children, who exerted exemplary patience during the hours I spent writing; and to my special friends, Betsy and Maggie for their continued support and encouragement.

INTRODUCTION

Life and times are ever changing. Sometimes adjusting to the changes can be difficult, even if the changes are for the better.

I grew up in a small town in southern Ohio; raised by an alcoholic mother who was rarely home. When she did come home, she was either drunk, hungover, or both. She was emotionally unavailable to me. I didn't know my father because he allegedly deserted us when I was an infant. My mother refused to talk about him so I knew nothing about him, not even his first name. I also was not certain if my mother was married to him or if I carried her last name. My mother absolutely refused to tell me anything about him.

By the standards of the average middle class American our living conditions were deplorable. Our home was a rented house that was barely standing. There were holes in the walls and the floors. Even the furniture was tattered and worn. Others in the community looked down upon us and labeled us 'poor white trash.' The clothes I had to wear only helped to facilitate the label.

In my early teens I decided that no matter how difficult, I would work hard to have a better way of life as an adult. I also vowed that I would never touch a drink of alcohol. It didn't take long for me to realize the reason we lived so poorly was due to my mother's obsession with alcohol and men.

Now, I don't want to paint a completely bad picture of my mother. She was once a very beautiful woman. I always believed her drinking was the result of a broken heart. She was always out searching for a man to take my father's place, or at least I thought that was her excuse. She frequently brought men home from the bar with her, some stayed for a couple nights, others only one night. Most "dates" ended in a violent episode, either verbally or physically. My mom wasn't physically abusive to me as often as she was verbally and emotionally, but she was always easily angered. I lived in fear that she would strike me; most of the time she was just verbally abusive. In fact, I don't ever recall her being kind to me. Some say verbal abuse is worse than physical abuse. *That* I am inclined to believe. With physical abuse, the wounds heal, but my emotional wounds never will. No one ever asks you, "How bad are you hurt?" when the injury is emotional, like they do with physical wounds. I will carry the invisible scars with me for the rest of my life. Over time I learned the less I said and the less mother saw of me, the less chance I had of agitating her. Some nights she would come home so drunk that she would pass out and leave me alone. I was never certain which was better, being alone with no one at all to talk to, or my only human contact being her abusive threats and sneers. Either way, I was well aware that she hated me, and I was nothing more than a burden to her. And if by some chance I managed to forget, she was quick to remind me, "You're nothing," or, "You will never amount to a pile of …" I heard one of those phrases at least once a day.

Mother passed away when I was just seventeen, the direct result of long-term alcohol abuse. As an only child with no other living family, I was left to fend for myself. I was forced to quit school and go to work to survive. I had never driven a car and could not afford to keep my mother's old car. So my options were limited. I managed to convince the owner of a small diner in town called Mongo's Diner to give me full-time work. The pay was small, but with tips I thought I could make it on my own.

The owner of the diner, Mongo, had known about my mother and her habits. In a small town there are few secrets. He said he understood my plight as he had hard times when he was young as well. Mongo agreed to give me a job at his diner on the condition that I temporarily resided with him and his family. They didn't want me to live alone until I was of legal age, and Mongo feared I would have trouble with the authorities. They were very kind to me. So, even though Mongo was difficult to work for, (he was a demanding perfectionist) I will always feel a loyalty toward him and his family.

By living with Mongo and his family for a few months, I was able to save enough money to rent an upstairs apartment just a couple blocks from the diner. The apartment was small with a kitchen and living room combination, and one bedroom and a bathroom. It was simple in décor with light-green carpet and creamy white painted walls. The kitchen had the old-fashioned, wooden cupboards and a small counter. I felt like I was in Heaven because there were no holes in the carpet or the walls, and of course, no drunken dates coming home with my mom.

The owners of the apartment lived downstairs. Their names were George and Kathy. They were very kind to me, and even left a sofa and chair in the apartment for me to use because I couldn't afford to purchase my own furniture. The apartment was also furnished with the other necessities: a small breakfast table, refrigerator and stove. Kathy even brought me a care package with food and cleaning supplies when I moved in. They charged me $300 a month and paid the utilities. I was overwhelmed by the kindness I had experienced from Mongo and his family, and George and Kathy. I vowed someday I would repay the kindness by helping others in need.

A few months after I settled into my new apartment, I managed to begin night classes to work on obtaining my GED. Education was always important to me, and to keep my promise to myself for a better life, education was a must.

When I was nineteen I had achieved my first goal and earned my GED. My next goal was to begin college classes. I knew it would take some time to save enough money to even get started. Even though I could qualify for loans, I needed transportation to get to the local college and to be able to decrease the number of hours I worked each day. The closest university was over 12 miles away. Since I had never driven a car, I would have to pay for driving lessons before I could even purchase one. I knew this would take several years to do.

I continued to work at the diner for the next three years … My income was small, and there wasn't much left over after I paid my rent and purchased a little bit of food. If I had any extra, I stashed it in the bank. Other luxuries were limited. But my life was comfortable. I worked six days a week and went to church on Sunday. I had little time for a social life or dating because I worked ten or more hours each day, or so I convinced myself. It was easier to live with the loneliness if I believed it was the life I had chosen. With very few exceptions, I went home after work and cleaned my apartment or washed my clothes. The only hobby I had was reading. And then I met Joshua …

PART ONE

~ CHAPTER 1 ~

MEETING JOSHUA

CHERIE:

The icy winds cut through Cherie's thin and tattered coat as she walked to work Monday morning. March weather was unpredictable in southern Ohio and evidence of the weekend's brutal snowstorm remained on the streets and sidewalks. The bitter cold and the ashy, gray appearance along with the barren trees sent a wintry chill through her as she thought, *sometimes a five minute walk can seem like an hour.* Cherie was not unaccustomed to the cold weather, but for some reason today seemed to be worse than usual. She hugged her coat tightly around herself in an attempt to keep warm as she unlocked the door to the diner.

Every morning, Monday through Saturday, Cherie left her apartment at eight-thirty and walked to Mongo's Diner to work. This particular Monday morning was no different. Cherie routinely arrived at the diner before eight forty-five every morning in order to be ready to open the diner by nine. She was always the first to arrive and then Sam, the cook, would come in by nine.

Mongo's diner was the local "greasy spoon." It was located in the center of the only business street in Dryville. The outdated décor and old-fashioned, metal tables and booths gave the appearance of a restaurant in the 1950's. The walls that were once light pink had faded to look almost beige and were accented by a dull and worn cream-colored, linoleum floor. Vinyl seats covered the metal, claw-footed booths and chairs. The few scattered pictures on the walls were actually original pictures from the 1950's. Overlooking the décor, the food was excellent and all homemade. If Sam couldn't make it, Mongo's Diner didn't serve it. There was nothing frozen or from a box.

Sam and Cherie were the only two in the diner until nearly lunch time. It was not uncommon for them to have no customers at all until ten-thirty am or later. In a small town like Dryville there aren't many people out in the early morning.

But on this day, Cherie's typical Monday changed drastically with the early appearance of her first customer. No sooner had she turned over the open sign on the door when the most handsome man Cherie had ever seen walked in. Cherie caught her breath as she watched him saunter over and sit alone in a booth. He was breathtakingly gorgeous. He was dressed in a red and green, plaid flannel shirt and blue jeans, with tan work boots. He looked to be at least 6'2" and quite well built. Thick, black hair lay in waves across his head, and his coal, black eyes sparkled and accented his high cheek bones and slightly pointed nose. As she approached him, she noticed that his hands were strong and muscular, the hands of a working man. He looked up and smiled softly at her.

Cherie, having had little dating experience and virtually no self-confidence with men, found herself becoming increasingly anxious as she got closer to the handsome stranger. Cherie looked around the diner in vain. She knew there was no one to help her; she would have to serve this customer in spite of her unfounded anxiety. *He's just another customer*, she told herself as she tried to maintain her composure. Cherie could not understand why the appearance of this handsome stranger had such an affect on her.

As she began to speak to him, she felt a shiver run up and down her spine. It was difficult to breath and even more difficult to speak without stuttering. The man seemed to understand her discomfort and politely initiated the conversation. "Good morning miss, how are you today?" When their eyes met at that moment, Cherie felt another shiver, this time it was so obvious that she was afraid the stranger had noticed. She was completely taken back by the gentleness in his voice and suddenly felt like a giddy school girl. Her hands trembled slightly as she placed a menu on the table in front of him and offered him a cup of coffee. She surprised herself with her behavior. She served as many as one hundred or more customers on some days, and never before had she reacted to anyone in such a manner. Cherie was so preoccupied with her anxiety about the customer that she didn't realize Sam had come in the back door. When she finally looked over and saw him, it appeared he was watching the entire interaction from behind the counter.

The handsome stranger was so kind and patient with her as she struggled to take his breakfast order: steak and eggs with home fries and coffee. Sam smiled and winked at Cherie when she placed the stranger's breakfast order. Cherie had hoped there would be other customers in the diner when she returned from placing the order with a Sam, but as usual the diner remained empty.

JOSH:

Josh was visiting Ohio to purchase a farm owned by an ailing uncle of one of his employees. He had chosen to remain in Ohio until the transaction and all other arrangements were complete as opposed to dealing with issues from his home in Montana. When not working with real estate agents and lawyers, Josh spent his spare time exploring southern Ohio. One morning while driving to an attorney's office, he decided to take the scenic route and came across a small diner in a town called Dryville. Feeling a little hungry and tired of fast food, he decided to stop for breakfast.

Josh took an instant notice to the shy little waitress when he walked into the diner. He immediately felt something stir inside of him. She was small in stature, perhaps 5'2" and maybe weighed about a hundred pounds. Her thick, auburn hair was neatly pinned up and even with no evidence of makeup she was beautiful. Not the glamorous kind of beauty, but wholesome and pure. She dressed in her light pink waitress uniform yet she was surprisingly attractive. It was obvious she was quite a bit younger than Josh, but he still felt the need to get to know her better.

Two years ago, Josh's wife was killed in a tragic automobile accident. Since then he hadn't been able to find an interest in any woman. But there was something different about this young woman. She seemed so honest and sincere. It was obvious that she was uncomfortable with him, but she made no attempts to hide her discomfort. In spite of the intense love he had felt for his late wife, Josh knew he didn't want to marry another woman like her. Leona was quite beautiful and glamorous, but it was all superficial. Her interest was with the high society functions and social status that his money could provide her. Her extramarital activities had caused Josh a lot of pain and he didn't care to relive that type of life. When he looked at Cherie, he saw a woman with an inner beauty as radiant as her outer beauty. Deep inside Josh hoped her uneasiness meant she was taken with him also.

He tried to ease her discomfort by making small talk with her. He introduced himself. She quietly told Josh that her name was Cherie Taylor. "Cherie, what a beautiful name," he told the petite young woman. He could see that his attempts to make conversation were making her increasingly uncomfortable so he decided not to push to hard. After he finished his breakfast he paid his bill and left quietly, but had already decided he would revisit the diner the following morning.

The following morning Josh did revisit the diner. He arrived promptly at nine, with the hope that he would once again be her only customer. Cherie actually smiled when she saw him enter the diner so he took the opportunity to try and talk a little more with her. Josh invited her to sit with him for a few moments and asked her if he could buy her some breakfast or at least a cup of coffee.

Nervously, Cherie explained that she was not permitted to socialize while she was on the job due to her boss's strict rules. Josh accepted her explanation, but was he was strong willed and determined. He told himself he would try again the following day. He thought to himself, *if we can just get an opportunity to talk a little, perhaps I can make her be more comfortable with me.*

Each morning for the remainder of the week, he visited the diner at nine. Cherie seemed to become a little more relaxed with each encounter, but continued to refuse to sit and talk with him. On Sunday, the diner was closed. Josh considered attending the local church, but decided if Cherie was there, she may view his presence as threatening. The day dragged on as he waited impatiently for another opportunity to see her. He didn't want to take any chances of scaring her away before he had a chance to get to know her.

Finally on the following Monday morning, Josh got his opportunity to get to know Cherie better.

CHERIE:

The handsome stranger who introduced himself as Josh was her first customer every day for the next week. Each day he would try and talk with her and each day she would feel the same flutters in her heart and butterflies in her stomach. Cherie would have given anything to be comfortable enough to get to know him, but her voice betrayed her each and every time she tried to talk to him.

At the age of twenty-two, Cherie had only ever had one date which turned out to be a nightmare. When she was a sophomore in high school, a young man in her class named Dean asked her to go out with him to see a movie. Dean was attractive and seemed nice enough, so she reluctantly agreed to go out with him. They never went to a movie. Instead, he took her to a deserted dirt road several miles out of town and began to make rough sexual advances toward her. When she fought against him and pleaded with him to stop, he became angry with her and told her she was nothing but a whore like her mother. He continued the assault by telling her he was treating her the way she deserved to be treated. After he struck her several times in the face, he forced her out of his car and drove away. She was left alone and afraid in the black of night, forced to find her own way home. To add to the trauma, there wasn't even moonlight so Cherie had to sit along the roadside and wait for the sunrise so she could see to walk home, her body in terrible pain from the battering Dean had given her. It was late morning when she finally found her way home. Her mother met her at the door with a blinding blow to the side of her already bruised and swollen face followed by hours of screaming obscenities and accusations. Cherie was left to bear the pain and humiliation of the assault alone, forced to believe it was her fault.

After that date, Dean spread vicious rumors about Cherie throughout the school. Of course people believed him over Cherie, because she was the 'poor white trash' and he was 'the banker's son.' Even the bruises on Cherie's face brought her no sympathy. Things went downhill for Cherie after that. Not only was she chastised for her social status and impoverished living conditions, but people began to call her filthy names based on Dean's allegations. For a while, several guys asked her out with intent of getting the sexual favors Dean claimed he got, but Cherie never took another chance. Even if someone would have had good intentions, Cherie couldn't have trusted them. It appeared that the boys her age knew about her mother's activities and expected the same out of her. Now that Cherie was grown up and on her own, she didn't have time for a social life, nor did she trust the men in her community not to hurt her again.

So for the first time in six years, Cherie found herself interested in a man. And she couldn't trust herself or him. Yet he seemed to persist. Cherie had to admit to herself that she looked forward to his visits every morning and actually felt a sense of emptiness each time he left. The truth was, even though his gazes and presence made Cherie very nervous, she really enjoyed Josh's attentions.

The following Sunday, after Josh had been coming in for over a week, Cherie found that she missed him terribly. On Monday morning, Sam was already there when she arrived at the diner. He took her by the arm and said, "Look Cherie, I have watched you every day for the past week. You look for that dark-haired man every morning, and you two can't keep your eyes off of each other when he's here. You like him and he likes you. I can feel the tension in the air. I've heard him invite you to join him for a cup of coffee and over and over you turn him down. Today, you sit and talk with him for a little while." Cherie's felt her face turn ten shades of red with embarrassment as she argued with Sam that Mongo would never permit such a thing, but he insisted. "I'll cover for you, and I'll let you know if Mongo comes in. Besides, how often does he get out of bed this early in the morning?"

Sam persisted until Josh walked in and even threatened her that she would either talk to the man, or he would personally escort her over to his table. Reluctantly, Cherie agreed to sit with him, "If he invites me again. Maybe he doesn't want to talk to me," she added. Cherie's embarrassment was enhanced by the realization that if Sam noticed how she was acting, then Josh must have too. Her heart pounded with anticipation as she approached Josh.

Their usual interaction began with the cordial 'good mornings' as Cherie served him coffee. Josh could tell that Cherie was more nervous than usual as she struggled to find the words to tell him she could sit and chat with him for a while. It would have been so much easier if he would have extended the invitation, but she feared that as a gentleman, he wouldn't. "Josh, uh, the cook, Sam, he said…" she stammered, *Oh, I can't do this*, she thought hopelessly.

As she put her head down with embarrassment and started to excuse herself Josh gently said, "Can you sit and have some coffee with me?"

Relieved, Cherie smiled and replied, "Well, uh, Sam the cook, he heard you ask me yesterday. He said he would cover for me, but just for a few minutes." Her anxiety suddenly got the best of her and left her completely speechless. Josh recognized her nervousness and offered her a cup of coffee. Cherie declined, she was afraid her trembling hands would create even more embarrassment for her.

Neither of them realized that she hadn't taken Josh's breakfast order. Sam smiled to himself. Josh's breakfast order had been the same every day since he had been visiting the diner, so he began to prepare the usual. When it was ready, he took it out to Josh and also took a cup of coffee for Cherie. He smiled and winked at Cherie as he served the meal.

Josh and Cherie talked for about fifteen more minutes. Or, Josh talked and Cherie listened. Josh was sympathetic to her discomfort, so he asked her a little about herself then spent time telling her about him. Cherie was grateful that he didn't push her to talk much. She knew she wasn't good enough for this man, but she didn't want to drive him away with their first conversation. Josh told her he was staying at a motel in a town nearby while he closed a deal on a farm he was purchasing down near the Ohio River. Cherie began to relax a little and really enjoyed listening as he talked about his horses and the ranch he lived on in Montana. It seemed as though the time flew by while they were talking.

Cherie knew she was drawn to him. She really liked the way he talked to her and the attention he gave. He was so kind and gentle and didn't seem to know about her past. There was a softness in his eyes that made her feel warm all over. Josh told her he would be in Ohio for a few more weeks. She actually felt a little sadness at the thought of him not coming into the diner every morning. She hoped she could keep her past quiet and not ruin things during his visit. The two of them both seemed to be enjoying the conversation when out of the blue they heard Sam say, "Twenty-two up!" Cherie recognized that as Josh's table.

"Sam must be trying to tell me that Mongo is here," she said aloud then abruptly excused herself.

A few moments later the diner began to fill with customers. Josh finished his breakfast then went up to the counter to pay his bill. Since the other help hadn't arrived yet, Cherie was very busy and was quite rushed when Josh paid his bill. He asked her what time her shift ended and could he take her out to dinner. "I would like to continue our conversation," he added. Cherie attempted to beg off by telling him that she didn't get off until seven. He replied, "Great, I'll pick you up here at seven." Then he promptly left the diner before she had a chance to decline.

Oh, what have I done? Cherie berated to herself. She wasn't ready to date this man, or any other man. She felt anxious and fretful for the remainder of the day. Since there was no opportunity to talk with Sam again, she had no way to alleviate her anxieties. The day both dragged on and flew by at the same time. Over and over she explored in her mind options to get her out of going on this date. *What if he's like Dean? What if he knows Dean, does he know what Dean did? What if he hurts me worse than Dean did?*

Some of Cherie's customer's noticed that she wasn't herself and asked her, "Are you alright? Are you sick, Cherie?" The only explanation she could offer them was that she was very busy. What else could she say, 'I'm going on a date and I'm scared to death?'

By the end of the day, Cherie had decided she would bolt out the door as soon as the clock struck seven. With any luck Josh would be just a couple minutes late, and then she could tell him she thought he changed his mind.

~ CHAPTER 2 ~

DATING JOSH

Josh arrived a few minutes before seven, and left Cherie no opportunity for escape. He looked even more handsome than he had in the morning. Cherie feared others could hear the thundering of her heart pounding, and thought it may thump out of her chest as she watched him walk into the diner. If there was ever a time when a woman could describe a man as stunning, that was it. He was wearing a black and white western shirt which accented his sparkling coal black eyes, and black jeans. He also wore a black leather jacket and black laced cowboy boots. When their eyes met, his gaze was so warm that Cherie thought she would melt. She was certain he could see her anxiety because her entire body was shaking. As she gathered her tattered coat and purse and prepared to leave the diner, Sam smiled and winked, "You have a good time girl," he said.

Josh gently took Cherie's coat. Cherie felt her pounding heart skip a beat when Josh's hands brushed against her shoulders as he helped her don her coat. *Oh, I don't know how I am going to do this without making a fool of myself,* she fretted.

Josh gently took her arm and led her to a shiny, black pick-up truck. He opened the door and helped her up into the truck. Cherie's skin tingled with his touch. When he climbed into the truck he gently said, "Cherie, you're shaking. Are you that nervous?"

She was too embarrassed to answer. "What can I do to make you more comfortable?"

Oh, how embarrassing! Cherie thought in shame. It was bad enough to be this nervous, but to have him see it. Cherie couldn't respond to his question and was grateful for the darkness. The heat of her face assured her that she was turning a bright shade of red. She wanted to open the door and run from his presence, but before she could react, Josh reached over and gently squeezed her hand, "Cherie, please don't be nervous. I'm not going to hurt you. You are a beautiful woman. I just want to take you out to dinner and spend a little time getting to know you."

"I'm sorry, Josh. I … uh … I don't have a lot of time for a social life. And,

I haven't dated much." She was so angry with herself. She had really added to her embarrassment. If it wasn't already bad enough, she had just admitted to a complete stranger that she was inexperienced with dating. *What must he think of me!* her brain screamed.

In attempts to help her relax, he gently brushed his hands across her upper back and reassured her, "Look, I don't date much either. In fact, you're the first woman I've been attracted to since my wife died. I did try to date a couple times, but it wasn't comfortable for me." He remained silent for just a few seconds then added, "There is something about you that makes me feel good. Now let's just relax and have a good time." He paused again for a couple seconds. When she still didn't speak he then added, "Besides if you find out that you don't like me, I live on the other side of the country. You'll never have to see me again."

Cherie realized that Josh was trying to make her more comfortable, but the memories of how Dean took her out of town then assaulted her and left her to walk an isolated road in the night flooded her consciousness. But then again, if she made a fool of herself, she would never have to face him again. She felt so confused. But she could not imagine never wanting to see him again. Sensing that she had been hurt in the past, Josh tried again to appease her anxiety. "Look, if at anytime you decide you're not enjoying yourself, all you have to do is say so and I'll take you directly home. I promise. If it'll make you feel better, I'll go and ask your friend to join us."

He seemed to be sincere. She remembered that Dean had seemed sincere until she got into the car with him. Then she was helpless. She thought it over and decided Josh was worth the risk. He had been so consistent, "Okay, Josh, I'll try. Thank you for being patient with me." After a couple minutes of silence between the two, Josh asked Cherie if there was anything else that she was worried about. Being so shy, Cherie was embarrassed and had to gather the courage to ask him to stop by her apartment so that she could change clothes "Would you mind if we stop at my apartment? I've been working all day, and I…"

Josh interrupted before she could finish. "Of course Cherie. I thought you may want to freshen up, so I made the reservation for 8:30. I found a quiet little Italian restaurant just a few miles away from here; I hope that's okay with you," Josh stated as he started the truck and began to drive. She directed him to her apartment.

The haunting memories from her childhood never let Cherie down. As a child living with her mother, she could never have brought friends or dates home. The home she lived in with her mother was unsightly and should have been condemned. She suddenly felt another chill of fear about taking Josh into her apartment. Other than the owners, George and Kathy, and Mongo's wife, Cherie had not invited any other guests into her apartment. Josh seemed to have sensed her apprehension about inviting him in. "Cherie, can you direct me to a drug store? I need to pick up a couple things. If you don't mind, I can do that while you change?" Relieved, she directed him to the local pharmacy. He promised he would be back to pick her up in half an hour.

Sheltered within the safety of her own four walls, Cherie willed herself to calm down and relax. *Josh has been a perfect gentleman*, she told herself as she showered. Then as if she didn't have enough to worry about, she really didn't have anything suitable to wear. With little extra time for a social life, and little money, there wasn't a lot to choose from in her wardrobe. She did manage to find a decent pair of blue jeans and a white cotton blouse. For the second time that night she noticed that Josh was a very punctual person. She heard him knocking on her door in exactly one half hour. When Cherie opened the door, Josh's massive presence towered over her, strikingly handsome, as he presented her with a card and a single pink rose. He asked her to please wait until after their date to read the card.

Cherie was embarrassed about the condition of her worn and tattered coat so she deliberately left it behind. Josh made a mental note as he noticed what she had done.

Josh kept her occupied with superficial conversation as they drove to the restaurant. Cherie felt a little relief as she noticed that Josh took all of the main roads and did not attempt to turn off to any back roads. Even though she had remained silent about her fears, it appeared that Josh knew, or was very intuitive. She began to relax and was beginning to love listening to him talk about his ranch and working with his horses.

Other than eating an occasional meal at Mongo's, Cherie had never eaten out in a restaurant. Josh recommended the Lasagna and told her that he had eaten it there a few days ago and it was excellent. Cherie permitted Josh to order the same thing for her that he was having. They both had the Lasagna, a salad and garlic bread with mozzarella cheese melted on top. Josh was constantly attentive to Cherie, and seemed to be one step ahead of her. If her soda glass was half empty, he asked the server to refill it. When she quietly looked around for the restroom, he pointed her in the right direction. They, or rather Josh talked almost constantly while they ate. Cherie sat and listened intently. She wasn't sure if it was the food or the company she enjoyed the most, but she found she was truly grateful she agreed to go out with him. He spoke more about the ranch he lived on and his horses. He told her colorful stories of how he and his ranch hands broke in young horses and trained them for riding.

Occasionally, Josh would slip in a question about Cherie. He noticed her hesitation to talk about herself, so he just tried a little at a time. He did manage to get her to tell him that her mother had passed away when she was seventeen and that she lived alone. Otherwise, she appeared to avoid any conversation about herself.

When they left the restaurant, Josh slipped off his black leather jacket and placed it around Cherie's shoulders. She gave him a puzzled look so he told her it was too cold for her to be out without a coat. "I'm sorry," she said. Attempting to cover her embarrassment she added, "I was in a hurry so I would be ready when you arrived, and I forgot," she stopped abruptly; once again she had embarrassed herself.

He held the door open on his side of the truck and gestured for her to get in. Before she could slide over to the passenger side of the truck, he placed his hand on her arm, "Stay here beside me," he insisted. She didn't protest. It felt good sitting there next to him. When he wrapped his right arm around her shoulder and began to drive her home, he felt her tense again. "What is it Cherie? You seemed relaxed for a little while, and now you are tense again." Cherie blushed at his noticing but didn't speak for a few minutes.

After she thought about it for a few minutes she spoke. "I'm sorry, Josh. I had a bad experience on a date a few years ago. I guess that's why I get a little nervous."

Fearing she had said too much, her voice trailed off and she fell silent.

Josh squeezed his arm a little tighter around her shoulder. "Cherie, I did promise you that I won't hurt you. And I won't ask you to do anything you don't want to do. I promise you that."

They drove the rest of the way to Cherie's apartment in silence. Josh kept his arm around her and she began to relax against him. She quietly cursed Dean for making her forever fearful of dating, and hoped she hadn't destroyed her chances of getting to know this man better.

When the couple arrived at Cherie's apartment, Josh walked her to the door. He gently brushed his lips across her brow. "Cherie, I had a wonderful time tonight. I'd like very much to see you again tomorrow night. That is, if you didn't decide you never want to see me again." Cherie admitted that she, too, had a wonderful time and agreed to see him again Tuesday night after work. Josh kissed her brow again and opened the door for her. Cherie had never been kissed by anyone before, so the warmth of his lips lingered on her forehead and created a tingling sensation that spread throughout her entire body.

After he left, Cherie remembered the card. When she picked it up off the table to open it, she felt the warmth of his presence. Inside the envelope was a beautiful card with pink roses on a cream background. She sat on the sofa for several minutes just looking at the front of the card, with her finger tracing around the rose. She was almost afraid to look inside. What if he said he never wanted to see her again? What if he said this was all a joke? When she finally managed to get the courage to open the card, she saw that Josh had written a short message:

> *Cherie,*
>
> *I know you were very nervous tonight. I understand that you have dated very little. That's ok with me. The only thing I want from you is that you be yourself. You are a beautiful woman. For the first time since my wife died, I feel alive. You make me feel that way. Please don't feel afraid of me or frightened of what you're feeling. Unless I am completely wrong, I suspect you like me a little, too. I will not ask anything of you that you don't want to give.*
>
> *Josh*

Cherie was crushed when Josh didn't appear at the diner for breakfast Tuesday morning. It was the first morning in weeks that he wasn't the first customer of her day. Cherie watched for him for most of the morning and the pang of disappointment grew when he didn't appear by lunchtime. She felt as anxious as she did all day Monday after he had asked her out to dinner. *What did I do wrong, I've chased him away,* she thought, or even worse, she feared he had heard the truth about her and wouldn't want to be with her again. The day dragged on and on. Sam tried to get her to talk about her date, but she felt irritable and humiliated, and refused to talk.

Cherie was grateful when it was nearly seven o'clock; relieved that she could finally get out of the diner – the place where they had met, and go home to feel miserable in peace. She went into the back room to gather her coat and purse. When she walked back into the dining room, her heart fluttered and skipped a beat as she looked over and saw Josh standing at the counter talking quietly with Sam. When he saw her walking toward him he ended the conversation, and with a smile that could melt an iceberg, walked over and took her hand. "Hi. I was afraid I had missed you."

Cherie smiled back and permitted him to help her don her coat. "I have a surprise for you when we get to the truck. I hope you don't mind," he told her as they walked outside. Josh looked back over his shoulder at Sam and winked as they walked out the door.

Cherie noticed there was a gift wrapped package on the front seat of the truck when he helped her into the cab. Josh closed the door and walked around the driver's side to get in. He asked her what she would like to do for dinner. She shyly told him she really didn't mind, and whatever he wanted to do. Josh told her that he had found a nice steak house and would like to take her there. He drove her to her apartment to permit her to change clothes. As she opened the door of the truck to get out, he took her hand. "Wait a minute, Cherie. I have something for you. I know this is only our second date, but, well, please just open this and I'll explain then."

In all of her life she had never received a gift. Her mother didn't even buy her new clothes for school. She received hand-me-downs from the neighbors. She bought her first new outfit after she was living on her own and self-supporting. Her look of confusion surprised Josh. "Please," he said. "Just open it and tell me if you like it."

Feeling nervous and embarrassed, she carefully opened the package. The package contained a black leather coat much like the one Josh was wearing. She held it up and admired it, then folded it back into the box. "I, uh, I don't understand."

"Cherie, last night when I loaned you my jacket, I thought how nice it looked on you, against your beautiful auburn hair. I really wanted you to have one, so I bought you one.

"Oh Josh, I can't accept this. We barely know each other, please understand," she pleaded.

"You're right, this is only our second date, but if I have my way, it's the second of many dates. I can't take the jacket back; it was one of those sale deals where all sales are final," he lied, "It would mean a lot to me if you would keep it."

Cherie looked at Josh, her expression baffled. She felt trapped, like she had no other choice but to accept his extravagant gift. She also felt nervous, *what does he want in return?*

As if he read her mind, he added, "There are absolutely no strings attached. It's yours, and if you choose to walk away from me right now and never speak to me again, it is still yours. I expect nothing in return."

Quickly Josh changed the subject before Cherie had a chance to argue any further.

"Do you want me to wait out here while you change?" he asked.

Cherie knew if they kept going out, she would eventually have to ask him into her apartment, "It's okay, you can come in," she responded, timidly. "Please don't expect much," she cautioned him. "My apartment is very simple."

Josh grabbed the box containing the jacket that Cherie left behind. They walked up the stairs to the second floor apartment together. Cherie felt embarrassed as she let him in.

Josh noticed her embarrassment. He closed the door of the apartment and took her by the shoulders. He turned her to face him and brushed his lips across her brow, "Your apartment is fine. It looks very comfortable. I'm grateful for this chance to get to know you." Not quite knowing what to do or say next, Cherie smiled and turned toward the bedroom. Fortunately the bathroom was located on the other side of her bedroom, so she didn't have to face Josh again until she had showered and changed. She desperately needed some time to recover from the embarrassment.

She hadn't had time to do any laundry, and the only other pair of jeans she had were quite worn. She donned the jeans and found a pale green sweater, then brushed her thick auburn hair and let it flow down over her shoulders.

Josh sat quietly on the sofa as he awaited her return. He turned on the television, but noticed its poor condition and that she didn't have cable. He flipped off the television and sat quietly. There were several library books on the table next to the sofa so he quietly flipped through them while he waited. He made a mental note that if he was fortunate enough to continue dating this lovely young woman, she would have a better television set and cable. He realized he had overwhelmed her with the leather jacket so he would have to take it slowly.

When Cherie emerged from the bedroom she looked beautiful. He loved the way her thick auburn hair curled slightly at the bottom. Her green sweater accented her green eyes and there seemed to be a slight glow about her when she smiled. He smiled and raised from the sofa. "You look beautiful," he told her as he helped her don the leather jacket. Cherie didn't offer to protest the jacket.

The couple drove in silence to the steak place he had told her about. It was a little farther away than the restaurant on Monday night, but Cherie felt more relaxed. She was not nearly as afraid that he would beat her up and leave her on an abandoned road as she had been on the previous evening.

At the restaurant they both engaged in conversation while they waited for dinner. Once again, Cherie allowed Josh to order for her. He ordered the large porterhouse steaks with baked potatoes and salad. Cherie's eyes grew very large when she looked at the size of the steak she was served. Josh had ordered the same size for her that he had for himself. "Relax," Josh told her. What you're not able to eat, you can take home and have for your lunch tomorrow." A puzzled look from Cherie prompted further explanation. "When people pay a lot for a meal, it's acceptable for them to request a container to take home the uneaten portions. Just eat what you are able to eat."

Immediately Cherie felt bad. "You had to pay a lot for this. I'm sorry. Josh, I don't want you to spend a lot of money on me."

"Cherie, please, just relax. If I didn't want to bring you here, I wouldn't have."

He changed the subject again before she had a chance to fret about the meal.

"I had to fly to Chicago early this morning. There was some urgent business I needed to attend to. I was afraid I wasn't going to make it back here in time for our date. I'm sorry I missed you at breakfast this morning."

"That's okay, Josh. I'm just glad you made it back."

He was careful not to say any more on the subject. The truth was he had noticed that her coat was thin and unsightly. He could not tolerate this pretty young woman not having at least the bare necessities. The air was cold, so he called his assistant, Stephen, to meet him halfway in Chicago with the jacket. The jacket came from his western store in Montana. He had not yet told Cherie about the stores. Because he recognized her sensitivity about her financial limitations, he didn't want to scare her away by letting her know too much about his financial status too soon.

Josh concentrated a little more on Cherie that night. He tried to get her to talk a little about herself. She remained very guarded, still harboring the fear that if he knew the truth about her, he wouldn't want to see her again. Josh did manage to get her to talk some about her plans for the future. He noticed how her eyes brightened when she told him about her dreams of going to college and studying to be a nurse.

Josh and Cherie continued to be together every night for the next few weeks. Her comfort level increased and she became more at ease with him. It was no longer an issue to invite him in to wait while she showered and changed. Josh took her to several different restaurants in the area, some close by, and some a longer distance away. On the following Saturday night, he took Cherie bowling, and then on Sunday he joined her for church, then the couple drove several hours to visit the zoo.

At the zoo, Cherie was like a young child in a toy store. She marveled at all of the animals, some she had never heard of, and some she had only seen on television or read about in her books. Even though Cherie was an adult, Josh was doing things with her that she had never had an opportunity to do as a child. More than the fun opportunities, Cherie truly enjoyed his company. They talked for hours each night. Little by little, Josh managed to get Cherie to tell him the story about her childhood, her mother's abuse, and about how Mongo, and George and Kathy helped her. Josh told her more about his marriage; that he and his wife, Leona were married for five years, and she was killed in a tragic accident two years ago. Cherie could see the pain in his eyes when he spoke of her, so she didn't press for more information. He was very sympathetic about her childhood.

ONE MONTH LATER:

Josh always kissed Cherie's brow and told her good night at the door after their dates. Even on weekends he left as soon as their date was finished. So Cherie was surprised when one Saturday night after several weeks of dating, Josh walked Cherie to the door and asked if he could come in for a while. "I need to talk to you Cherie." It was after eleven, but since she didn't have to work Sunday she agreed to let him stay for a while. Fearing the worst, that he was going to tell her he didn't want to see her again, Cherie stalled by offering to make him coffee, but he stopped her. "Please Cherie, let's talk first. I have something to tell you."

"What is it, Josh?" Cherie asked. She felt her heart quicken because she was afraid he was going to tell her it was over.

Josh sat down on the sofa next to her. "Cherie, the time has come when I'm going to have to return to Montana." Cherie felt a sudden pain in her heart as he continued. She was right, he was leaving. "I completed my business here several weeks ago and have been staying here to spend time with you. Now my business at home needs me and I can't put off returning home any longer." Cherie suddenly felt a lump forming in her throat and a hollow pit in her stomach. She had known he was only visiting for a short time and didn't expect to become this attached to him. Josh continued, "I know it has only been a few weeks, but I have fallen in love with you." As Josh continued to speak, he slid off the sofa onto the floor in front of her, on one knee. He took both her hands into his and they looked into each other's eyes, Josh said, "Cherie, there is much to tell you, but first, I have something to ask you." He hesitated a few minutes to give himself time to choose his words carefully, "As I said, I am in love with you. I want to spend the rest of my life with you. I want to give you a life of joy and happiness. We can build our dreams together." After another moments hesitation, "What I am trying to say is … will you marry me?"

Hot tears of joy and confusion streamed down Cherie's face. She didn't know how to respond. It was only a few weeks that they had known each other, barely one month that they had dated. But, on the other hand, she loved the way she felt when they were together, and she longed for him when they were apart. Josh must have sensed her confusion, "Cherie," he added as he cupped her face in his hands, "I know this is a lot, and it is soon," his voice gentle and soothing. "I don't expect you to answer me right now. I just ask if you will consider marrying me."

"Josh, I … I uh … I don't … I don't know what to say. I knew the day would come when you would have to leave, but I didn't expect to feel this way. I've never felt this way before. I'm not even sure what I'm feeling. I'm not ready to marry you yet. I have dreamed of going to college and becoming a nurse. There's so much we don't know about each other. I don't even know how old you are, but I suspect you are a few years older than me. I need to think about this," she blurted out, with words racing as quickly as her thoughts.

Josh sat up on the sofa beside her and wrapped his arms around her, "It's okay, Cherie. I'll give you all the time you need." He gently kissed the top of her head, "But, please do, think about it. I love you, and I want to spend the rest of my life with you. And as for us barely knowing one another, we could date for years and still not know each other until we live in the same house."

"But, Josh, I'm confused. How can you give me all the time I need when you have to leave in the morning?"

"Cherie, I'll leave you my home phone number and you can call me. I'll come for you if you decide you want to come out west with me. But understand, I will not harass you or keep asking you. I'll wait for you to call me. I don't want you to decide to marry me because you feel pressured."

"Okay, Josh, I'll think about it, I probably won't think of anything else for a long time."

Josh decided it was time for him to leave. "May I take you to breakfast in the morning before I leave to go back to Montana?" Cherie agreed to go to breakfast with him, and he stated he would pick her up at nine. He then told her his plane would leave at noon.

So, I'll have just a couple more hours with him, Cherie thought to herself. Josh rose to leave and for the first time since they had been dating, he kissed Cherie passionately. As his soft hot lips pressed firmly against hers, she felt her body melt into his arms, his kiss causing sensations in her that she never knew existed.

After Josh left, Cherie sat on the sofa to think. The memory of her mother's harsh words flooded her mind. She sat and cried in despair. Mother had always told her if it's too good to be true, then it's not. Josh was too good to be true, and now he was proposing to her. She had really grown attached to this handsome stranger. He pampered her and made her feel cared for—for the first time in her young life. Never before had anyone treated her the way he did. She had never been hugged or kissed, and no one had ever told her they loved her, not even her own mother. The tears spilled, and continued to fall even when she went into her bedroom to prepare for bed. She couldn't seem to stop crying as she listened to the echo of her mother's voice, "You're worthless! You're not good enough for him!"

Then she heard footsteps and a knock on the door. "Cherie, it's me, Josh." Cherie quickly dried her eyes before she opened the door. Josh apologized for coming back, "I think I left my wallet here."

Cherie couldn't look at him. She didn't want him to know she was crying. *What will he think of me if he knows I am crying after he asked me to marry him?* she thought to herself.

As usual Josh seemed to know something was wrong. He stated, "Cherie, I lied. When I went down and got into my truck, I noticed your light was still on. I waited a few minutes and you still didn't turn it off. That's not like you; you usually turn the lights of as soon as I leave here, so I thought something might be wrong. I came back to see if you're alright."

Continuing to keep her back to him she told him everything was fine and she was just getting ready to go to bed. Sensing her dilemma, Josh gently took his young girlfriend by the shoulders and turned her to face him. When he lifted her face to meet his gaze Josh saw the tear streaks and reddened eyes. He held her face in his large hands and gently brushed her tears away with his thumbs. With a sympathetic voice, "Oh, Cherie, I didn't want to upset you." He held her tight next to his chest while she sobbed uncontrollably. For Cherie, being held close to Josh's warm body seemed to be permission to release all of the emotions she had been feeling.

After a few minutes Cherie was able to regain a little control. Josh released her and cupped her face into his hands. He gently kissed her and said, "I didn't mean to upset you, Cherie. Does it make you feel sad that I proposed to you?"

"No, not that you proposed. I feel bad that you have to leave and I'm not ready to say yes and go with you."

Josh brushed her hair back from her face then took her by the hand and led her to the sofa. On the sofa he cuddled her on his lap and continued to stroke her hair.

"Tell me what it really is that upsets you so, Cherie."

"I just feel sad that you are leaving tomorrow," she sobbed.

Josh didn't believe his young girlfriend. Sensing there was something deeper, he prodded further, "Come on, talk to me. I know you can't be this upset because I am going back home. I didn't break up with you, I proposed. Now, talk to me."

"It's just memories from my past," Cherie said, choosing her words carefully.

"Go on, tell me more."

"I can't tell you more."

"Look, Cherie, I know something is wrong. Now I want you to talk to me about it," Josh insisted.

"Josh, if you really knew the truth about me, you wouldn't want to marry me. You wouldn't even want to be with me. I can't marry you. I'm not good enough for you. I'm just white trash."

Irritated, Josh questioned, "Where on earth did you get an idea like that?"

"It's the truth, Josh," she sobbed.

"Does this have anything to do with your mother?"

"Yes," Cherie wept.

"Look little one, your mother is dead and gone. Now why don't you let her go and go on with your life? I'm in love with you, and I don't care who or what your mother was. It's you that I love."

"But most of the people in town say I'm poor white trash," she cried.

"Well, those people don't know you like I do, do they?"

Cherie continued to cry softy. Josh held her and stroked her hair until she fell asleep. She knew it was wrong to have him there while she slept. But lying in his lap as he held her felt so good that she couldn't force herself to get up and ask him to leave.

When Josh awoke several hours later, he realized he had fallen asleep too. He gently picked Cherie up and carried her into her bedroom. After he laid her on the bed, taking care not to awaken her, he contemplated leaving and going back to his motel room. With careful consideration, he decided to remain there on the sofa until morning. He didn't want her to awaken and think he had left her after she had confided about her mother and her feelings last night.

The next time Josh awoke the sun was coming up. He looked in on Cherie and she continued to sleep soundly. He decided perhaps he would prepare breakfast for her but when he looked in her refrigerator and cupboards, he found only a couple of dry good items and coffee. Unfortunately there were no markets open in Dryville at six on Sunday morning so he had to drive several miles to the nearest town where he found a twenty-four hour supermarket. Remembering the scarce amount of food in her kitchen, Josh not only purchased breakfast food, but he filled the shopping cart full of fresh fruit and vegetables, salad fixings, and dry goods, and even some snack foods, then went and selected a beautiful romantic card for her.

Josh returned to the apartment about an hour later. Quietly he carried the grocery bags up the steps to the apartment, and then looked in on Cherie. She still slept peacefully.

The groceries he bought filled her refrigerator and freezer, and her cupboards. He did not want to see the woman he loved without food. He hoped she wouldn't notice until after his plane was in the air. He knew her pride would cause her to be embarrassed and make her argue that he shouldn't have spent money on her.

Making breakfast was not without challenges. It appeared that Cherie only had two small pans. Josh proceeded to make bacon, eggs, and home fries; but abandoned the idea of making pancakes. He had also bought orange juice and fresh melon.

Cherie awoke to the wonderful aroma of bacon frying. Bacon was a rare treat for Cherie, but one that she loved. She went into the bathroom to wash her face and brush her teeth. Then she brushed her thick auburn hair until it lay in waves around her shoulders.

Cherie felt embarrassed to face Josh. She had never been so emotional before. In fact she had not cried since she was a young child. She had learned early in her life that her tears only proved to agitate her mother further. If she even looked like she would cry when she was a little girl, her mother smacked her harshly across her face, "There, now you have a reason to cry," her mother would scold. Her legs trembled as she walked to the kitchen to face Josh. *Will he be angry with me like mother was?*

Josh gasped when he looked up and saw her standing in the kitchen behind him. "Wow! You look absolutely beautiful!" he exclaimed as he wrapped his arms around her and kissed the top of her head. "How'd you sleep little one? Do you feel a little better?"

"Yeah, Josh, I do. I … I uh, I'm sorry for last night. I'm sorry that I acted so stupid."

Josh placed the spatula on the stove and turned down the heat on the burners. He walked over to the small kitchen table and sat down on one of the chairs. Then he pulled her over to him and lifted her gently on his lap. "Little one, you don't have to apologize for last night, or for anything. I'm in love with you and I accept you for the person you are. But I do think we need to talk."

Cherie lowered her head and avoided eye contact with him, but nodded her head. Sensing her embarrassment he tried to divert her attentions. "Look, I'm going to burn breakfast. I wanted to surprise you and bring you breakfast in bed, so you march right back in the bedroom and get into bed, and I'll bring your breakfast into you. And at least pretend to be surprised," he joked.

"How about I just watch television, or maybe I could help you," she replied.

Doing his best to appear stern, he pointed to the bedroom and insisted, "Bed!"

Obediently, Cherie went off to the bedroom and lay quietly on the bed. She closed her eyes and permitted herself the luxury of imaging what life would be like if she were married to Josh. Initially she felt the same feelings of despair that she had on the previous night, but she quickly tuned them out.

Some time later, Cherie startled out of her daydream when Josh entered the room carrying two plates and two glasses of orange juice. She thought she must have dosed off briefly and just entered into a most wonderful dream about married life with Josh. Josh bent down and kissed her forehead. "I thought this would be nice instead of driving to a crowded restaurant. This way we can be alone and talk a little more before I have to leave. Is that ok?"

Cherie smiled and nodded in approval. She had already begun to enjoy the wonderful breakfast he had prepared for her.

"Josh?"

"Hmm"

"How old are you? You never did answer me when I asked you before?"

"You're right, Cherie, I didn't answer you. I didn't want to give you another reason to worry. I'm thirty."

"But I'm only twenty-two. Do you think that's too much of an age difference?" Cherie asked.

"Well," Josh responded, "It hasn't bothered us so far, has it?"

"No, I don't think so, but it might later."

"Well, little one," Josh said between bites of food. "If you're still that concerned about our ages, I'd like to introduce you to my parents. My father is ten years older than my mother, and they still act like a couple of newlyweds," Josh boasted.

When the couple finished their breakfast, Josh set the dishes aside and looked at Cherie, "You and I, we need to talk. We need to talk about all these issues that made you cry last night."

Cherie swallowed hard, knowing the moment of truth had come. He was going to make her tell the whole truth about her past, and then he would hate her like everyone else in town did. "It's really hard for me to talk about," she managed to say.

"Look, it appears to me that you need to talk about it. Now, talk to me, little one."

"Josh, there's really nothing more than I told you last night. I just can't imagine that you want to marry someone like me."

"Cherie, do you really think I am that shallow of a person."

Cherie knew he had her there. He was definitely not shallow. She feared she had insulted him, "I'm sorry, I didn't mean, uh, I…"

"Talk to me, Cherie."

"I don't know, it's just that every time something good happens to me, I have the memory of my mother words going through my head, telling me that I'm not good enough. She says I'm not good enough for you, and you're too good to be true."

"Well, she's wrong. And I strongly suspect the past you are referring to is not your past, but rather, your mother's. Now, I want you to tell me everything. I want to know who and what these ghosts are that keep you from allowing yourself to be happy."

"Josh, I can't."

Sternly Josh looked into Cherie's eyes and insisted, "It's not an option. I'm not leaving here until you tell me the whole truth."

"But, what about your flight?" she challenged.

"Start talking," he demanded.

Avoiding eye contact, Cherie proceeded to recap the story of her younger years with her mother, the home they lived in and the slander of the town's people, labeling them 'poor white trash.' She talked about her mother's drunken dates and their violent behaviors. She managed to omit the part about Dean and the filthy rumors he spread about her. That was something she could not bare for Josh to know about.

"So you see, Josh, I really am not good enough for you. You deserve someone much better than me."

Josh pulled her a little closer and wrapped his arms more tightly around her. In nearly a whisper he told her soothingly, "Cherie, look, I understand that you've been a victim of abuse for most of your life, and I'm sorry about that, but please don't place me on a pedestal. I'm just a man, not a saint, and not without faults. As for the kind of woman I want or deserve, you are everything. When I married Leona, she knew I was wealthy, and that was exactly what she was after. Even though she came from a 'high classed' family, she was selfish and wanted more. You are so different than that."

"But what do I have to offer a man like you?" she said, almost whining.

"Just your love. The only thing I want from you is for you to love me, pure and unconditional love. Everything else will come naturally," Josh answered.

When it was time for Josh to go, Cherie asked him, "If I decide I'm not ready for marriage, will I ever see you again?"

"Yes, Cherie, if you want to. I'll fly out and see you whenever I can get away. It may only be about once a month, but we can still see each other. But, I still will not pressure you into marriage until you're ready." Josh kissed Cherie passionately before he left to catch his plane. A kiss long and lingering. The feel and taste of his lips remained with her for hours after Josh was gone.

He had given her his toll-free phone number and told her to call him anytime, even if just to talk. He told her that if she decided to join him in

Montana he would come for her. Cherie knew she loved this man and wished she had someone to talk with about her decision. Part of her wanted to drop everything and leave with him that very moment. But she was being asked to give up her home and all that was familiar to her, to move to Montana, amid total strangers. The only person she would know would be Josh. But even at that, Josh was virtually a stranger. She barely knew him. If only she had someone wiser and more experienced to talk with.

~ CHAPTER 3 ~

DAYS TO FOLLOW

Before Cherie met Josh, she was content being alone. But the time she spent with him and the intensity of her feelings for him left her with a feeling of emptiness she had never before experienced, not even after the death of her mother. Monday morning came and Cherie prepared for work as usual. But she had no enthusiasm, nothing to look forward to. For several weeks, Josh had been her first person she saw every morning, and the last person she saw at the end of each day. Cherie knew Josh wouldn't be there this morning. It was now the end of April, and the air smelled of spring. The trees were filling with leaves, flowers blooming, and the birds chirping. But Cherie was cold and lonely inside.

By the end of the week, Sam noticed the dark circles under her eyes and commented on her depressed mood. "You're tired girl. Why aren't you sleeping?"

It was early morning and the diner was still empty. Cherie, needing desperately for someone to talk to, took the opportunity to confide in Sam. "Oh Sam, I'm so confused. You know Josh had to return to Montana. Before he left, he proposed to me. I miss him terribly, but I just don't know what to do." She further stated that they had only known each other for a few weeks and she didn't feel ready to commit to marriage.

"Cherie, do you love him?" the old man questioned.

"Yes, Sam, I do. I have never felt anything like this before. And now that he's gone, I feel lost without him."

"Then what is it you are afraid of, Cherie?"

"Sam, you know I have only ever had one date other than Josh. My life has been this diner. And now this strange man I barely know has proposed to me. And if I accept, I will have to leave the only place I've ever called home. What if he's not what he seems to be? What if he's a mass murderer or something?" Cherie was shocked with herself that she had just made that statement, but in reality, Josh was a virtual stranger to her. She realized that the fears implanted by her past experience and her mother's influence still prevailed within her.

"Cherie, you have been alone with him both in his truck and in your apartment. Has he given you any reason to be concerned?"

"No, Sam, he has always been a perfect gentleman. I guess that's what frightens me the most. My mom always said, 'If it's too good to be true, then it is.' How could someone like him want me, 'poor white trash?'

"Girl, you're letting a few people's lame opinions and foul mouths shape your entire life! I hope I have heard that statement from you for the last time!" Sam shouted angrily. "You have got to give up on that notion. Yes, your mother was a drunk, and you were poor." Softening his voice he added, "But, you have done well for yourself since you've been on your own. You live in a small town where people are narrow-minded and unforgiving. If they want to continue to believe that about you, then why would you want to stay here?"

"I'm sorry, Sam. I didn't mean to anger you."

Sam sighed heavily, "Cherie, I'm not angry with you. I just want you to stop putting yourself down. And for crying out loud, stop apologizing for everything you do or say … Listen, I have a friend on the police force. I can ask him if he can do a background check on your Josh. You give me his last name and I'll check him out for you. Then maybe you will feel better about marrying him. Because you know you want to marry him."

"Sam, how do you know that?"

"Girl, I'm an old man, and I've seen a lot in my day. I saw that way you looked at him, and I saw the way my wife used to look at me. I see the way Mongo's wife looks at him. You're in love with him. Now, you just have to learn to trust him. Perhaps that will take some time, since you haven't had many in your life you could trust."

The diner began to fill with customers so their conversation ended. Cherie felt a little better after talking with Sam. *He's right*, she thought. She did cling to the idea that she was still 'poor white trash'. And maybe that was why she had trouble accepting Josh's love. How could he love white trash if he was a wealthy man?

Later that same afternoon, Cherie received two dozen roses of assorted colors in a beautiful pink glass vase – delivered to the diner. With them was a card:

> *Cherie,*
> *I love you and I miss you.*
> *I will call you soon.*
> *Love, Josh*

Cherie's mind was racing with thoughts of Josh saying he would call her soon. She didn't have a telephone and he couldn't call her at work. Just as she finished setting the roses in a safe place on the counter a delivery truck stopped outside of the diner. Sam and Cherie looked at each other, wondering what they could be delivering to the diner. To Cherie's surprise, the driver delivered a package to her. Her hands quivered with excitement as she signed for the package. Sam waited on her next customer so she could open the box. The package contained a cell phone and a card. Still shaking, she opened the card:

> *Cherie,*
> *If I can't see you, I at least want to be able to talk with you. The phone is activated. Your number is written inside the box. I'll call you tonight at 9:00 your time.*
>
> *I love you,*
> *Josh*

Josh must really love me, she said to herself. She was grateful the day was almost over because she could hardly wait to hear his voice. It seemed as though they would never get finished so she could go home and await Josh's call. Sam and Cherie were not able to talk anymore but she knew he would give her the quiz tomorrow.

Cherie's new cell phone rang at exactly 9:00 pm. Her heart raced as she answered the call. Cherie's hands were trembling so much that it was difficult to press the buttons. When she answered, it sounded like he was in the very next room. "Hello, this is Cherie," she said, feeling anxious and unsure of herself.

"Cherie, how are you? I'm so glad to hear your voice!"

"Oh, Josh me too, I'm so happy to hear your voice. How are you?"

"Cherie, you don't sound okay. Is everything alright?"

"I'm just a little nervous, that's all."

Concerned, Josh asked, "What is it that makes you so nervous?"

"Oh, I guess the phone, and oh, I don't know."

"Does it upset you that I sent you the phone?" Josh quizzed.

"It doesn't upset me, but I, I'm just nervous, and I really can't afford..."

Josh stopped her, "Cherie ... little one, you will never have to worry about paying for anything you and I do together."

"But Josh," she argued, "I can't let you do that. It wouldn't be right."

"Look, little one. I know your financial situation is tight. I have plenty of money, and if I choose to provide you with gifts, then *so* be it. And who said anything about you letting me!" Josh retorted.

Okay, Josh. I'm sorry. I didn't mean to upset you. But…"

"What, little one? I'm not upset. But I don't want to spend our time on argument about who is paying for the phone. Just relax and enjoy the gift. It's yours to use as you wish. I would like to be able to talk to you every night though."

"Won't that be expensive, Josh?"

"No, little one. It's a cell phone. I have service all over the country. Can we stop worrying about the phone, and you tell me what you have been doing since I left?"

"Just working, nothing much. I have to confess though, I have really missed you," she sniffed.

"Cherie, are you crying? What is it, little one?"

"I'm okay, Josh. Maybe just a little overwhelmed. I don't know. Everything that has been happening the past couple months, I just don't know how to handle it or what to think."

"Cherie, I'm hopeful that you will get more comfortable telling me what you are feeling. I can't put your fears to rest if you don't share them with me. Now, tell me exactly what it is that is bothering you," Josh demanded.

"It is hard for me to talk about with you."

"We've had this discussion before. You can tell me anything. Besides, all good relationships start with good communication. Just tell me," Josh insisted.

"I told you that I grew up poor, but I don't think I ever told that the other folks in town called me other names besides white trash. They labeled me because of my mom's nighttime activities. You tell me you are a wealthy man. I am having a hard time believing a man like you would want to marry someone with a reputation like mine."

"You know, I am so sorry for all you've had to endure. I can only imagine how hard it is for you to trust, but there are a couple things you must understand about me."

"What's that?" Cherie asked.

"Well, first of all, young lady, I'm not from your town, and even if I was, I would make my own decisions based on the person you are. And second of all, I don't give a damn about the opinions of some shallow idiots who judge people on the basis of their wealth. You work hard and take care of yourself, and have done well at it. How can you even think of yourself as 'white trash, or those other names?"

"Now I've made you angry. I'm so sorry." She had never seen or heard him angry before. It was a little frightening.

Josh's voice softened, "Cherie, I love you. I want to marry you because I love you, and I wish you could see yourself the way that I see you. You are a genuine person. I see nothing fake or insincere about you. You're beautiful and fun to be with, even when you are worrying too much..." He hesitated for a couple seconds then added, "Look, I told you before that I have dated a couple women since my wife died. They were dating me for my possessions or the social status. My wife got caught up in the social status stuff. That's not real, and that's not how I want to live my life. When I am with you, I feel like you are there because you want to be with me. You see, maybe we both are a little alike, in an opposite sort of way."

"Josh, I am with you because I love you. I know you tell me you have money, but I've never even seen where you live. I can't possibly want you for your money. But, I have another question. But, I don't want you to get mad, or yell at me again."

"Little one, I'm not mad at you. I just get a little frustrated with you and your obsession with your perceived social status."

"Josh, promise you won't yell at me if I ask you this"

"I'm not going to yell at you again little one. What is it?"

"You are eight years older than me. That still worries me. And, until I met you, I never even really dated a man before."

"Cherie, yes, you are young. But, we love each other, and we can learn to live with the age difference. It hasn't bothered us so far, has it?

"Well, no, I guess not"

Remember, I told you about the age difference with my parents. It has never caused them any problems. If anything, their marriage is stronger than most."

"Okay, Josh. I'm still thinking a lot about marrying you, but..." her voice trailed off.

"Then tell me what you are really worried about. And stop dancing around all this nonsense that we have already discussed!"

"There you are, mad at me again."

"So that's what it is. You are afraid of me ... or maybe men in general?"

"Well, yes, I guess. I never knew my father, and the men my mother brought home, well, you know … they were drunks. Sometimes they would hit her and knock her around and stuff. One of them hit me in the face and knocked me on the floor when I walked in the room while he was beating up my mother. And I told you I had a bad experience on a date once. I never tried to date again. That is, until I met you."

"Cherie, this is really a conversation we should be having face to face. I wish you would have told me before, so I could have put you worries to rest. I rarely ever drink alcohol. For one thing, I don't have time for that kind of nonsense. And, for another thing, I don't like not being in control of my thoughts and actions. I told you I run the horse ranch, but I also own a chain of western stores. I have to be able to respond to problems any time of the day or night. There isn't room for alcohol in my schedule. And as for the men knocking your mother around, I'll never do anything to hurt you. I love you, and I want to take care of you. I knew there was an issue with you and dating, because you were so frightened at first. I promise you, I will never do anything to hurt you."

"Oh Josh, I love you so. But, I have one other fear that I guess I should tell you."

"Yes, little one. I want you to always be honest with me.

"Well, I will have to move out there. And give up everything I know here?"

"Is there something keeping you there?

"No, the only people I have are Mongo and his wife, and Sam. My grandparents are dead, and I have no brothers or sisters. It's just those who have helped me over the past few years, since my mom died. But it's scary."

"I know you need some more time to think and that's okay. But, if you want to marry me, yes, you will have to move out here. And, you will not be working as a waitress!"

"Then what'll I do?"

"Cherie, you won't have to work, I'll take care of you. I can provide more than everything you need."

"But, what about going to school to be a nurse?"

"Is that what you wanna do?" Josh asked.

"Yes, Josh, it's been a dream of mine since I was a very young girl. If I marry you, do I have to give up my dream?"

"No, Cherie, you don't. If you decide to marry me, you won't have to give up your dream. In fact, you can count on that dream becoming a reality. The only thing I ask is that you wait for one year after we're married. I want us to have sometime together first. And, you will not have to work while you go to school."

"Thank you, Josh. You know, my mom always cautioned me, 'If it sounds too good to be true, then it is.'"

"Well, it sounds too good to be true to me too. You see, trust isn't as easy for me as it seems to be. After my wife was killed, I didn't think I would ever be able to love again; especially after she was found with another man when she was killed. What a time to learn your wife is having an affair. And it is all happening so fast. Maybe we were meant to be together. Let's look at it that way. Why else did I just happen to go out of my way and end up in Dryville that day?" Josh said insightfully.

"Josh, I love you. I'm going to go to bed now. "

"Very well, little one. I'll call you tomorrow night at 9:00. Unless you'll be busy with another date?"

"No, you're the only one. I'll be waiting for your call."

Cherie's mind was spinning after Josh's call. There was so much to think about. More and more she was leaning toward marrying him. But, it was so frightening to think of leaving everything that was familiar. She decided she would wait to see what Sam learned from the background check. Cherie didn't sleep at all that night. This time, her mind was racing with thoughts of Josh, and memories of their phone conversation. By no choice of her own Cherie had always been an independent person; she only had herself to rely upon. She had the feeling Josh was going to strip her of all independence. She wasn't sure if she could handle that, but she knew she didn't want to live her life without him. Whatever decision she made was going to result in tremendous sacrifice. Josh was a very powerful man, and she was seeing more of it each time they talked. But, Josh made her feel safe and loved. She really liked that. Maybe she could get used to being under his control. She didn't think she had ever been so confused about anything in her entire life. That night she prayed for guidance and placed her trust in God to lead her in the right direction.

Josh and Cherie talked on the phone every night for the next four days. Finally, on the Saturday morning, Sam arrived with the results of the background check. Cherie knew when he was a few minutes late, which was not like him, that he must have news. That added greatly to her anxiety. *What if it's bad news?* she feared.

When he came in, Sam took her arm. "Cherie, I had my friend, the police officer, run a check on your Josh."

"Tell me, Sam, is there anything I need to be concerned about? Please, I can't stand the suspense!"

"Relax, Cherie. Except that he owns half of Montana, your Josh has a clean record. His was married for five years and his wife was murdered two years ago. According to the police records, they still don't know who did it. It appears there was another man in the car with her. There was a car accident, but an autopsy report said she was dead before the impact. They don't know any more than that. There are no children. When my friend talked with his contact out there, they said he is active in public service and is a man of integrity. Cherie, if you love him, why don't you ask him if you can go out there for a couple months to see how you like it before you decide whether or not you want to marry him?"

"But, what about my job here, what about the diner? What will I do if it doesn't work out?"

"Girl, Mongo loves you like a daughter. I'm sure the diner will be here if you decide to come back. But, I doubt that you will."

Cherie was so excited that she hugged Sam. "Thank you, Sam. Josh is going to call me tonight. I'll ask him and see what he says."

~ CHAPTER 4 ~

ACCEPTING

Cherie felt as though a ton of weights had been lifted off her shoulders. Of course she didn't want to live her life alone, and here was a man who wanted to marry her. She loved him, but still couldn't get past the fear of the unknown. She vacillated between telling him she would like to visit him in Montana and avoiding the subject as she awaited his call. Josh called at nine. She was so anxious and excited when she answered the phone that she could barely catch her breath. Immediately, she heard the alarm in Josh's voice when he heard her breathless speech.

"It's okay, Josh, I am just a little excited and afraid, I have to talk to you about something. Will you listen and not be angry with me?"

"You're not breaking up with me, are you?"

"No, silly, but I have to ask you something. Please hear me out," she pleaded.

"Of course, Cherie, tell me?" Josh replied.

She could hear excitement in his voice, which made her even more nervous. *What if I disappoint him?* she silently feared.

"Josh, I've been thinking about everything and I have talked to Sam a lot. Sam came up with an idea that I would like for you to consider."

On the other end of the phone line, Josh waited in anticipation. He had missed Cherie terribly since his return home. He struggled to get through each day, having only their evening phone calls to look forward to. He tried with all of his heart to be patient as she carefully chose her words. Wild ideas raced through his mind – was she going to accept his proposal? Never before in his adult life had he felt so helpless. His entire world depended upon what Cherie was about to say.

"Would you consider letting me come out there for a little while … you know, to see how I like it, and to get to know you better and stuff. I could get a job as a waitress, and a small apartment…"

Josh stopped her in the middle of the sentence, "Cherie, I'd love to have you come out here! Of course little one, it only makes sense that you would want to get to know your new home and surroundings before you commit to marrying me."

"Thank you, Josh. It makes me feel so much better to know that I can come out there and then be free to return home if I'm not happy. Not that I think I'll be unhappy, but, well, uh, you know what I mean, don't you?"

"Yes, little one, I do know what you mean. And I truly hope you will be happy and want to stay. But I will understand if you decide to return home. That's the purpose of this, a trial run. Just on thing though."

"Yes, what's that Josh?"

"I will not hear to you working as a waitress or getting a small apartment. You can stay right here. I have plenty of room. I'll still give you all the time you need. And you can keep your apartment for a couple months, just in case you're not happy.

"Josh, I don't want to upset you, but how can you tell me that you won't hear of me working as a waitress? We're not married yet, and I have always taken care of myself."

"Look, little one, you're correct, we're not married. But, if you come out here as my guest, it would be acceptable for me to provide for you. I would much rather you spend your time getting acquainted with your new environment, and of course, spending time with me."

"But Josh, I've never lived off of anyone in my entire life, or at least since my mother died. I can't do that now. Besides, what would people say about me just living with you?"

"Well, as for what people will say, they won't know unless we tell them. I live far enough out of town that there are no nosy neighbors to interfere in my private life. You'll have a suite of your own. And I have two employees who live in my home, so we'll have plenty of chaperones. Look, let's try a compromise. How about if you are my guest for one month, then if you choose to stay on with me, we can talk about finding you a job? You could even work in my store if you would like to. Does that sound fair?"

"Yes, Josh, I can live with that."

"Cherie, I'll pay for you apartment for three months. That way, if something happens that you're not happy with me, you'll have a home to return to."

"Oh, Josh, you don't need to do that. I understand the risk I'm taking. I don't expect you to buy me out of it if I get myself into a mess."

"Well, it's not an option. I insist we do it this way. I want you to stay with me and decide to marry me because you love me and are happy with me, not because you feel trapped in any way."

Cherie could see that Josh was not easily willing to give up control. "Okay, then I guess I have no choice in the matter," she retorted.

"Cherie, I don't want us to argue. We can work this out. When do you want me to come for you? I can probably be there in a few days, if that's okay with you?"

"I'll need to give Mongo two weeks notice. I can't just up and leave him without giving him time to get a replacement for me."

"Okay, how about if you give your notice tomorrow. And, ask for Saturday off, so we can have some time together. I'll make arrangements for the store and the ranch to be covered and I can be there Saturday morning. I can help you get everything ready. I'll see you in a couple of days. Good night, Cherie, I love you. You've made me a very happy man."

"Good night Josh, I love you too." She pressed the end button on the cell phone and sat on the sofa. She had just committed to giving up her life here and moving to Montana with Josh (at least temporarily). Tomorrow morning she would be telling Mongo that she was leaving the job and the life she had for nearly five years. There was a lot to digest and think about.

Another sleepless night. Cherie's mind whirled with thoughts of what the future would bring. On one hand, here was a man who said he loved her, and could offer her a much better way of life. On the other hand, she was leaving all that was familiar and safe to her. She really did love Josh, but she had reservations about his controlling personality. Although, so far he had given in to her on most issues.

Because she was so tried from several sleepless nights, Cherie was late for work the following morning, for the first time in five years. When she arrived at work, she was surprised to find Mongo and Sam already there. *Oh great*, she fretted, *the one day in five years that I'm late and Mongo has to be here. And of all days, the day I have to tell him I'm leaving.* Cherie and Sam exchanged glances. Sam gave Cherie a reassuring nod. He had covered for her and completed all of the morning detail. The diner was ready to open. Cherie had already warned Sam that she was going to talk with Mongo about leaving the diner if her conversation with Josh went well. He smiled and winked when she asked Mongo if she could talk with him privately. The two went back to his private office. "You're a little late this morning, Cherie. Is everything okay?"

"Yes, Mongo…"

"I certainly hope this type of tardiness won't become a habit," Mongo scolded.

"No, sir, it won't. But, Mongo, I have something to tell you. It's like some good news and some bad news."

"Okay, what is it?" She could tell he was already irritated with her. Mongo was not a man of many words.

"Well, I'm sure you've heard that I have been seeing a man. He came in here a couple months ago. One thing led to another, and, well, he uh, I'm going to Montana in a couple weeks. I'm sorry to leave the diner, and I'm so sorry if it will make trouble for you. Please don't be mad at me." Cherie looked up to Mongo with pleading eyes. She was quite anxious about telling him her news and trembled as she talked with him. Cherie could never stand to have someone angry with her, and especially not Mongo. He and his family had done so much for her.

"It's okay, Cherie. I'm not mad at you," Mongo promised. After thinking for a couple minutes, "Cherie, are you going to marry him? I don't like the idea of you just going to live with a man," Mongo questioned in a fatherly tone.

"He has proposed to me. I'm afraid, all the changes and stuff. He has agreed to let me visit for a few weeks to see how I like it out there. And, of course, for us to get to know one another better."

"Where will you be staying, Cherie?"

"We are still debating that. He says he has plenty of room. I think I should get an apartment of my own. We'll talk more when he gets here Saturday. Oh, and he wants me to ask for Saturday off, so we can spend some time together. Is that possible?"

"Well, Cherie, I'll have to learn to run this diner without you anyway. I'll work Saturday morning. I'm not real crazy about you going out there with a stranger, but, you know how Katie and I feel about you. You're like another daughter to us. We'll be here for you if you need us."

"Thank you, Mongo. I want you to know I appreciate everything you and Katie have done for me. You made it possible for me to survive after my mom died. I'll never forget you for that."

"You know, Cherie, you made it possible. The only thing we did was give you a job, and a place to stay for a little while. You have worked hard to make a life for yourself with what you had to work with. You still carry the scars that your mother left you with. I hope your gentleman friend will help you erase those scars. You need to see yourself for the person you are, and not your family history or the words of some illiterate townspeople. I knew about your relationship – Sam talked with me. I think your Josh probably sees you for the kind of person you really are. You go and be happy."

Cherie's eyes filled with tears as Mongo talked with her. She didn't realize that the scars from her mom's alcoholism and verbal abuse had been so visible to others. She knew that Mongo cared about her, but not so much. It was still difficult for her to accept that people could like or care about her. Mongo hugged her quickly then told her, "Now get to work, you're already late."

Later that day, Mongo's wife Katie came into the diner and asked Cherie to sit and talk with her. Mongo came out from his office and nodded in approval. Katie told her that Mongo and Sam had advised her of the plans. She questioned was there anything she could do to help. Katie was tall and thin, and so beautiful, with her long wavy brown hair and blue eyes. Cherie knew she was deeply in love with Mongo. When she stayed with them, Cherie noticed that they were always finding ways to be alone, and they were always doing nice things for each other. Cherie thought Katie appeared to really worship Mongo.

"Katie," Cherie asked, "It seems like you still really love Mongo. How do you know when it's right? I mean, I really love Josh, but I'm so scared?"

"Oh Cherie, every woman is afraid of this step in her life. Whether you are staying here, or moving far away, your life is going to change completely if you marry Josh."

"Well, there is one thing that bothers me. Actually there are a lot of things, but one is most pressing right now."

"What's that?" Katie asked.

"Well, Josh is kind of controlling, I am afraid I'll lose all of my independence."

"Cherie, you will lose your independence, at least to some degree. Once you marry, you are sharing your life with someone else. He sounds like a very strong and virile man. That can be very sexy you know."

"Well, it frightens me. You know how those men knocked my mom around."

"Yes, I remember that. But, this isn't the same. I mean, it's not okay for any man to slap a woman around, but many men want to be in charge of their houses."

"I guess it's just a fear of the unknown."

"You know, Mongo is 'the man of the house' in our home. And he can be quite controlling. But, as a woman, you learn how to control them without

47

them knowing they're being controlled. It's all about sharing and learning where you fit in with one another. It'll take some time, but trust me, if you love this man and he loves you, he's worth the time."

"What if it doesn't work out?" Cherie asked, still not convinced completely that she was doing the right thing.

"Cherie, if you weren't a little afraid, I'd be concerned. It's normal to be anxious when you are facing a major life change. Mongo and I will be here for you if you need us. In fact, we're always just a phone call away," Katie pledged.

Josh arrived on Friday evening, a day sooner than expected. Cherie had been sorting through all of her belongings, trying to decide what to take and what not to take with her. So consequently, her apartment was a mess. And of course, she was a bit disheveled, with her hair tied back in a bandana. She hadn't planned on company after work, so she just took off her work uniform and donned a pair of old sweats and a stained and worn t-shirt. She nearly panicked when she heard footsteps coming up the stairs, then a knock on the door.

Cherie opened the door and there he stood, his huge presence gazing down at her. "Oh, Cherie, I'm so glad to see you!" He lifted her off the ground, then hugged and kissed her.

"Josh," she exclaimed as she hugged him tightly, so excited to see him. "I thought you weren't coming until tomorrow. I'm sorry, everything is such a mess."

"Cherie, you're more worried about how you apartment looks than you are happy to see me?" Josh asked.

"Honest, I'm delighted to see you. I've missed you so much! I'm just a little embarrassed. I'm a mess, this place is a mess."

"I can see I still have a lot of work to do to get you out of that shyness. Have you had dinner yet?"

"Know, I haven't even thought of it," she admitted. The real truth was she still ate one meal a day. Years of not being able to afford much food were engrained within her, even with the generous supply of food that Josh had left her. Cherie knew it wasn't a good idea to tell Josh that she was still only eating once a day.

"How about if I order us a pizza and we sit and catch up. Do you think you house work can wait? I can help you later."

The couple ate pizza and salads and talked for hours. Josh told Cherie he wanted to take her to see the farm he had purchased on his last visit. He mentioned that he needed to check to see how things were running. He also remembered her interest in horses, and offered to take her riding.

"Perhaps we can take a lunch and ride into the woods for a picnic." Josh held her close as they talked late into the night. It was after midnight when he decided it was time for him to go back to his motel room. He kept his promise and helped her straighten up the apartment before he kissed her good night. They made plans to get started about eleven in the morning.

After he left, Cherie thought to herself, *yes, I do want to marry him. I know he's the man for me.* She decided to tell him while they were on their picnic the following day.

Unfortunately, it was raining and thundering when Cherie awoke Saturday morning. Josh arrived as planned, dressed for riding. She didn't question him but simply finished getting ready, and off they went.

The farm was located near the Ohio River, about 30 miles southwest of Dryville. Cherie sat close to Josh in the truck. The two were quiet for most of the ride. Cherie was content just to be next to him and feel his strong arm around her. Finally, Josh asked, "You're quiet today. Is something wrong?"

"No, Josh. I'm just enjoying the sights and the company."

The rain continued as they arrived at the farm. She was surprised that the house wasn't in good repair, and the grounds were not as well kept as she had expected. She knew there was trouble when she saw the veins in Josh's neck bulge as he looked about the grounds. "This is what happens when you pay someone to do a job, and you don't supervise them ... Cherie you'll find out soon enough. I have no tolerance for people not following my orders. I hired two men to have this place cleaned up and manicured. It looks no different than the day I hired them."

"What'll you do now?" Cherie asked, almost afraid to anger him further.

"Well, they are fired. I'll tell them as soon as I see them. And if the horses aren't cared for, I'll file charges against them. There are half a dozen quarter horses in that barn. When I purchased this farm they were healthy and fit. I hope to find them that way today. I realize it hasn't been very long and I shouldn't expect perfection, but I see no progress at all. I don't pay for people to not do their jobs. Josh thought it over and realized he was frightening Cherie with his display of temperament. "Oh, I apologize little one. We came here to have a good time. Let's go into the house. Because of the rain, we'll have to have our picnic inside. I hope you don't mind."

"No, Josh, I don't mind. I'm sorry you had to find your farm this way."

Josh swatted Cherie's bottom as she climbed out of the truck. "You need to learn to stop apologizing for every misdeed that occurs, little one," he exclaimed. Not knowing quite what to say, Cherie just kept silent for a few minutes. His irritation frightened her.

The inside of the farmhouse was antiquated. The baseboards and hardwood flooring appeared to be the original. The kitchen was old-fashioned with the high wooden cupboards, painted white, much like the cupboards in Cherie's apartment. With a little work it could be beautiful. As they entered into the living room, Cherie noticed the old worn furniture and a fireplace with a stone hearth. Josh set the picnic basket down in the middle of the floor then spread a blanket in front of the fireplace. He lit a fire then took Cherie by the hand and led her to the blanket. "I thought we could have our picnic here since it's raining out doors. Are you hungry, my love?"

Since Cherie hadn't had any breakfast, she replied, "Yes, I am. How about you?"

Josh opened the picnic basked and pulled out enough food to feed a dozen people. There were several types of cold cuts, chicken, fruit, salad, sodas, and potato chips. Josh had thought of everything. He was so thoughtful and caring. Cherie suddenly realized that she loved him so much it hurt. She planned to tell him she was accepting his proposal after their meal.

They ate until they were both ready to burst, then lay back on the blanket. Josh reached over to pull Cherie close, but instead she sat up. Cherie wanted to look him in the eyes when she spoke. She wanted to see the expression on his face.

"What is it, Cherie? Why are you moving away from me?"

"I have something I want to tell you, Josh."

"Okay, but can't you lie down with me while you talk."

"No, Josh. I'm serious. I have decided I want to marry you. I don't want to wait three months. That is, if the offer is still there?"

Josh's entire face lit up. He smiled and reached up and grabbed her, then pulled her over to lie on top of him. His lips burned hot against hers as he kissed her fervently. Cherie felt his tongue probe to explore the inside of her mouth. Her lips suddenly had a will of their own and parted to allow him to explore every inch of her mouth. Without thinking about it, she found her tongue exploring the inside of his mouth too. She felt her entire body shudder as his hands explored through her clothes, caressing up and down her back then cupping her bottom and pulling her close to his male passion. She felt his hands unbutton her sweater. Josh's hot fingers reached inside her bra to stroke her ample breast. As he flicked his finger over her nipples, the sensations she was experiencing were so intense she thought her entire body would explode. She pressed harder against him, wanting to feel every inch of him. Josh released her from his grip and removed his shirt. Inexperienced and confused, Cherie wasn't sure what she should do next. Josh sensed her anxiety and pulled her close to him. "Are you okay, Cherie? I don't want to push you too far?"

"Josh, I, uh, I never..."

"It's ok, I know that. If you're not ready, we'll stop."

"I don't think I want you to stop. But, I'm not prepared." She felt so embarrassed talking with him this way, and with her sweater halfway off. As he held her against him, she felt the hard bulge of his passion again. Cherie knew it wouldn't be fair to make him stop now. She loved him, she wanted to show him how much she loved him.

Josh pulled Cherie back to lie next to him. "I got a little carried away. The thought of you being my wife just drives me crazy. What made you change your mind?"

"Well, I talked with Katie, Mongo's wife about some of the things I've been afraid of. She told me that every woman who is about to be married has the same fears. And my final decision was when I saw you last night. You didn't seem to mind that I was a mess or that my apartment was a mess. You just acted happy to see me. And then I remembered how good it feels to be with you. I just decided I don't want to be away from you ever again."

Josh interrupted Cherie with a kiss then told her, "I don't want to have to be away from you again, my love,"

After careful thought, Cherie added, "You know Josh, Sometimes you make me feel like a woman, but other times you make me feel like a little girl. I still worry about our age difference."

"Cherie, I love you. Yes, I do pamper you. But in part, it's because I love you so much. If it makes you feel better, until the last year or so, I pampered my first wife. Then when she got caught up in the social limelight, everything changed. She lost interest in my attentions. On the other hand, you haven't had much of a life up to this point. So, what will it hurt if I pamper and spoil you a little?"

"Well, I do kind of like it. But, I don't want to lose all my independence."

51

"You won't, my sweet. But, you do need to remember, if I tell you to do or not to do something, you need to respect that. I didn't get where I am today by letting others have control of my life."

"That's the part that frightens me," Cherie confided.

"I'll never be an abusive husband. And, I'll do everything I can to make you happy. But, some of that happiness will have to come from you. And I understand that you getting over the scars of your past will take time. My guess is with time and an opportunity to build up some self confidence; you will grow into a secure and self-sufficient woman. But, don't fear, you are everything I want in a woman. You don't paint your face and pretend you are something you're not. That's what is important to me, not social standards. I know I have told you this before, you just need to believe me. My only hope is, if the high society people get a hold if you, it doesn't change how you feel about me. My days are very busy with my business and my ranch. I don't wanna be expected to have a nightlife to. You see little one, I have fears of my own. After a long day, I want to come home to a loving wife and a lot of attention from her. But with my first wife, she wanted me to attend this affair, and that dinner party. That kind of thing is okay once in a while, but I prefer not to do that on a daily basis. Leona wasn't happy, and she sought the attentions of another man. She was with another man when she was killed. … enough of that talk. I think you have made me the happiest man on earth!"

"I'm very happy too. You won't mind if I am afraid?"

"No, I'll still love you."

The hours had passed and it would be getting dark soon. Josh sat up and helped Cherie fasten her sweater, and then re-donned his shirt. "I want to show you the horses before dark then I want to take you out to dinner. We have some celebrating to do."

He held her hand as they walked out to the barn. The rain had stopped but the mud was thick. Cherie's only pair of shoes was ruined, but she was too happy to care right at that moment.

Cherie had never been close to a horse before. Their sizes were intimidating. Josh showed her around the barn and told her each horse's name while he looked them over for signs of abuse or neglect. The horses appeared to be well fed and exercised, and the barn was relatively clean.

Dusk began to fall. Josh took Cherie's hand and led her back to the farm house. "We'll clean up our lunch and I'll take you back to your apartment. I want to take you to dinner, and we both need to clean up a bit first. What do you think about CHEZ _ Marzeys?"

"Josh, you have to really dress up to go there. I don't have appropriate clothes for a place like that. Since we are celebrating our wedding plans, would you consider that Italian restaurant we went to on our first date. I had such a nice time that night."

Josh smiled to himself that Cherie was beginning to let go of some of her shyness. "Okay Cherie, we can go there. It actually would be quite fitting to celebrate our engagement at the scene of our first date. I see your shoes got pretty muddy. Do you have another pair?"

"No, I can clean these ones. It'll just take a little while."

"You have to get used to the fact that you don't have to live with the bare necessities any more. From now on, you will not go with out anything. You have committed to marrying me. That gives me the right to buy you things. We're going to stop at the mall and get you some new shoes. And I don't want to hear any argument."

Josh and Cherie stopped at a mall on their way home. He bought Cherie three new pair of shoes and insisted that she buy something to wear that night. He got a little angry when he caught her looking on the bargain racks. Cherie left the store with a new pair of jeans, a new blouse and the shoes. Her emotions in confused turmoil – she felt like a child at Christmas time, and embarrassed that he had to buy her clothes. Instead of leaving the mall when they finished their shopping, Josh took Cherie by the hand and led her into a jewelry store.

Despite her protests, Josh insisted she look at engagement rings. He had the jeweler pull a few from the showcase for her to try on. Cherie was too overwhelmed to admit to truly liking any of them. Josh was satisfied with his accomplishment. He had learned what size ring to buy so he could surprise her at a later date.

By the time they finished at the mall, it was nearly seven o'clock. He dropped her at her apartment and asked that she to be ready by eight. Then he drove off to his motel to shower and change.

Dinner was wonderful. In celebration of the new beginning and in honor of their first date, the couple ordered the same meal they had on their first date – lasagna, salad and garlic bread. They talked at dinner about the wedding plans. Cherie only wanted a small wedding, "Since I don't have any family." The only people she wanted to be there were Mongo and Katie, and Sam, of course, and George and Kathy. Josh agreed that they should get married in her church. The couple planned to talk with Pastor Mark after the Sunday morning service. Cherie didn't want to wait. She wanted to be married before they left for Montana. She had made her decision that she would make a home with Josh.

Josh explained that he would not be able to contact his parents to tell them about the wedding. "They were currently doing mission work in South Africa."

Josh attended Sunday morning church services with Cherie. After the service, Cherie asked Pastor Mark if she and Josh could talk privately with him.

Alone in Pastor Mark's private office, Cherie and Josh explained their desire to be married before they were to leave for Montana. Pastor Mark agreed to marry them, but only if they completed three pre-marital counseling sessions with him before the wedding ceremony. He made clear that if he had any reservations about the union after the sessions, he would not perform the ceremony. "Fair enough," Josh agreed.

Pastor Mark then, with a concerned expression, asked to speak with Josh in private. The two men then left Cherie sitting alone in the Pastor's office and went walking to another section of the church.

It seemed to Cherie that they were gone for an incredibly long time. About twenty minutes later the two men returned, both smiling. Josh sat down next to Cherie and whispered that everything would be okay. The trio set up times for their sessions and parted ways.

Josh suggested the couple spend the day lounging in her apartment. Josh wanted have a home cooked meal. Cherie was suddenly quiet. She wasn't ready to bare the embarrassment of telling Josh that she couldn't cook.

"What is it, Cherie," Josh asked. Cherie remained silent, uncertain how to proceed. Would he rescind his wedding proposal when he found out that she wouldn't be a good wife?

"Look, I know when you're not comfortable. I want you to just tell me when something troubles you. I don't want to have to fish it out of you. Now give it up!" he scolded.

"Well, if you want me to cook, well, you see, uh … I'm not a very good cook. I live alone, and I don't cook for myself," she explained.

"Cherie, I wish you would stop worrying. But then, that's not your way. I understand. As for your cooking abilities, when we get home you won't need to cook. I have a maid who lives on my grounds. She cooks and cleans six days a week. You really won't have anything to worry about."

When they arrived at Cherie's apartment Josh stopped and kissed her softly, "Please forgive me when I lose patience with you. I know you've been severely traumatized throughout your young life. I just want you to learn to trust me and tell me things as they come up. Will you please try to do that for me?"

"Okay. I'll try."

"You know, when Pastor Mark asked to talk to me in private, he wanted to be certain I wouldn't hurt you. In fact, he all but threatened me. He said you've already had enough pain in your young life to last forever. He talked to me a little about you mother and the prejudices of the town's people. I promised him, just like I am promising you, that I will never hurt you."

Embarrassed, Cherie closed her eyes. She couldn't bear to look at Josh right then. Josh understood and hugged her close. He held her for a few minutes then said, "Look, you haven't been sleeping, and you've had a lot of stress. Why don't you go and lie down while I prepare dinner. Once I get it all together and in the oven, I'll come in and rest with you for a little while."

Cherie obeyed, thankful for a little time to recover from the humiliation of Josh talking with Pastor Mark about her horrible past. She said a silent prayer that Pastor Mark didn't talk to Josh about Dean. She couldn't bear for him to know about that.

Later that evening, before he left Cherie, Josh reached into his wallet and pulled out a Visa card. He placed the card in Cherie's hand and told her, "I'm not sure if this is the right time to do this, I mean, after what we talked about earlier today. But we don't have a lot of time to prepare for our wedding. I know you don't have extra money for a pretty wedding dress. I got this card for you, to give to you after we are married. It has a $5000 limit. It's yours, you can use it for what ever you want or need. Yes, I will pay the bill. The only thing I ask is that you don't go over the limit."

"Josh, I can't accept this."

"Why can't you, Cherie? You're going to be my wife in just a few days. It's yours, and I don't want to see you in the church for our wedding without a wedding dress, and all the trimmings that go with it."

"Yes, sir," she replied.

"Look," he added, "Once we are married, everything that is mine is yours too. I am just giving you a little advance. Please don't be upset about it."

Cherie couldn't help herself and she had to ask him, "Josh, why are you so nice to me? Are you always going to be this nice? I know I'm not supposed to say this, but you are too good to be true."

"Cherie, I don't know what happened when I met you, but I fell for you almost instantly. I can't explain it. Perhaps it was your timid demeanor, but I think it was your honesty. I told you yesterday, I did pamper my first wife, until she found another man to spend her time with. Her dissatisfaction, as far as I know, was my lack of willingness to accommodate her social life. You will find that I am a man of my word. Honesty is very important to me. But I am also not a pushover. If I want something done, then I mean it. I can't reassure you enough that I will always love you … Look, I understand that you have been a victim of abuse. I want to help you heal those scars. And I'm sorry if this offends you, but I do have this desire to take care of you."

"So you do think of me more as a child? Because sometimes I feel like you treat me that way."

"No, Cherie, you are very much a woman to me. Someday I'll be able to show you."

"Yesterday, you started to love me then you stopped? I thought I did something wrong."

Josh's voice softened, "Cherie, you weren't ready yet. You were confused and obviously uncomfortable. When we make love, it will be your first time ever. I don't want it to be uncomfortable for you. The first time is hard enough for a young woman. I want to make you as at ease as I possibly can. I did get a little carried away, but then I didn't think lying on a blanket in that old farm house was the ideal setting for our first time.

"Sometimes you treat me like a China doll. I'm not going to break, and I'm not a little girl. I have been on my own for most of my life. I feel like you think I am incapable of taking care of myself," Cherie retorted, feeling just a little irritated.

"I am well aware that you have been on your own. I am also aware that you have not experienced much happiness in your life. Maybe I have this primitive desire to give that to you. It is okay for you to just settle down and relax for a while. That doesn't make you a bad person."

"You keep saying that, but really my life wasn't all that bad. I was getting by."

"Yes, Cherie, you were doing fine before I came. But it's still obvious that you never knew real love."

"You know it's hard to let go of years of hearing how worthless and useless I was. Either my mom or the town's people were always putting me down. With my mom, I fantasized it was the alcohol talking but even when she was sober, she didn't have anything nice to say to me. There are times when I still have nightmares about her drunken rages. Sometimes, if I did absolutely nothing to agitate her, she would fall asleep. But, I never knew what it was that would set her off. I keep trying to shake it off. After I moved into my apartment, I decided it was the one place that no one could put me down or make me feel bad about myself. It became my safe haven. Now, I'll be living in your house. I love you, so please don't take this the wrong way, but it still makes me anxious."

"Your new home will be a safe haven for you too. I do have hired help there, but we can make certain you have a place to call your own," Josh vowed.

"You'd do that for me?" Cherie asked.

"I'll do anything, within reason that I can do to help you adjust to your new lifestyle."

"I still don't understand Josh, why you or anyone else would want to go to so much trouble for me," Cherie stated sadly.

"Let me try to explain this a little differently," Josh responded. "Look little one, your youth and inexperience does have certain advantages to me. I've told you that I have my own fears about marriage. I don't see you interested in the social scene. I want a wife who will be my best friend, there at my side most of the time. I understand you will sprout wings when you start school, but we can still be best friends. As for your concerns about living with me, I will never scream and yell at you. And, I will never put you down. I can't erase the scars your mom embedded into you, but I promise I won't make new ones."

"I don't know what to say. I've never been able to talk to anyone like I do you. And I've never had a best friend. I was the "poor white trash" and the other girls would have nothing to do with me, except to make fun of me." Cherie stopped herself. She knew Josh became irritated with her when she spoke that way. "I'm sorry. I know you don't like me to say that."

Josh's heart melted. He realized the years of abuse were deeply embedded within her. "It's okay Cherie. I shouldn't make you feel bad about expressing your feelings. When I do that, I just make you more uncomfortable. You need to understand, I proposed to you because I love you. The few weeks we were apart I thought I'd go crazy. We will have some obstacles. Because we're getting married early in our relationship, we'll be getting to know one another even after we are married. But it'll work if we both want it to."

"What if you decide after you live with me for a while that you don't like me?"

"You know, that's a chance every couple takes when they get married. If I make a commitment, I stick with it. You will learn when you meet my parents. That's how I was raised. And I guess I'm sort of an old fashioned guy. You know, that country living and all."

"There must be something about you that is less than perfect?"

"Baby, I am far from perfect. I'm strong minded and set in my ways. And can be demanding and I have a temper. Over the years I've learned to control my temper, but it's still there. Those who work for me may tell you that I'm difficult to work for. I think you've already seen that I have no tolerance with people not doing what they are supposed to do."

"What if I don't do what you want me to do? Will you fire me too?"

"No, little one. I told you, I'm very committed to you. I'll be right up front with you. It won't happen very often, but if there is something that I see fit to tell you to do, or not to do, I do expect you to comply. But you are going to be my wife. I will always love and cherish you."

"I can't believe I am saying this, but Josh, you are controlling. And that frightens me."

Josh was shocked at her new found ability to be so candid. "Well, little one, you are probably right. I'll have to watch that."

~ CHAPTER 5 ~

WEDDING PLANS

Cherie reluctantly returned to work on Monday morning. After spending the entire weekend with Josh she began to understand why he didn't want her to work in Montana. With so many preparations for their wedding in less than two weeks, Cherie didn't know how she was going to manage everything. The premarital counseling sessions were to start Monday evening after work. She needed to purchase a wedding dress ... Cherie's mind raced as she walked into the diner. *How am I going to get everything done?* she thought to herself. She would have preferred a simple ceremony with only Josh and herself, but Josh insisted that his bride would have a beautiful wedding regardless of the size.

Cherie barely noticed that the diner was already set to open for the day, until Mongo greeted her from behind the counter. "Good morning, Cherie, we need to talk before you get started," he told her. After all the years she had known Mongo, he still presented as somewhat intimidating to her. She'd never known of him to be angry with her, but had seen him irate with fellow employees who didn't do their jobs correctly. Puzzled and a little anxious, Cherie followed him back to his office. *Have I done something to make him angry with me, maybe I shouldn't have taken Saturday off,* she worried. When they entered Mongo's private office, Katie sat quietly waiting for the two of them.

"Cherie," Mongo began, "you know we have always cared a lot about you. From the time you lived with us we have thought of you as family. Katie and I have something we want to talk with you about."

Katie added, "Because you're like a daughter to us, we want you to know that we'll be here if you ever need us. All you have to do is call. I know I have encouraged you to marry Josh, but the truth is we are going to miss you terribly."

While the two women talked, Mongo reached into his top desk drawer and pulled out a sealed white envelope then handed it to Cherie, "Here Cherie, this is from Katie and me. It's kind of an early wedding present. Go ahead and open it."

Cherie gasped in surprise as she read the note written on plain white paper.

One week paid vacation, effective immediately!
Congratulations!
We Love you,
Mongo, Katie, and family.

"But, I owe you a notice of resignation?"

Mongo placed a loving hand on Cherie's shoulder. "You have fulfilled your obligation to the diner. I told you I would have to learn to run the diner without you. You go on and take care of your wedding preparations. Gripes, I remember what Katie was like the week before we were married. Now, go on, I have work to do!"

"Thank you, sir. But I really can't go shopping for a dress yet. Josh left me off here and went out to his farm. There are no wedding shops within walking distance."

Katie jumped in, "Actually, Josh knew we were going to do this. I told him I would like to take you shopping for a dress and all of the other necessities, that is, if it's okay with you?"

"I'd like that very much, Katie."

Shopping for a dress proved to be more of a chore than Cherie had anticipated. She looked at dozens of gowns before she was able to narrow down four favorites. After trying each gown on at least three times she decided on a completely different dress: a tea length white lace gown with a scalloped hemline. The entire dress was made of delicate white lace with a V-cut neckline, which was worn over a white satin slip. The sleeves were long and slightly puffy at the shoulders. Initially Katie tried to dissuade Cherie from buying the dress, "Cherie, don't you think you should have a traditional long wedding gown with the train and veil?"

Usually Cherie would avoid confrontation but she was absolutely certain this was the dress she wanted. "Let me try it on, maybe you will like it then," she coaxed.

The dress was a perfect fit and complimented Cherie's petite figure. She looked absolutely stunning in the dress. "Okay, okay, you've convinced me. The dress is perfect for you!" Katie exclaimed. "But I have to tell you," she added, "I received strict orders from Josh to make sure you bought the dress you wanted, with no worry about the price."

"Trust me, Katie, this is the dress I want. I fell in love with it the first time I saw it. I looked at the other dresses, you saw that. I didn't like any of them as well as this one. It has nothing to do with the price."

"Very well, but if *your* Josh gets mad at me before the two of you are even married," Katie quipped.

"Relax, we'll be leaving for Montana the day after we are married. He can't do too much damage in that amount of time. Can he?"

Before they drove home, Cherie asked Katie, "Do you mind stopping at the jewelry store? I'd really like to get a wedding band for Josh."

When they finally finished their shopping, Cherie realized it was after six o'clock. In a panicked voice Cherie exclaimed, "Katie, oh, no! We have our first counseling session tonight. I have to be at the church by seven."

"It's okay, Cherie. Don't worry. We have about at forty-five minute drive. We can make it."

As fate would have it, they came upon a large group of motorcyclists. "Oh no," Katie moaned. "It's a poker run. There are thousands of them. I'm sorry Cherie. This will really slow us down. I'm sure Josh will understand."

"Yeah, but what will Pastor Mark think? We had to convince him to marry us on such short notice. He said he would marry us as long as he was comfortable with the idea after we completed all three sessions."

"Well, I'll help you explain. They'll have to understand."

"But whatever either of us says, Katie, we can't tell them we were late because of the ring. I want that to be a surprise," Cherie pleaded.

Katie weaved in and out of traffic, passing one small group of cycles at a time. When they were finally out of the congestion Katie sped up to try to make up for lost time. Both women knew they were in trouble when they passed a rest area as a highway patrol car was pulling out. Instinctively, Katie slowed down the car but it was too late. The red and blue lights were already flashing.

Katie pulled off to the side of the road. The officer approached her car, "Good evening ma'am. May I see you license and registration?" He politely accepted the two items and quizzed, "Do you know why I pulled you over?"

"Yes, sir. I guess I was going a little fast," Katie replied.

Ma'am, I clocked you at ninety miles an hour, before you started to slow down."

"Please sir, may I explain," Katie pleaded. Katie began to explain their dilemma as the officer nodded his head in approval.

"That's all well and good ma'am, but I have no choice but to give you a citation. Legally I could take you in to jail for going twenty-five miles over the speed limit. I won't do that unless I catch you speeding again. But you will have to appear in court and pay a fine."

"Could I just pay the fine?" Katie asked. I would rather not go to court, and I certainly can't contest the fact that I was speeding.

The officer told Katie she could call the court to find out how much the fine would be and avoid having to appear in court, then he sent them on their way with a warning to watch their speed.

Cherie rushed into the church at half past seven. Josh and Pastor Mark were shaking hands and about to abandon the idea of having the session when they heard her running through the church. Josh stepped out in the hallway to greet her, "Cherie, thank God you're alright. We were so worried about you!" he exclaimed as he rushed over to hug his future bride.

"I'm sorry, Josh. We had an eventful trip home. Can I tell you about it later?"

"Eventful how? Is Katie okay? Where is she?"

"She went home to talk to Mongo. Please, can we talk about it later? Shouldn't we get in there with Pastor Mark?" Cherie questioned breathlessly. Josh relented and wrapped his arm protectively around his fiancé as he escorted her into Pastor Mark's office.

After the initial greeting and Cherie apologized for being late, Pastor Mark asked Cherie if she would mind talking to him alone. "I've already had an opportunity to talk privately with Josh." Josh took the liberty of excusing himself. He bent down and gently kissed her brow, "I'll be waiting outside in the truck when you're finished little one."

Cherie failed miserably in her attempts to hide her anxiety and frustration. Pastor Mark could clearly see that she was disturbed, "What is it Cherie, what upsets you?"

"Are you still going to marry us," she asked.

"Well, Cherie, we talked about that. Nothing has changed as far as I can see. Now Cherie, do you want to tell me why you were so late for our appointment?"

Cherie recapped the details of their ride home. "So you see," she explained, "it's all my fault. If I wouldn't have wanted to go to the jewelry store before we came home, we wouldn't have been so pressed for time, and Katie wouldn't have gotten stopped for speeding. And now Mongo is going to be mad at her and me."

"Cherie, I wouldn't worry much about Mongo. He may grumble a little, but he adores Katie. He won't stay upset with her for long, if at all. And I don't think I've ever seen him angry with you. Now, how about we talk about you and Josh for a while. Tell me why you want to marry him?"

Cherie nervously stumbled with her words in attempts to answer Pastor Mark's question. "Oh," she said in despair. "I don't know how to explain it. He just makes me feel so good, like no one else ever has. And I've never felt this way about anyone."

"Cherie, I have to ask you some questions. It is part of the counseling so please don't be upset or embarrassed. You told me why you were late for you appointment, but is there anything I should know? Do you have any doubts?"

"No, sir. Like I told you, I just wanted to get a ring for him. He does so much for me and I wanted to surprise him."

"Okay, is there anything else I need to know? Is there a reason you're not telling me for getting married so quickly?"

"No, if you are asking what I think you are, we never, you know ... Oh, I'm sorry Pastor Mark. I'm just really nervous. I don't want to say the wrong thing and then you won't marry us."

"Cherie, I hope your future husband can help you develop some self-confidence. You have got to learn to give up the ghosts of your past." He continued with the counseling session then reassured Cherie that he saw no reason for him to refuse to perform the wedding ceremony.

When Josh and Cherie were back in her apartment, he took the liberty of ordering them pizza and salads, then insisted Cherie sit and talk about her day while they waited their delivery. "Tell me little one, what happened to make you so late?"

Cherie could see the veins in Josh's neck start to bulge as she talked about the speeding ticket. "Please don't be angry Josh," Cherie pleaded. "We were trying so hard to get home on time for our session with Pastor Mark. It just seemed like it was one thing after another kept detaining us. I'm sorry, really I am. I didn't want to make you angry with me."

Josh put his arms around Cherie and gently pulled her onto his lap. He hugged her close to him and said soothingly, "It's okay. I'm not mad at you.

I just don't want anything to happen to you. Driving that fast for any reason is not safe and it put both of you at risk. I hope Mongo has a serious talk with Katie."

While they were eating their dinner, Josh brought up the subject of witnesses for their marriage ceremony. "I haven't even given that a thought," Cherie admitted.

"I was wondering, did you want to ask Mongo and Katie?" Josh suggested.

"I would love to ask them. Katie was so wonderful today, helping me try on dresses, and trying to get me to buy the most expensive one. We had such a great time! Yes, yes, if it's okay with you, we should ask them."

"Well, now that we have that settled, who do you want to give you away?"

Cherie thought for a few minutes, then asked, "I would have asked Mongo, you know, since I lived with them and all, but since he can't do both, what do you think if I ask Sam? He was the one who pushed me to come and talk with you that first day we talked?"

"Okay, then we will ask Sam. Can you think of anything else we need to do?" Josh asked Cherie.

"Well, no, not really. This is my first wedding ever, so I'm kind of following your lead." The couple decided they would go down to the diner for an early lunch the following day and talk with their future wedding party.

Josh arrived at Cherie's apartment with a small gift wrapped package. Cherie, becoming a little less intimidated with Josh's generosity accepted the package and smiled. "What's this? Josh you don't have to keep giving me presents. I feel bad, I can't give you anything?"

"You can make that up to me later. Now open it," Josh insisted.

Cherie opened the box and found a beautiful gold watch inside. She took it out of its box and looked at it. The engraving on the back of the watch read, "To Cherie, all my love, Josh." Cherie's eyes filled with tears as she looked up at him. "Josh, it's beautiful. I love it, but is this because you were angry with me last night for being late?"

"No, little one, I was not angry with you. But I was worried. And I noticed you never wear a watch, so I assumed you don't have one. We have much to do over the next few days. I just thought you could use one. Now, we need to get going." Cherie reached up and hugged Josh then kissed him softly. Josh responded with a kiss and a light pat, "um, we're making a little progress.

Now come on. We have to get going if we want to talk to Mongo and Katie before the diner gets too busy."

It was just before eleven when Josh and Cherie walked into the diner. Mongo was working behind the lunch counter. "Hey, my little speed demon, how are you?"

Cherie smiled uncomfortably in response, "Mongo, I am so sorry. I hope you weren't too mad at Katie. It was all my fault. I got upset because we were going to be late for our counseling, and then the motorcycles and…"

"Cherie, Cherie, it's alright. You'll learn after you and Josh are married. Husbands and wives learn to be forgiving of those types of things. Now don't get the wrong idea. I don't condone driving dangerously. She put the two of you at risk for an accident. We talked about it. She knows I don't want her taking chances like that, but I am not mad either of you. So relax."

"Will she be coming down her, Mongo?" Cherie asked impatiently. "There's something we want to talk to the both of you about?"

"She's here, in my office helping me with payroll. I'll go and get her."

Cherie's mind wondered while she and Josh waited for Mongo and Katie to come back out of his office. *What will it be like living with a man who loves me? Will Josh adore me the way Mongo adores Katie? They always seem so happy together,* she thought.

Katie and Mongo walked out into the dining room together. Katie, smiling as usual, "Good morning guys," Katie said cheerfully.

"Good morning," Josh and Cherie both returned. Then Josh added, "Katie, Mongo, Cherie and I have something we'd like to talk with you about." Josh nodded to Cherie.

"Well, you see," Cherie began nervously, "We were wondering if, uh, you know, if, you two would be, uh, well you know willing to stand up for us for our wedding?"

Katie beamed with excitement. "Of course Cherie, we'd love to, right Mongo?"

"Mongo smiled and put his hand on Cherie's shoulder, "I'd like nothing better. I'm so grateful that you have found someone who loves you and makes you happy. Besides that, once you're married I won't have to worry about you any more."

Cherie looked a little hurt and confused. "He is just kidding with you. Of course we're happy for you. But, if I'm going to be your matron of honor, we need to so some more shopping." Katie looked at Josh and asked, "Josh, do you mind if I borrow Cherie again today? You know, I just have to find a new dress now."

"That would be up to Cherie. I can go to the farm alone. And I'll catch up with you in time for our second session with Pastor Mark."

Mongo, standing at his wife's side added, "And I trust the two of you will be traveling at the recommended speed limit."

"Yes, dear," Katie answered mischievously. Then she looked at Cherie, "How about it Cherie, are you up to shopping again today?"

"That sounds like fun," Cherie responded, barely controlling her excitement. She still couldn't believe this was all happening to her. For 22 years of her life she had lived essentially alone, or at the mercy of her drunken and abusive mother. Now, she was beginning to realize that some people actually cared about her. Sometimes it was all so overwhelming.

"Oh, wait, Sam, we need to talk to Sam."

Mongo smiled, guessing what it was she wanted to ask Sam. "I'll go and get him for you."

Sam followed Mongo out of the kitchen. His face lit up with a smile when he saw Cherie and Josh. "Hey there girl, I hear there's good news going around here. Is it really true?"

"Yes, it's true Sam, and I have something to ask you."

"Well, come on, get on with it. What is it you want?" Sam replied.

"Well, you know how most brides have a father to give them away. And Mongo, I know you have been like a father too, but you can't be two places at once. I, I mean we would love it, Sam, if you would give me away … you know, since you were the one who encouraged me to talk to Josh in the first place, Sam, please say yes?"

"Oh sure girl, you go ahead and tell them all that this is my fault!" he chuckled. "Of course, I'd be honored to give you away."

While Josh and Cherie were waiting for their lunch, two young men Cherie had known in high school walked into the diner. One of them was Dean, the young man she went on the date with, and his friend Jeff. They both ridiculed and made fun of her every time they saw her. Cherie felt her heart sink with dread as she saw them walking toward their booth. *Just keep your head down*, she told herself, hoping they wouldn't notice her. Cherie didn't think she could bear the embarrassment if Josh heard them say the things they said about her.

To Cherie's despair, the two men stopped at their booth. Looking directly at Josh, Dean exclaimed, "Hey man, you new in town?"

Josh politely told Dean he was just visiting for a few weeks. Cherie hoped the conversation would end at that, but Dean couldn't let it stop. "Well, look man, I'm going to do you a favor and tell you what you're doing right now."

Josh, noticed his fiancé's discomfort but didn't know who the two were so he continued to be polite, "And what might that be?" he asked.

"Well," Dean started, "Do you realize you're slumming it with poor white trash here!" Dean and Jeff elbowed each other and laughed as they awaited Josh's response.

Josh didn't say a word, but the bulging veins in his neck signified his anger.

The two men took Josh's silence as a cue to continue, both shouted at the same time while pointing at Cherie, "The town slut! Man, you are sitting with the town slut!!"

The next couple seconds seemed like hours. The two young men stared and pointed at Cherie while they made several spiteful smirks. She wanted to crawl under the table. They continued to say malicious things about her to her fiancé, telling him how filthy she always was, recapping all of the rumors they had spread about her during high school, and then prodding Josh, "What are you doing with white trash like her? If you only knew what a slut she was in high school! And I'll bet she gives you this goody two shoes routine. I went out with her once you know … what a…" Finally Cherie couldn't take it any longer. She rushed from the booth and ran into the women's restroom. As Cherie was running away she heard one of them say to Josh, "Oh man, what are you doing with that girl? She is from the trashiest family in town."

By the time she entered the restroom, she could no longer fight back the tears. Cherie's world was shattered. She knew she could never face Josh again. Since Josh had come into her life, she had hoped that he would never have to hear the awful things they said about her. And now he had heard everything, every filthy, disgusting thing Dean and Jeff said about her. Cherie was in the bathroom crying her heart out and trembling violently when Katie came in. Katie placed her hand on Cherie's shoulder and tried to comfort her, "Cherie, honey. You can't let those guys upset you like that."

"I'm s- s-so- sorry, she sobbed. I n- never wanted Josh t-to hear what those two say about me. I feel so hu-hu- humiliated! It's true. I am from the trashiest family in town. I don't deserve to be with Josh!" Cherie sobs increased.

"Cherie, listen to me," Katie insisted. "Josh called the police. He and Mongo are going to file charges against them for harassing and slandering you. He is furious with them for upsetting you. And Mongo is livid because he threw them out of here the last time they did that to you, and told them never to come back."

Now Cherie was crying even harder. "I thought I was just being treated the way I deserve. That's what Dean always told me, he just treated me the way I deserve to be treated," she cried. Katie reached over and hugged her. "Honey, you're going to have to learn to trust somebody, sometime. That man out there loves you. Haven't you figured that out by now/"

"How can he l-love 'p-po-poor white trash' like me?"

"Cherie, do you understand that the reason they treat you the way they do is because you didn't give in to them. Have you forgotten what started all of this harassment?"

"No, I haven't forgotten, Dean was the only guy I ever had a date with. He, he thought b-be-because my m-mother slept with his dad, that he could do the same with me. Just then there was a knock on the door and Josh walked in.

"Everyone decent in here?"

Katie looked up and saw Josh with his head peaking in the doorway. She nodded to him then exited the room to leave Josh and Cherie alone.

Josh saw how upset Cherie was and walked over to her. He wrapped his arms around her and hugged her to him. "It's okay, little one? They're gone now. Why don't you come back out and eat your lunch?"

"Josh, I- I j-ju- just want to go h-ho home. I am n- not in the mood for anything else now."

"Cherie, I called the police. We have to go down to the station to complete some paper work. We are filing charges against them. I promise you, they will never speak to you that way ever again!"

"I h-h-oped you would n-n-never hear what they say about me. H-how can you want to be with someone like me? Don't you understand what I am? They'll never let me forget it either!" She managed between sobs.

Josh continued to hold Cherie close as he tried to comfort her. But she was beyond comfort. Cherie was ready to give up on the fantasy of marrying him. "I can't marry you Josh. I'm just poor white trash. You can certainly find someone better than me!" she cried. She thought to herself, *what gives me the right to think that I deserve a man like Josh?*

Josh pulled away from Cherie and led her over to a small bench in the corner of the restroom. Cherie kept her head down to avoid eye contact with Josh. "Look at me young lady," he insisted sternly as he lifted Cherie's face to meet his gaze. "Just what makes you think those two have the power to change how I feel about you?" Still not able to face him, Cherie closed her eyes and continued to sob.

Aware that coddling her would make things worse at that time, Josh remained quite stern. "Come on, I want an answer and I want it now. You are going to talk to me."

"I can't Josh. Please don't make me. Please just leave me alone."

"No, I won't!. You're not going to get away with hiding behind self pity young lady. I'm going to be your husband in less than a week and we have to be able to work through any problem that comes up. Now talk to me or else," Josh demanded.

Cherie dried her eyes and attempted to contain her sobs. "Or else ... what?" she managed to ask.

"Let's just leave it at that for now, Now, tell me why you think those two have the power to change how I feel about you. Why do they affect you so?"

"Well," Cherie answered, her speech broken from her spasmodic breathing, "Do you remember I told you about the only other date I had?"

"So that was him, huh?"

"Yeah, the bigger one. And you heard all of the things he said about me. I never did any of that. I swear I didn't!" she cried. "But he told everyone in town, and they all believed him. They started calling me a whore and a slut. For a long time people would whisper and stare at me when I walked to work or to the store. And when they came into the diner, I could hear them talking about me from across the room."

Josh pulled Cherie onto his lap and hugged her tight. "Look, little one, I have known you for just a few months and I can tell none of that is true. You don't have any of the qualities of a woman with that kind of experience. If you're worried that I will believe them or be influenced by what they say, don't be. I formed my opinion of you the first time I laid eyes on you. And I haven't been wrong."

Cherie dried her eyes and hugged his neck. "Please, can we go home now?"

"No, we need to go down to the police station. They're waiting for us. After that, if you still want to go home we can."

While Josh paid their uneaten meal, Cherie went to talk with Katie. She wasn't in the mood for shopping. Katie understood and they agreed they had a date for the following day.

The police seemed to have a thousand questions for Cherie about Dean and Jeff's behavior. She had not been aware that she had the right to file charges against them. It seemed as though her future husband had some sort of power over people. But the charges were filed and Josh was promised a court date by Friday.

Cherie still didn't feel like socializing, or anything else. Her experience at the diner and the police station left her emotionally drained. Up to then, the only familiarity she had with the police, other than serving them breakfast, was when her mother's dates beat her up.

Back in Cherie's apartment, Josh filled her bathtub with hot water and lavender bath beads. He then turned off all the lights. Her small bathroom had no windows, so he lit a candle and set it on a shelf, then placed a small radio\CD player on the same shelf. After inserting a CD of soothing music, he went to the living room and took Cherie by the hand. He led her to the bathroom and instructed her to take a long, hot bath. When Cherie started to protest Josh responded sternly, "Either you get undressed and get in there on you own, or I will help you."

Cherie waited for Josh to leave the bathroom, and then she undressed and climbed into the hot bubbly tub. She was surprised that she was able to allow herself to relax. She laid her head back against the back of the tub and rested for nearly half an hour. When the water became too cool for comfort, she regained hers senses. She quickly finished her bath and dressed in casual sweats.

Josh kissed her softly when she come out of her bedroom, "You look a little better. Do you feel better my love?"

"I think so, a little," Cherie responded shyly, still embarrassed over the afternoons events.

Josh had prepared a light lunch for the two of them, sandwiches and salads. Cherie argued that she didn't feel much like eating, but Josh insisted.

After lunch Josh flipped on the television and they sat on the couch. He motioned for her to lay her head on his lap. Gently, he stroked Cherie's forehead and back. Feeling safe in his arms, she slept most of the afternoon. Josh woke her up just before seven.

Cherie was dreading the therapy session. She had already been grilled by the police and certainly didn't feel like being questioned any further. When they arrived at the church, Josh asked Cherie if she would mind if he went to speak with Pastor alone. "It will give you a few minutes to get your bearings," he suggested. Cherie nodded in complacently.

When Josh appeared from the Pastor's office, he hugged her and motioned for her to go in, "your turn," he said.

Pastor Mark greeted Cherie with a concerned expression. "Cherie, you've had a bad day I hear. This is supposed to be a happy time for you. Let's talk about why those two guys upset you so."

"Pastor, I have listened to the people of this town put me down for most of my life. I have always just taken it because I thought it was true. I guess I had some bizarre idea that I could keep Josh from knowing what they say about me. I was so embarrassed when the said all of those awful things for Josh to hear."

"How did Josh react to them?"

"Well, he didn't speak to them, but after I ran into the ladies' room, he called the police. Then he made me go down to the police station to file charges against them."

"Cherie," Pastor Mark interrupted, "Was he upset with you at all, or did he question you that made you think he believed them?"

"No, he said he didn't. But, I- I n n-never wanted him to know. How can he care about me now that he knows? How can anyone care about me?"

"Okay Cherie, you're a bundle of nerves."

"I know I am, but why? I have cried more in the past few weeks than I have in my entire life? I don't understand it."

"Do you think it could be because you haven't allowed yourself to feel for so long? And now, Josh has broken down that protective wall you've had for so long. This brings me to another issue I want to talk to you about." Cherie nodded, so Mark continued, "Someday you will learn to trust. I'm going to recommend that you attend counseling meetings for people with family members who are or were alcoholics once you get settled into your new home. I've already talked to Josh about it, and he is willing to go with you. Remember Cherie, I was there. I have watched you grow up. I know you have many of the qualities of the child of an alcoholic. And you have a real issue with trust. I'm surprised you're actually letting Josh into your life."

"Thank you Pastor. But I feel so out of control of my life. I just don't know what to think right now. Just like those meetings. You talked with Josh before me. And for my vacation from work, Mongo and Katie talked with Josh before me. I love him, but I am so confused!"

"Cherie, look at me." Pastor paused and waited for Cherie to lift her gaze to him, "Josh is trying so hard to make things easier on you. Maybe you should tell him how you feel. Communication and honesty are the basis of a good marriage. Begin now, and talk to him. Do you want to tell him here, would you like me to bring him in?"

"Yes, sir."

When Josh entered the room, Pastor spoke first, "Josh, Cherie has something she needs to share with you."

"Yes, of course," Josh promised.

"I've been talking with Cherie about being open and honest with you. She's afraid to tell you what she's feeling right now. I have assured her that the key to a successful marriage is communication and honesty," added Pastor.

"I agree. I've been trying to encourage her to talk with me. What is it Cherie?"

"Josh, I'm dealing with a lot of strange emotions right now. Pastor Mark says it's because I have opened up feelings I didn't permit myself to experience because of my mother hurting me all the time. But I also don't feel like I have any control over my life. And that really bothers me."

"What can I do to help, Cherie?"

"Well, you knew about my vacation gift from Mongo before I did. And now you were in here talking to Pastor Mark about me going counseling meetings before talking to me about it. I still feel like you're treating me like a little girl."

"You're correct. But let me explain something, okay?" Cherie nodded in approval, but didn't speak. Josh continued, "I did tell Mongo that we were going to marry. It was after Mongo pulled me aside last week and asked me what my intentions were with you. He was concerned about me taking you to Montana to live with me, and us not being married. When I advised him of our plans, he was elated. A short time later he pulled me aside and asked if I thought you would accept his gift. He and Katie wanted it to be a surprise. I was sworn to secrecy. I did not manipulate it in any way, other than I thanked him for the opportunity to spend this time with you. Yes, I did talk with Pastor about how you have difficulty trusting others. My uncle was an alcoholic, and I saw the effect it had on my cousins. So I asked Pastor Mark for his opinion. I was not trying to undermine you or treat you like a child. Cherie, I love you. And I need you as much as I think you need me. In every other aspect of my life, I must be in control. If I get a little carried away with you, please talk to me. And I promise I'll talk to you." Josh reached over and took Cherie's hand, then pulled her close to him.

As the couple walked out of the church, Josh asked, "How about I buy you some dinner?"

"There you go trying to get me to eat again. Are you going to love me when I'm fifty pounds overweight?"

"Little one, you have a long way to go. But as long as you are you, I'll love you." Josh kissed her then helped her up into the truck.

Late the following morning, Cherie decided to walk to the diner to meet Katie. On her way she stopped at the local drug store where she ran into Dean and Jeff. Hoping they didn't see her, Cherie abandoned the idea of shopping and attempted to quietly leave the store. But Dean saw her and the two young men followed her out of the store.

"Hey, slut!" Dean called to her. Cherie kept walking, hoping to avoid confrontation with them. "I said hey slut, and I expect you to answer me!" Dean called again, a little louder.

To her surprise, Dean then grabbed her by the arm and pushed her hard against the brick wall of the store. Trapped and shocked, Cherie didn't know what to do or say. She stared wide-eyed at Dean, flashbacks of the last time he beat her flooding through her mind.

He roughly slapped her face then again trapped her against the wall with both arms. "You are nothing, bitch, absolutely nothing without your big city boyfriend. Nothing! And you had better tell him to drop the charges on us, or I will beat you worse than I did a few years ago!" He then raised his hand in a fist to strike her again but his fist was caught in a firm grip. Dean gasped in shock as his body suddenly landed hard against a black pick-up truck.

Before either of the men could move or speak again, the sound of the police siren caught their attentions. The police chief's tires screeched as he brought the cruiser to a screaming halt. "All right you two," he shouted as he jumped out of the car. Hand cuffs in hand, he cuffed both Dean and Jeff and pushed them roughly in the back of the cruiser.

Chief Baker looked at Josh and Cherie, "I was at the traffic light on the corner. I saw the whole thing, from the time he raised his fist to her. I'll press formal charges, but I need the two of you to come down to the station and make a statement." Then realizing his rudeness, "I'm sorry Cherie, are you alright?"

"Yeah, I think so," she replied, still in shock as she rubbed her aching cheek. After the chief and Josh exchanged a few words about how Cherie had been treated, Chief Baker left with the two tormentors.

Josh and Cherie remained standing alone on the sidewalk. Josh gently stroked her already bruised cheek, "You really okay, little one?" he asked, his tone sympathetic. "I'm sorry. I shouldn't have let you walk alone."

"Why shouldn't I be able to walk alone in my own home town?" Cherie asked, nearly in tears.

"How often do they attack you like that?"

"This was the first time since I went out with him in high school," Cherie responded.

"He attacked you the night you went out with him?" Josh quizzed.

"Yeah, but I don't wanna talk about it right now," Cherie said.

"Okay, you've had enough for now, but we will talk about it later. Did he say why he was attacking you this time?"

"Yeah, he told me we better not file charges against the two of them. He said if I don't make you drop the charges, he would beat me worse than the last time." By then she was trembling.

"Come on, let's go and get some ice on your face. It's already starting to swell." Josh put his arm protectively around his fiancé and helped her into the pick-up. "Let me get you home, then I'll go and tell Katie that your shopping expedition will need to be delayed for another day."

The next morning Katie and Cherie prepared to shop for Katie's dress. The two women talked constantly as they drove back to the bridal shop. "Was Mongo mad because you got a speeding ticket?" Cherie inquired.

Katie threw her head back laughing, "Of course, he was as angry as he could pretend to be. He puts on a good front for those who don't know him the way I know him. Naturally he was concerned for our safety, but he knows I don't make a habit of driving like that … at least not anymore."

"What do you mean by that?" Cherie asked.

"Well, I had several speeding tickets when we were first married. He did get a little angry back then. And he brought it up the other night, that he hopes I won't get back into that pattern again."

"What made you quit speeding?" Cherie asked, curious as to how this forgiving relationship thing worked.

"I became a mother. The last thing I ever want to do is leave my little girls without a mommy."

Katie chose a light-peach colored, lace dress made similar to Cherie's. It seemed appropriate for a May wedding.

Cherie was getting more and more excited about the wedding. However, lurking behind her excitement was her fear about the wedding night. She was quiet most of their trip home, trying to gather up the courage to ask Katie about it.

Katie noticed that Cherie was exceptionally quiet on the way home and quizzed her. "What's on your mind Cherie? You're not still upset about the other day are you? I thought you and Josh talked through all of that."

"It's not about that. I'm just a little, well a lot nervous about, well, you know, after we are married."

"I understand that. I remember how frightened I was when Mongo and I first got together. But don't worry too much about it Cherie. Josh is a gentle man and he loves you. But you need to be prepared. It will hurt like crazy that first time."

"That's not what I am worried about, Katie."

"Then what is it?"

"Well, I never uh, I don't really know what to do."

Katie reached over and placed her hand on top of Cherie's, "You don't have to worry about that. Mostly it comes naturally, but Josh will lead you through everything."

"Thank you, Katie, thank you for being here for me."

"Cherie, you have always been very special to Mongo and me. And the girls just love you."

"I guess I never realized..."

"No, Cherie, you didn't. You were so busy hiding behind that wall you built around yourself. Mongo and I just hoped and prayed that someday soon, someone could come along and tear down that wall. You just went through the motions each day."

"I was that obvious:"

"More than you will ever realize. Josh has something really special about him to be able to break through. But Sam said he wasn't about to give up, that he tried for weeks just to get you to sit and talk with him. I think he's exactly what you needed."

"Yeah, you're probably right. But I still get a little afraid. He really can be controlling," Cherie declared.

"Well, what is it about that that makes you so uncomfortable? Are you afraid of him?" Katie quizzed.

"Well, like the other day when I was so upset. I didn't want to talk. All I wanted to do was go home and be miserable in peace and he wouldn't let me. And I did not want to talk about it, but he actually threatened me if I didn't talk"

"Good for him!" Katie commended. "Now tell me, did you feel better when you were done talking?"

"Well, yes, I did?"

"And how would you have felt if he had let you go home and curl up inside yourself. Would you have felt better about things today?"

"No," Cherie answered. "I actually told him I couldn't marry him. He could have walked away and made a clean break, but he refused to."

"You have a man who really loves you."

Cherie was totally stressed by Friday. There was so much to do on Friday and Saturday that she was afraid she would never catch up. And to top it off, just two days before her wedding was the court hearing for the charges Josh had forced her to file against Dean and Jeff. To call Cherie a nervous bride was an understatement. And the thought of facing her two tormentors in court had her terrified. "Can't we just drop it Josh, please," she begged, "We'll be leaving for Montana and I'll never have to see them again."

But Josh stood firm that they would not go unpunished. "Just trust me," he encouraged as his fingers gently stroked her tender cheek, "It'll work out okay, I promise." Josh was unrelenting once he made a decision.

Cherie wasn't convinced, "How can you be so sure? They've gotten away with it all of these years and no one has ever said they were wrong. I always thought I was the one who was wrong."

"Cherie, I have a plan. But I don't want to discuss it with you until I know if it can be done legally. We'll talk after I talk it over with the judge."

Cherie gave up. It seemed no use to try to argue her point with her fiancé. He had made his decision that the two young men were going to face his wrath and there was no changing his mind.

Josh left Cherie to sit alone in the courtroom while he talked with Judge Curtland. There were no attorneys, *aren't there supposed to be lawyers?* she thought, *and where are Dean and Jeff?* Josh returned from the judge's chambers after being gone for about ten minutes, and asked Cherie to join them.

Judge Curtland stood up to introduce himself and shake Cherie's hand, then explained what he and Josh had been talking about. "Cherie," the judge started, "Your future husband has an idea that just might solve two problems at one time. It's a little out of the ordinary, but I think we could make it work. The two men you have filed charges against have a lot to lose. They'll definitely be found guilty of the charges of assault and battery and will likely be convicted of harassment as well. They may be willing to agree to Josh's proposition in lieu of jail time and a hefty fine. Additionally, you have a right to file a civil suit against them, and we'll lay that card on the table as well."

When the judge stopped talking, Cherie looked around the room, confused. "I don't understand what you're talking about, sir. They're not even here. And what possible charges could there be?"

"Well," the judge began, "our police chief was an eye witness to Dean putting that bruise on your face, and there are several witnesses to the years of verbal abuse and harassment they have inflicted upon you. Additionally, Mongo has filed trespassing charges against them. The problem is that they have the right to request a jury trial. If they do, it could delay your return home, or else you and Mr. Tolsten will have to fly back here in a couple weeks for the trial. So, your future husband has proposed a possible solution.

"So, I don't have to face them today?" Cherie asked.

"Yes, unfortunately you will, but I'll be right beside you," Josh interrupted.

"But they aren't here?" Cherie questioned again.

"They're here, Cherie. But I didn't want you in the same room with them yet. They're being held in a room down the hall," Josh interjected. What incredible power her future husband had, that he could actually control a court hearing.

Judge Curtland continued, "Cherie, your husband has a plan for these two young men who have hurt you. For all the charges, I can definitely impose a jail sentence. But we need to know if you approve of Mr. Tolsten's plan before we proceed. After all, it was you that was hurt by them."

Josh attempted to explain his plan to his future wife, "Cherie, as Judge Curtland already explained, those two are facing a definite jail term for assaulting you, and a possible sentence, if not a stiff fine for harassment and trespassing. They have no other criminal record. Plus, if they don't cooperate, I plan to serve them with a civil suit for the way they have slandered you and defamed your character. I think they need to learn a lesson, and I think we can teach them, if you will agree?"

"What is it, Josh? I really don't care what you do to them as long as they don't humiliate me again," Cherie responded, becoming irritated at them for keeping her in the dark. "I just want to get this over with."

"Well, I think a little humiliation on their part might be a good lesson. We're going to offer them a chance to work for me for six months by contract, in exchange for jail time and a civil suit." As Cherie opened her mouth to speak, he cautioned her, "Now hear me out. You remember the condition of the old farm house and the amount of work that needs to be done. The offer will be for them to live and work on the farm, caring for the horses, and doing all of the other repairs. I will pay them just enough to get by on, basically food money only. The expectation will be that they work at least 10 hours a day six days a week and six hours on Sundays. Judge Curtland will monitor their progress while we are in Montana but we'll need to fly back periodically to follow up too. The restrictions will be tight so they may prefer jail time. If they break the contract, then they will go to trial. What do you think?"

Cherie, picturing the unsightly farm house and the condition of the grounds, broke into a laugh that proved to be contagious. The three laughed heartedly for several minutes. When they settled down, Josh asked Cherie if she wanted to be in the room when the judge summoned Dean and Jeff into his chambers. Cherie agreed to stay, "But what about Mongo," she asked, "you said he filed charges too?"

"Mongo has agreed to go along with us if you agree," Josh responded. He kept his arm around her protectively as the two young men entered the chambers.

"Gentlemen," Josh began, "On Saturday, this lovely young lady will become my wife." He relished in pleasure at the expressions on their faces as he announced his engagement to them, "Two times this past week I have had the opportunity to witness for myself the profound abuse you have inflicted upon her, and I find that intolerable. As you well know by now, Cherie and I have filed formal charges against the two of you. Now legally, there are ways that we can have a jail term enforced as well as a stiff fine. Additionally, I plan to file civil suit against each of you. It can and will cost you not only a lot of time but a lot of money as well. I will see to it that you will not be able to afford to live in much better conditions than those which Cherie was forced to live in as a child. I can and will make you the towns next, 'poor white trash.'"

Dean opened his mouth to speak, but Josh held his hand up, "I suggest you hear me out, young man. Because if you don't, we will enter the Judge Curtland's courtroom and a formal hearing will begin. I have absolutely no patience with you and your haughty, spoiled brat attitude." Dean abandoned his attempt to speak and permitted Josh to continue, "I have an offer for you. My offer is in lieu of a jail sentence and a civil suit. However it will be a matter of court record, so if you default, we will be back in court.

After listening to Josh's proposal, Dean and Jeff looked at each other. "Why would you want to do this for us?" Dean asked suspiciously.

"Well," Josh stated, "Neither of you have a criminal record and truthfully I think you're a couple of spoiled little rich kids that don't have enough to do with your time. I did my homework on both of you. You were big men on campus in high school. Others listened to you, so when you condemned Cherie the rest of your peers followed. I also know that you're both a couple of losers now and you both still live under your daddy's wings. Your fathers will be very unhappy with you if you end up in jail. They also won't like the negative publicity the papers with give you when I'm finished with you. In fact, you may even get to experience some of what you inflicted upon Cherie a couple days ago if you anger your fathers," Josh said as he gently touched his fiancé's cheek. "And, I think a little humbling and character building will do you both a lot of good. Therefore you have your choice. And you both have to agree."

Jeff asked, "What is the longest jail sentence we can get?"

"Two weeks to six months in county. Now that doesn't sound like much, but some of the inmates are pretty rough. Of course, maybe you need some of them to rough you up a bit. They all hate women beaters you know ... And you will have jail time on your permanent record," the judge informed them.

"But you said if we accept this offer, it will be on record with the court too. So we still have a record. What's the advantage of serving six months in his prison over two weeks in county jail?" We'll still have a record," Jeff mocked.

"Well, "the judge responded, "I said two weeks to six months. And it is likely that I will impose the maximum penalty based on the number of witnesses we have on both counts. And, I can write the harassment and trespassing charges up as a community service sentence, if you accept Mr. Tolsten's offer. If you don't default, I will have the harassment and trespassing records expunged. This offer can keep you out of jail, but I cannot and will not erase the assault and battery charge. Regardless of your decision, you will have that on your record.

"Well, I don't know man; I think maybe I should just take my chances with a trial and a jury. I do have my rights you know," Jeff smirked.

"What are you talking about?" shouted Dean. "Our dads will kill us if we end up in jail. And do you know what will happen if they sue us! Do you want to face your old man! I don't!"

Josh was irritated by this time. "Fine guys, if you want a trial, then let the chips fall where they may. I gave you a chance to make up for hurting my fiancé, but…"

"Wait a minute, please," Dean begged. "Can we talk to our dads for a couple minutes?"

"Are your fathers here?" the judge asked.

"No, we would have to call them," both young men responded at the same time.

Jeff spoke up, "Wait, right now our dads know nothing about this. If we take the community service, we can just tell them we took a job. They'll never have to know the whole story, right?"

"Well, it won't become a matter of public record unless you default. I'll keep it here in my desk for the six months of your sentence. And, you are of legal age, so no, as long as you complete the six months with a satisfactory work performance, they will not need to know about the charges," Judge Curtland promised, then added, "but you need to remember, I can't hide the assault and battery charges. You struck her in front of a police officer. Cherie does have a right to sign an agreement if you accept Mr. Tolsten's proposal. But, if you get arrested for assault again, that one will show up."

The two young men looked at each other and both stated they would accept. "My dad told me if I ever got into any legal trouble he would disinherit me," Dean added.

Cherie rode with Josh to deliver the guys to their new home and took great pleasure in the expression on their faces when the young men saw the old farm house. Josh pulled a picture out of his wallet and presented it to Dean and Jeff. "Look guys," he teased. "This is the house my soon to be wife will be living in. And see this farm house? This is your life for the next six months. If you think you will be living easy, think again. You hurt and insulted the love of my life. Now you are going to work like horses to pay for what you have done to her! And, I trust you will be fully prepared to give Cherie a heart felt apology at the end of your six months."

Both Dean and Jeff gasped with horror as they stepped off the back of Josh's pick up truck. "You really want us to live here, man!" Dean exclaimed.

"Yep, Josh replied, "and you are to have this place looking like a new home, inside and out by the end of your six months. If I'm not happy with the results, I will re-impose the charges. So I suggest you don't give yourselves the luxury of thinking this is a paid vacation. You are to work seven days a week, ten hours every day except Sundays, when you will work at least six hours, just like the agreement you both signed. And I will expect to see a log of each day, the hours you worked and what you did. It better be good enough to convince me that you did do the time. I expect the log book to be reflective of the progress too."

Cherie smiled to herself. She was already too familiar with the sternness in her fiancé's voice. She knew her two tormentors were in for a long six months. "May I say something Josh?"

"Sure Hon, what is it?"

"Well," she began, "I just wanted to let them know that I saw your anger, and what you did to the other two, the last time we came out here … You know, when the other two guys didn't do their job."

Josh smiled back at his young bride. *She has come a long way*, he thought to himself. *She's really come a long way.*

~ CHAPTER 6 ~

THE WEDDING

Immediately following the Sunday morning church service, Katie began to help Cherie dress for the wedding. Cherie normally tied her hair back or pinned it up neatly, but Katie insisted that Cherie wear it down for the wedding. Katie brushed it and added a special touch with the curling iron until Cherie's auburn hair lay in perfect waves around her shoulders. When she was almost ready, Katie presented Cherie with a new Bible, a blue garter and a pearl necklace. She recited, "Something old, something new, something borrowed, something blue. The necklace is a family heirloom. It will be the something old and borrowed. The garter is blue, and the Bible is new. I bought you this type of Bible because this is really a precious time and you will always have a special place in our hearts. Cherie and Katie hugged briefly then they heard the music begin to play. "Wedding music, I hadn't even thought about that," Cherie stated, puzzled.

"Josh did, he wanted you to have a real wedding. Now come on, it's time to find Sam."

The two women found Sam waiting for them in the corridor outside the sanctuary. "Sam," Cherie gasped, "I … I don't think I have ever seen…"

"I think what she is trying to say," Katie interrupted, "is you dress up nice."

Sam gently hugged Cherie and whispered, "You look beautiful girl. I'm really going to miss you," then he turned to the table behind him and picked up two bouquets. There was a small bouquet of peach carnations with white baby's-breath for Katie, and a larger bouquet with peach roses and white carnations with baby's-breath for Cherie. The bewildered look on Cherie's face made Sam laugh a little, "Your man, he wanted to surprise you, now come on, let's get this over with."

Yet another surprise awaited Cherie. When Sam opened the Sanctuary door, Cherie couldn't believe her eyes. The entire Sanctuary was flooded with beautiful flowers. There were roses, carnations and many other flowers that Cherie couldn't identify. On each end of every pew was a large bouquet, and flowers covered the entire length of the altar. Cherie thought her heart skipped a beat as she stood and stared at the sight, but was even more surprised when she saw Josh walk into the sanctuary and take his place at the alter. He looked incredible, wearing a black suit with a white dress shirt. *So this is it*, she thought, "I really am going to marry him," not realizing she had spoken out loud.

"Yes, Cherie, you really are," Katie said quietly. The wedding march began and Katie walked slowly down the aisle. She looked so beautiful in her peach lace gown. Cherie was mesmerized with the sight when Sam nudged her back into reality.

The music changed and Sam took Cherie by the arm. This is our cue. We need to start walking down the aisle. Are you ready to do this?"

"Yes, Sam, I truly am." As they began their procession down the aisle Cherie began to tremble, her heart pounded as she gazed lovingly at the wonderful man she was about to commit her life to. Cherie could see the twinkle in his coal black eyes from the back of the church.

Even though they had rehearsed the entire service on Saturday night, Cherie was terribly nervous. *What if I do something wrong*? She thought, *What if I mess everything up and disappoint Josh or embarrass my friends?*

Sam squeezed he hand gently as if reading her mind, "Relax girl, it's your wedding, you can't do anything wrong." She managed to smile at her only other guests: Pastor Mark's wife – Sherry, and George and Kathy, as she walked past them and approached the altar.

"Who gives this bride away?" asked Pastor Mark.

Sam responded, then backed away to sit in the first pew.

Josh reached down and took Cherie's hand in his, "You look absolutely beautiful," he whispered to her.

Cherie handed the Bible and the bouquet off to Katie, and then Pastor Mark initiated the ceremony. Josh took both of Cherie's small hands in his. When their eyes met, Cherie's eyes filled with tears of joy. She could see the love in Josh's eyes as he listened intently to Pastor Mark.

They were halfway through the ceremony when Pastor nodded to Josh to the church pianist. The music began and Josh started to serenade Cherie with one of her favorite love songs. She couldn't hold back the tears as she heard his lovely voice sing the beautiful words of the ballad.

When the song was finished, Pastor Mark asked for the rings. Katie handed Cherie the golden band she had purchased for Josh. His unsuspecting eyes displayed sincere surprise and Cherie thought she even saw tears. Josh presented Cherie with a beautiful gold wedding band, delicate but with a full carat diamond in the center, and full baguette diamonds inlayed on each side.

When the rings were blessed and placed on each of their fingers, Pastor Mark gave permission for Josh to kiss his new bride. As he kissed her gently he held her close and whispered, "You are so beautiful. I love you so much. You've made me the happiest man in the world.

"I love you too, Josh. I really do.

When the ceremony was over, Mongo approached Cherie and asked her, "Would you mind coming by the diner on your way home this afternoon. I need you to clean out your locker and pick up your belongings."

Cherie felt the pang of hurt feelings but agreed to comply with Mongo's wishes. When Josh and Cherie were alone she complained, "It makes me feel bad that Mongo is in such a hurry to be rid of me."

"Did you tell him that?" Josh asked.

"No, I could never do that."

The diner was just a few doors down from the church, so the newlyweds walked hand in hand, enjoying the moments alone together. Cherie, completely unsuspecting of the final surprise planned for her wedding day, opened the door to the diner fully expecting to find just a few customers and Mongo, whom at that moment she believed didn't want to see her anymore. "SURPRISE!" she heard at least a dozen or more voices yell.

"What? What's all this," Cherie gasped.

Josh placed his arm lovingly around his new bride and spoke quietly, "This is why Mongo wanted you to come down here right away. They're having a surprise wedding reception for you."

"Did you know about this?" she demanded to know, but there was no opportunity for Josh to answer. Cherie was flooded with hugs and "congratulations" from Mongo and Katie and the girls, Pastor Mark and his family, and Sam. Then her former co-workers, the other waitresses smothered her with hugs.

"I can't believe all of this!" Cherie exclaimed. "All of these years, I thought no one cared about me. I always thought they believed the rumors."

"Cherie, these people know you for the wonderful person you are." Josh continued. "They all wanted you to have a wedding day you will never forget. They also don't want you to forget them. Now, I say we get on with the party so we can get out of here and be alone."

The thought of being alone aroused the butterflies in Cherie's stomach again. At the age of twenty-two she had never made love to a man and was completely unsure of herself. *What if Josh decides after tonight that he doesn't want to be married to me, what if I'm not able to please him*? she worried.

As if Josh knew what she was thinking he put his arm around her, "Relax little one. It'll be okay, I promise. Now let's go and have a good time. Your co-workers spent a lot of time trying to make this event memorable for you." He bent down and kissed her lips softly. Just then there was a bright flash of light. Someone had caught their kiss with the camera.

Even though the hour was still early, Cherie was exhausted by the end of the festivities. Josh and Mongo loaded up the truck with all of the gifts. When the couple arrived at Cherie's apartment, Cherie proceeded to help Josh unload the gifts from the back of the truck. Josh stopped her and told her to go upstairs and relax. "Josh, please, don't treat me like I'm helpless. I have carried my laundry baskets and groceries up there for over three years now."

Josh laughed quietly and said, "I don't think you're helpless. But today is your day, and I don't want you lifting a finger. You relax and be pampered for once in your life. He bent down and kissed her brow then swatted her bottom. "Now, upstairs."

Obediently Cherie went upstairs empty handed. Cherie thought that she loved this man so much, and anticipated being pampered for a long time to come. The pang of anxiety returned. *He deserves for me to give something back. I hope I can live up to his expectations tonight.*

"And stop worrying," Josh called after her.

It took Josh two trips to carry all of the packages up the stairs. Cherie jokingly told him, "Now see, if you would have let me help, you would have only had to make one trip." Josh swatted her backside again for her teasing comment then pulled her close and kissed her. His lips pressed hard against hers and forced them apart. Cherie felt his tongue explore inside her mouth and returned the kiss with equal hunger.

Josh's hands traveled up and down her back and buttocks causing those strange sensations that Cherie still wasn't accustomed to. As he pulled her tighter into his embrace she felt the firmness of his passion and he whispered, "Cherie, I want to make you happy the rest of your life. I adore you."

"Oh, Josh, I love you so. But you are spoiling me terribly."

"This is your life from now on, Cherie Tolsten. You are my wife, and you will be treated like a princess. You will always know you are loved, and you'll never want for anything. I'll spend my life determined to make yours better than it was as a child or even as a young adult. I'll never let anyone hurt you," he vowed. Anticipating Cherie's protest Josh changed the subject before she could speak, "Now what do you say we open our gifts?"

"Okay, Josh," she responded–confused. Once again he had started to love her then stopped. *What am I doing wrong*, she wondered. Hoping to conceal her embarrassment she added, "I just can't wait to get into them! I have never had so many presents at one time before!"

Together the newlyweds opened all of the gifts and read each and every card. One card of particular beauty was from Mongo and Katie, was inscribed with words of love and wisdom. Katie gave Cherie a short white negligee with a low cut v-neck and she gave Josh a new Bible. Most of the other gifts were small and of a personal nature. Everyone knew the couple would be leaving for Montana on Monday and gave them gifts that would be easy to pack.

After the last gift was opened, the couple decided it was time to get some sleep. Cherie excused herself to shower and change. Anxiety got the best of her and even after she completed her evening routine she sat in the bathroom, contemplating what to do next. Other than Josh, the only sexual encounter Cherie had ever had with a man was the night that Dean tried to force himself upon her. He had not only humiliated her that night, but he had hurt her physically as well. *Will Josh hurt me tonight*? She questioned as flashbacks of Dean pushing her down against the seat of the car and forcing himself on top of her. He had torn her clothes as she struggled against him and pleaded for him to stop. Cherie remembered feeling like she would suffocate before Dean finally relented and pushed her out of his car after striking her several times in her face.

Sensing his new bride's first time anxiety, Josh went to the bathroom door. He quietly rapped on the door and called to her before he entered. He gently wrapped his arms around his new wife, "Oh Cherie, you look beautiful."

Cherie smiled nervously at her husband. "You're trembling little one. Please don't be worried. I promise you it'll be ok … but, if you want to wait until another night, we can. I want you to be comfortable.

"It's okay, Josh, I'm just a little nervous."

"Cherie, this is more than a little anxiety. You are scared to death. I'm going to take a shower then you and I are going to sit down and talk about this."

Moments later Josh returned from the shower to find his young bride sitting quietly on the bed. He sat down next to her and gently massaged her shoulders and upper back. "Talk to me, Cherie. There is something you're not telling me," he insisted.

"I told you, Josh, I'm just a little nervous."

"Who hurt you?" he questioned.

The couple bantered back and forth for several minutes before Cherie finally relented and told Josh the rest of the story about her date with Dean.

"Cherie, you should have told me that sooner. I would never have let you go through all of this worry. Do you remember the afternoon in the farmhouse?" Cherie nodded, so Josh continued, "Did I hurt you then?"

Too embarrassed to speak, Cherie nodded. Josh went on, "Not all men hurt women. I know the first time is painful for a woman, but I'll do everything in my power to make it as easy as possible for you. If you tell me I'm hurting you, I'll stop."

"But what if I can't please you?" she asked.

"Young lady, you have got to stop worrying about everything. We are going to have many nights together. Tonight is your night."

Cherie put her head down in shame.

"Hey, please don't be embarrassed. We're going to spend our lives together and we have a lot to learn about each other." Josh gently kissed his new wife then lay her down on the bed. Josh bid Cherie to roll onto her stomach then began to slowly massage her back, gently kneading in slow circular motion, working his way from her shoulders down her back and to her buttocks. Cherie's anxieties began to dissipate as her body became tortuously aroused. When his hands reached her buttocks they lingered there, slowly messaging each area then working their way to her most private spot. Cherie jumped when his fingers touched the moist areas between her legs. No one had ever touched her there. She felt as though she may explode. Never before had she felt anything like she did with his touch. She suddenly wanted to touch and explore his body. She rolled onto her back and reached for Josh as he bent down to suckle each of her breasts. Josh's fingers worked in the same rhythm between her legs as his tongue on her breast. Cherie thought she may go mad, the sensations mounting until she let out a scream of delight. Josh climbed atop her and gently began to enter her. He felt her tense with pain and tried to ease away but Cherie placed her hands upon his buttocks and pulled him back. She cried out in pain when he entered, but refused to let him stop.

Cherie's mind began to wonder as they held each other close. Memories of her mother and the abuse from her and her dates crept back, the memory of how she had longed to be loved for all of her life. She began to weep.

"Tell me what you're thinking about that makes you cry?"

"I was just thinking that I've never had anyone love me before. Right now I feel more loved than I've ever been in my life."

"Well, my petite, you are more loved that you've ever been in your life. And I am going to love you for a lifetime. I promise nothing will ever change that," Josh swore.

"But, what if I get out to Montana with you, and totally let you down?"

"Are you going to stop loving me, Cherie?"

"No, but what if I'm not a good enough wife?"

"Cherie, I keep trying to reassure you, but you are so insecure that you won't believe me. I don't expect anything from you but love and fidelity. Anything else we can deal with as it happens."

~ CHAPTER 7 ~

MONTANA

Cherie stared in disbelief as she approached her new home. Josh had told her that he was a wealthy man, but if the sight if his home was any indication, he was far wealthier than she had ever imagined. The entrance to the estate was protected by huge wrought iron gates that opened after Josh entered a code into his security system. As they circled up the driveway toward the house Cherie could only gasp with shock. Josh pointed to an exceptionally large log cabin house with a veranda on the lower lever and French doors opening to individual balconies outside each of the upstairs windows. "This is your new home my love," he told Cherie.

She couldn't speak. Josh continued on, "This is our home and the main house on the ranch. There are several small cabins throughout the estate. We have over five hundred acres; most of which are fenced in. I will take you to the main barn after we get settled in.

"The main barn?"

"Yes, I have a barn for my own personal horses, there are ten in all, and another barn on the north eastern part of the ranch where we board horses for others, and we have some that we rent out for trail riding. There are also have a few that we are raising to sell.

Cherie felt completely overwhelmed. *How can I set foot in a place like this, I am not good enough to live here.*

As though Josh read her thoughts, "Don't even go there. You're my wife, Mrs. Cherie Tolsten. Then he added, "Come on, let me show you around your new home." He took Cherie in the front door then into a large receiving area. Josh called it a foyer. The interior of the cabin had finished walls, the entrance way had cedar paneling and was decorated western style. A man and a woman approached the couple before they could proceed any further into the house.

"Josh, welcome home. How are you?"

"I'm wonderful, Stephen. Stephen, Jeanie, I would like you to meet my new wife, Cherie."

"Your wife, Mr. Tolsten!" the woman exclaimed. "I didn't even know you had a girlfriend."

"Yes, Jeanie. Cherie and I met when I was back in Ohio buying your uncle's farm."

"Mrs. Tolsten, I'm very pleased to meet you. I'm Jeanie, Mr. Tolsten's housekeeper. And Stephen is Mr. Tolsten's right hand man, you might say." Jeanie took Cherie's hand in hers as she spoke to her. Cherie found herself feeling quite uncomfortable with a person who appeared to be at least ten years her senior referring to her as Mrs. Tolsten. Jeanie looked to be in her mid-thirties. She was quite attractive with blond hair tied up in a pony tail. She wore blue jeans that fit pretty tight, a t-shirt and an apron. Stephen appeared more stuffy and sophisticated. He wore a dark, western suit and tie. Stephen was not an unattractive man, but there was something about his eyes that made Cherie uncomfortable. He was tall, but not as tall as Josh, with brown hair and blue eyes, and a bit heavier than Josh.

Stephen welcomed Cherie but she felt an intense coolness from him. She made a mental note that she would spend as little time as possible around him.

Josh interrupted and asked Stephen to get their luggage and packages from the car. "Cherie, what do you say I show you our bedroom? Then if you want to freshen up or rest for a while you can. It's getting late but I would like to at least show you around your new home. I can give you the grand tour of the grounds tomorrow since it'll be dark by the time we have dinner." Then he turned to Jeanie, "Jeanie, would you mind making us some dinner?"

"Not at all, Mr. Tolsten. Did you have anything in mind?"

"Cherie, what would you like to eat?" Josh asked.

"A salad would be fine with me, Josh. I think I'm more tired than hungry."

Josh laughed and turned back to the housekeeper, "If Cherie had her way she would only eat once or twice a week. How about a couple steaks and a salad, maybe a couple baked potatoes?"

"Any desert," the blonde woman asked.

"Oh, surprise us," Josh answered.

"Yes, sir. I'll have it ready in an hour." Jeanie turned and left the room.

"Come with me, Cherie. I'll show you to our room." Josh took Cherie by the arm and led her from the entrance way to a formal living room. He laughed as he described the room as formal, saying, "How formal can you get in a log cabin?" The walls were also finished with heavy cedar paneling. Various pictures and outdoor themes were on the walls, most of them with horses. The wooden furniture enhanced the rustic appearance. Next, Josh led Cherie up a winding hard wood staircase to a suite on the far end of the hallway. He explained that there were four other suites on the second floor, all having a sleeping area, a sitting area, and a bathroom. "Our room is that last one on the left side of the hall. I moved down to this room after my first wife was killed. I hope you will be comfortable in here," he said as he opened the door. "Later on, we can work on choosing a room for you, like I promised, a room to call your own."

Just inside the door was a sitting area furnished with a small settee and chair, two end stands and a television set. The walls were deep maroon with animal pictures on each wall, again mostly horses. The couple walked through the sitting area and past a small doorway into the sleeping area. There was a huge four poster bed with a solid maroon comforter. The carpet was a thick and an off-white color. In the far right corner was a desk with a computer and a small library of books. The entire room was filled with the aura of masculinity. Josh directed Cherie to the bathroom and offered her time to freshen up before dinner. Before he left the room, he told her he would be waiting downstairs in the den. "The den is just off of the living room. You shouldn't have any trouble finding me. Make yourself at home. This is your home now too." He kissed her then left the room.

Cherie was left alone, to herself in her new home, an elaborate home far greater than anything she had dreamed of seeing. She sat down on the side of the bed and marveled at the huge room. *This room is actually larger than my entire apartment*, she thought aloud. Cherie couldn't believe this was her new home. She had gone from living in a small tar paper shack to a simple one bedroom apartment, and now to a mansion like this. After a few minutes of trying to absorb everything, Cherie went into the bathroom to wash her face. The bathroom was magnificent! The walls were black and white checked, and the carpet was white. There was a shower with a clear door, and a large, claw-footed bath tub. It looked big enough for two people. It was a scene Cherie thought she would only ever see in a magazine. The bathtub, commode and lavatory were all black with gold fixtures. It was strikingly beautiful. When she realized she had been completely awe-stricken for several minutes, she decided to move quickly and get back downstairs to her new husband.

As Cherie approached the den it was apparent that he was having a discussion with someone. She heard a male voice say, almost shouting, "Josh, just what the hell are you doing? She's just a child, and you barely know her! How do you know she's not just out to for your money?"

Josh's tone was irritated as he responded, "Well, first of all, Cherie has no idea of the extent of my wealth. I was afraid if I told her the truth it would frighten her off. Second of all, and foremost, I do not have to answer to you. If you remember correctly, you work for me. As for her age, she is young, but she is not a child. She is twenty-two years old, and have you forgotten that my parents are ten years apart? Now, I suggest you end this conversation. And further, you will treat my wife with the respect due the lady of this house."

"All right, sir!" the male voice said sarcastically, "But I thought you and I were friends, and I thought friends could speak openly to one another."

"You're right, Stephen. Maybe I was a little too harsh just now, but Cherie is timid enough, I don't want anyone making her uncomfortable here."

"I won't treat her with any disrespect. But I can't understand what you were thinking. And you didn't talk to anyone about this."

"I really don't think that is any of your business. Enough of this conversation. I would appreciate you getting our luggage from the car and taking them up to our room, just as I asked you to do twenty minutes ago."

"Very well. I guess you just expect us to accept the fact that you married on a whim?" Stephen demanded.

"It's not a matter of what I expect, Stephen. Remember, you work for me, and now you work for her. I expect you to treat her with the same respect that you treated Leona. And that is not an option! She has had enough hard times in her life. She will not experience any hard times as my wife."

Cherie couldn't bear listen any longer. As she turned to flee and go back upstairs to her hew bedroom, Stephen opened the door and bolted through. He gasped as he saw her standing there, "Mrs. Tolsten!" he exclaimed. Josh had been sitting on a black leather sofa, but rose and came to the door when he heard her name. He kissed her softly on the brow, and said, "Cherie, Stephen and I were just having a discussion about us getting married. He seems to have some difficulty accepting the fact. But you need not worry. You will be treated with all the respect the mistress of our home should be treated. Isn't that right, Stephen?"

"Yes, Josh, Mrs. Tolsten, I'm sorry that you had to hear that conversation."

Stephen excused himself and left Josh and Cherie alone. "Come, let's sit down and rest for a few minutes before dinner is served. Jeanie will call us when it's ready.

And don't worry. We're not formal around here."

"Josh, I'm sorry Stephen is upset about me."

"Cherie, please don't apologize for someone else's behavior. He works for me, and now he works for you. You will be accepted, but remember, they are the hired help. You are part owner of this house. Therefore, I don't want you to let the help get the upper hand."

"I know nothing about being in charge of other people."

"Actually you do. You ran the diner without batting an eye. I think when you are ready to, you will take over as mistress of our home without any difficulty."

"I hope I don't disappoint you, Josh."

"Cherie, remember what I told you. I don't expect anything from you except that you love me and remain faithful to me."

"I'm sure I can do that, I do love you, Josh. I'm just a little overwhelmed by everything. My whole life has changed completely, and it has happened in just a few months."

"But, my sweet, it has changed for the better. I'll do everything I can do to make you happy and to help you adjust to the changes."

Jeanie entered the room to advise the newlyweds that dinner was being served. Josh thanked her, and then sharply reprimanded her for not knocking on the door or announcing herself before she entered the room. Jeanie apologized and exited quickly.

"Josh, do you think you should have embarrassed her like that?" Cherie questioned.

"Little one, you have much to learn about managing hired help. Had I been in the den alone, Jeanie would have knocked before entering without any hesitation? Both she and Stephen are testing their limits. They need to remember who the employer here is. I believe I have told you before, I have no tolerance for disobedience to my orders. If they don't want to follow my guidelines, they're free to work elsewhere. And you may be surprised to know that they have both been with me for many years. So, I must not be too bad."

Josh led Cherie to an informal dining room (by his description). It looked pretty elaborate to her. There was a large oak dining table with eight high back chairs, and a matching hutch. The chandelier over the table was gold with hundreds of crystal teardrops. The dining room walls were covered with light mauve and hunter green wall paper, and plush hunter green carpet. The room was beautiful.

After dinner, Josh gave Cherie a tour of the remainder of the house. Cherie felt like she would never be able to learn her way around. They exited the dining room and he led her to the kitchen where Jeanie was busy cleaning up the dinner dishes. The kitchen was enormous with all black appliances and a black island counter in the center. The walls were white, and the flooring was black and white. Jeanie didn't look up as they toured through the kitchen. Josh didn't say anything, but Cherie could tell he was not happy about her rudeness. The remainder of the first floor of the house consisted of the den, the living room and a formal dining room, and an office. In the back of the house was an area that was kept for Stephen – "He is in charge of security," Josh explained. The basement was finished with a bar, and a game room. It was huge with a pool table, a ping pong table and several other game tables. In the back of the basement was an exercise room complete with all the equipment imaginable.

Cherie exclaimed to Josh as they traveled up the back stairway to their suite, "Josh, this house is beyond anything I have ever imagined. I can't believe I actually live here!"

"You not only live here, my sweet, you're part owner. Remember, we are married. Half of everything I own is now yours." Josh reminded.

"Josh, I can't possibly think that way. I have done nothing to earn this. This is all yours,"

"You'll get used to it little one. Pretty soon you will be spending my, our money without thinking twice about it."

"By the way, I did forget to tell you, Jeanie and Stephen live here also. The attic has been finished and Jeanie has a small suite up there, and Stephen has a room off of the security area." Cherie could not quite understand why that made her uncomfortable.

Cherie suddenly felt very tired, and began to yawn. Josh wrapped his arm around her, "Come on, let's get you into bed. You're probably exhausted."

It was nearly ten when Cherie awoke Tuesday morning. Momentarily disoriented, she looked around the room and tried to reorient herself to her surroundings. Josh wasn't in the room. She had a sudden uncomfortable feeling, but tried to brush it off and decided to get a hot shower then dress to go explore the rest of her new home.

When she returned from the shower, Josh was sitting on the settee waiting for her. "Ah, my beautiful wife, you finally decided to wake up. How did you sleep?"

"I slept well, Josh. And you?"

He walked over and kissed her. "I slept well. But now I'm famished. I was trying to wait for you to wake up so we could have breakfast together." With that, he turned to the small dining table in the sitting area and pointed to a huge tray of food. "I brought you breakfast."

"Josh, you have to stop giving me so much food. I'm going to look like an elephant!"

"Now we keep having this conversation over and over. It's not going to hurt you to gain a couple pounds. Besides, you now live on a horse ranch. I'm certain you'll be able to work off any excess calories you may consume. Since I've taken a wife, I've fired all of the ranch hands," he said with a grin.

"Oh, so I'm supposed to take their place? I don't know the first thing about horses."

"Well, you will learn quickly, I presume."

"Thank you. Is that why you brought me here?"

"Yes, of course, that and to look at your beautiful body," he said with a chuckle.

Cherie suddenly realized she was standing before him with absolutely nothing on. She felt her face turn many shades of red from embarrassment. Josh hugged her naked body and consoled, "Cherie, you're my wife. Try not to be embarrassed with me. And I do love looking at you naked body. Except, seeing you like this makes me want to do far more than look."

"Well, if you keep stuffing food in my, you are not going to feel that way!" she retorted.

"Yes, dear, I will, as long as you don't go over 200 pounds." Now please hurry and dress so we can eat. I'm starving. While you have been sleeping, I have been out working the horses. You know, doing your job."

"Okay, okay, I'm going already. I don't want you to have to do any more of my work."

She quickly donned a white terry robe that had been provided for her, and then the couple sat down to enjoy their breakfast. "Truthfully love, I would enjoy you much more without that thing on," Josh quipped.

"Well, your majesty, you are the one who told me to get dressed."

"Some day soon, Cheri, you won't be bothered at all by me seeing you without proper attire. You may even come to enjoy it."

"I enjoy all of the attention you give me, Mr. Tolsten. Now, what are you going to do with me today?"

"I thought I should take you on a tour of the ranch, since you are going to be my chief ranch hand."

The two continued to torment each other as they ate their breakfast. "I'm beginning to think you're serious. I really know nothing about horses."

"You will by the end of the day. I'm going to put you on the back of the wildest horse I have and slap his rump. You will learn to ride very quickly then."

"Gee, if you want rid of me that bad…"

"Well, seriously, little one. I do want to show you around. And introduce you to the ranch hands. There are four of them. Eventually, like next Monday, I am going to have to go back to work at the store. You'll have some time here without me. I want you to know our way around, and know who can help you if you develop an interest in riding."

"That'll be nice, Josh, but I have no idea how to ride a horse."

"When you're ready, we can teach you. Any of my ranch hands will be happy to be your instructor. It will be a nice reprieve from breaking and training the horses. I also want to show you around town, so you can do some shopping. You need to get some new clothes. Do you have any balance left on your Visa card?"

"Yes, Josh, most of it."

The mood suddenly changed. Josh's expression went from happy to an intense frown. Cherie felt her heart skip a beat as she sensed his irritation." How do you figure? You bought a new wedding dress and all of accessories?"

"Well, I did, but my dress didn't cost that much. It was only a couple hundred dollars. All of the other ones were nearly a thousand or over."

"So, you bought the cheapest dress you could find?" The tone of his voice was getting angrier and angrier.

"Well, yes it was the least expensive, but Josh, I tried on over a dozen dresses and I didn't like any of them. When I saw the dress I bought, I mean you bought, I fell in love with it. Katie kept leading me back to the expensive gowns, but I didn't like them. Honest."

"What about the rest of your attire, did you buy cheap too?"

"No, not really, I bought what I liked. Everything came from the bridal shop. I have the receipts if you would like to see them."

"Actually, yes I would. But not because I think you spent too much. It sounds like I'll never have to worry about that, at least not for a long time. But, because I do keep track of all our expenses. I handle all of my own accounting. I don't trust any one else to handle my financial affairs."

"You mean you don't trust me?" she asked as she retrieved the receipts from her purse.

"No, love," his voice softening, "it's not you I don't trust. I've known many people who entrusted their moneys to their accountants and they've been rendered virtually penniless. I will not allow that. I have worked hard to get where I am, and I will now expose myself to that possibility."

Josh's expression hardened again as he looked through the receipts. "You managed to purchase everything you wore for our wedding with under five hundred dollars. But what about the ring, I don't see it on here?"

"Well," she said nervously, "I didn't want to buy that with your money. I really wanted it to be my gift to you. I had a little saved up in the bank, you know, I told you I was saving to go to college. I used some of that money. I'm sorry, please don't be angry with me," she pleaded.

"It's okay, little one," he said, kissing her brow. "I just never want you to think you have to do without anything. In fact, later today, or sometime this week, I want to take you to get you a car."

Cherie was suddenly quiet again. It seemed she suffered so many embarrassments with her new husband. Apparently Josh had no idea that she couldn't drive. Her mind began to race with all of her insecurities. She had to tell him she couldn't cook, and now she would have to admit she couldn't drive a car. The simple things that most people take for granted.

"What is it, Cherie? I didn't mean to upset you," he said as he walked over to hug her. Cherie returned Josh's hug but didn't speak. She was afraid to. This crying thing was getting the best of her. For most of the years of her life she had kept her emotions under control, never letting others see that she was hurting or how she was feeling. Since she had met Josh, her emotions had complete control of her.

"Hey little one. The one thing I will demand of you is that you talk to me and tell me what is bothering you. I can't guess, and we can't resolve a problem if you don't share with me," he demanded.

"Well, you looked like you were angry with me about the dress I bought, and now you want to buy me a car."

"Yes, I think you will be needing one, don't you? If I am working and you want or need to go somewhere…"

"But I can't drive," she exclaimed. "I always have to tell you how inadequate I am and I hate to do that. You must think I'm pathetic!"

"No, I don't think you are pathetic at all, but I do think you need to stop feeling sorry for yourself. So you can't drive, do you see a reason why you can't learn?"

"Well, no."

While Josh was attempting to console Cherie he thought to himself, *this is going to take a long time to get her to have some confidence.* "Why don't you go ahead and get dressed, we have a lot to do today. Now I not only need to teach you how to manage the horses, but how to drive a car, and all in one day. We have to hurry," he teased.

Josh's teasing broke the tension of the moment. Cherie started to laugh and asked, "I just don't think I can master the horses and the driving all on the same day. Do you think you can give me two days to learn all of this?"

Later that morning Josh gave Cherie a complete tour of the ranch. Tolsten Acres was around 500 acres, most of which was fenced in. There was the main barn which was for personal use, and another in the north eastern part of the estate that was for more commercial use. Josh explained that his family, his grandfather, had always bred and raised Quarter horses. He elaborated that at that time he owned nearly one hundred horses. The smaller barn closest to the main house housed ten houses that were for his personal use.

Josh introduced Cherie to two of the ranch hands in the smaller barn and explained their positions. Sammy and Jed, he explained would be available to assist her if and when she chose to learn to ride. Cherie was immediately drawn to a small black filly. "She is just a baby, not quite a year old. It will be a long time before she is old enough to break and ride," Josh explained. Cherie marveled at her beauty, she was solid black without a spot of white anywhere. Her coat was shiny and glossy. The animal seemed to like Cherie as well. She allowed Cherie to rub her face and nose and even permitted Cherie to hand feed her some small sugar cubes. Josh stared in disbelief. The young filly typically shied away from people. "When she is ready, she can be your horse. But I want you to learn to ride on one of the older, tamer horses," Josh promised.

When Josh and Cherie returned to the house, Stephen had an ATV fueled and ready for their use. Josh explained, "It's impossible to cover all of the grounds on foot". As the couple got onto the ATV, Jeanie approached them with a small cooler. She smiled and told Josh that she had packed a small picnic lunch and some cold drinks for them. Josh turned to Cherie after Jeanie left, "Now see, I told you they would come around and accept you."

The couple set off to explore the ranch. There were several small cabins scattered about the ranch, each named based upon its geographic location. There was one small cabin on the east side of the ranch, hidden neatly in the woods and out of sight from the main house, but still within a few yards. The east cabin had only one bedroom and was very small. On the western part of the ranch was a larger two bedroom cabin with a kitchen and living room. It was by far the most elaborate of all of the cabins. There was plush light blue carpeting throughout and soft overstuffed furniture in the living room. The west cabin also had a television set with a satellite. "This is where my parents stay when they come to visit," Josh added, "Usually that's only once or twice a year." To the north eastern part of the estate, near the larger barn were two single bedroom cabins, "Sometimes the two guys I have working up there need a place to stay. In the winter time it's hard for them to get in and out. We keep each cabin stocked with frozen and canned foods as well as powered milk and some dry goods. All of the cabins have electricity and running water. Josh explained that at one time, the cabins were rented out to tourists. "When I married Leona, she didn't like the idea of having strangers on our grounds, so we stopped that practice."

Josh elaborated on his hired help, Jeanie was in charge of the main house, cooking cleaning, shopping etc. She also did the gardening and tended the lawn around the house. Josh had another housekeeper, Betsy, who worked two days a week to keep the cabins cleaned as well as to offer any assistance she could to Jeanie.

The tour had taken several hours when Josh decided he was hungry. Since Cherie was so infatuated with the West cabin, Josh decided that they would have their picnic lunch there. They both washed up then sat down in the dining area to enjoy their meal. Cherie was grateful to be indoors for a while. Because the weather was not as hot as in Ohio, she didn't use sunscreen. Her face and arms were beginning to get sunburned.

After they ate, Josh led his lovely wife into the living room and pulled her onto his lap. "Let's enjoy a little privacy for a few minutes." His lips searched for hers, brushing across her breasts then slowly traveling up to her neck. He stopped at Cherie's neck and suckled softly for a few minutes, causing her to want him more and more. When he reached her mouth, they both explored each other hungrily. Gently, but firmly his hands roamed to explore each of her breasts. Both of them were becoming more and more aroused. Josh proceeded to unbutton Cherie's blouse then unfasten her bra. Cherie moaned with pleasure as she felt his hot tongue flick each one of her nipples. Each flick of his tongue caused a shooting sensation to sizzle through her stomach and private parts. Cherie moaned again and let her hands travel to his male hardness. He drew Cherie to straddle his lap, and then pressed her clothed body against his bulging passion. Slowly they rocked against each other until they both felt as though they would explode. Suddenly Josh stopped and lifted her up into his arms. Cherie held tight as he carried her to one of the bedrooms where he laid her gently on the bed. Slowly Josh began to undress her, making her wait in anticipation as he removed her blouse and bra, then slowly and teasingly unzipped her jeans. He let his hands wonder as he slowly pulled her jeans down over her knees then tossed them onto the floor. Cherie reached to assist Josh to undress. He couldn't wait any longer when she reached for the zipper to his jeans. Urgently he removed them and tossed them into the pile with the rest of their clothing. Josh lay down on the bed beside her and they both explored each other's bodies hungrily.

Cherie's hands explored every inch of Josh's body, giving him the kind of pleasure he had almost forgotten. While Cherie was enjoying her new toy, Josh's hands found her most intimate area. Cherie thought she would never get enough of his hands exploring the soft moist area between her legs. His fingers were so gentle and seemed to know exactly what to do to drive her completely insane. When they were both ready to explode again, Josh pulled his young bride on top of him and entered her. When Josh initially entered her, Cherie realized she was still a little sore from her first experience. Josh noticed her reaction and stopped, "You okay, love?"

"Oh, Josh, I love you so much. Please don't stop." They both cried out in ecstasy at the same time as the rocked together. Then they lay and held each other until they both fell fast asleep.

Several hours later Josh woke Cherie with a sense of urgency. "Let's get dressed and return to the main house Cherie. It's difficult to get around up here in the dark. I don't have any outdoor lighting this far up." Cherie quickly dressed then attempted to clean up the mess they had made, but Josh stopped her, "The maid will clean up."

"But Josh," she protested. "Then they'll know what we've been doing."

"Cherie, we're married and this is my, I mean our property. It's not up to the hired help to judge what we do. Please don't worry about what they think. Remember, I sign their paychecks."

"Don't you ever worry that they may talk?"

"No, gossip is forbidden. They were all told upon hire that they will be terminated if they are caught gossiping, either on or off the ranch. You need not worry, my love. You will never be ridiculed here." Josh kissed her and took her arm to lead her to the ATV.

On the way back Josh asked, "Well, since we slept most of the afternoon, I doubt we will be ready to turn in any time soon. What would you like to do tonight?"

Josh seemed to understand Cherie's discomfort in asking people to do for her so he added, "How about we go into town? My store will be closed, but I would like to show it to you, then maybe I can show you around town a little. There is so much for you to see! I can show you Montana at night. Then tomorrow, we get you a new car and begin teaching you to drive."

PART TWO

~ CHAPTER 8 ~

A NEW LIFE

FOUR MONTHS LATER:

Josh and Cherie had settled into their new life. Two days a week, Cherie went to the store with Josh and worked as a sales clerk. She had adjusted well to her new position and made friends with the other clerks in the store. Josh was pleased that she was even showing a sense of leadership. He had been hopeful that Cherie would develop an interest in his business so he took every opportunity to teach her about it. Josh however, did not want his young bride working as hard as she had when she was struggling to support herself, so he insisted she only work a couple days a week The other days of the week, Cherie could either shop or spend time in the stables, learning to ride and care for the horses, or even just meander about the ranch. Even though it wasn't difficult for Cherie to keep busy, her time away from Josh seemed to drag on and on. When it was time for him to return home from work, Cherie was waiting impatiently for him at the front door.

Josh normally shared the same excitement for their reunion and greeted his wife with identical pleasure and passion. It was obvious the couple was madly in love. And Josh was ecstatic that he had found a wife who he could love and would return his love equally. However, this day was dreadfully different. Josh's coal black eyes nearly burned right through Cherie as he entered the front door of their home. Cherie had seen him talking briefly with Stephen when he drove into the driveway. The expression on his face gave Cherie a strange sense of panic that made her blood run cold. Never before had she seen her husband so angry, and from the way he glared at her, she only too aware that his anger was directed at her. Before he spoke to her, Josh barked an order at Jeanie, telling her to go to the grocery store and citing a list of items to purchase. Cherie's impending sense of doom was escalating.

Stephen, fully aware of the source of his boss's anger, had remained outside of the house after his brief encounter. Stephen had met Josh in the driveway to update him on Cherie's activities that day but was immediately sorry he had done so when his boss reacted so violently.

Josh turned to Cherie and growled. "What did you do today?" Before Cherie had a chance to answer, Josh fired another question at her, this time with more intensity than the first, "Did you leave the house without Stephen? And, did you bring a stranger back to our home?" he exclaimed. Cherie was certain now that Josh knew what she had done earlier that day, and he was infuriated with her. Her knees trembling so violently that she stepped back to lean against the wall for support. While Cherie was searching for the right words Josh violently interrupted her thoughts, "Why, Cherie? Why ... why did you blatantly disobey me like that?"

Two weeks ago, Josh abruptly decided that Cherie could no longer leave their home unless accompanied by either himself or Stephen. She was only permitted to walk alone on the grounds closest to the main house. The area with the tightest security. Even though she could not understand Josh's dictate, he refused to give her further explanation. Today she had gone shopping, and as instructed, she asked Stephen to accompany her. Cherie didn't particularly like to have Stephen along. She felt uncomfortable with him. He had made his disapproval of her quite clear from the day she came home with Josh.

While they were driving home from shopping, Cherie noticed a man walking a few miles from their home. Judging by his disheveled and unkempt appearance, Cherie assumed he was homeless and her heart went out to him. He looked so frail and weak, she thought. After she returned home she couldn't stop thinking about him. She even felt guilty unpacking packages of new clothes while a man was walking the streets alone and cold, without proper clothing. Cherie decided to go back for him. There must be something she could do to help the poor man. Cherie knew that Stephen wouldn't approve, so she left without informing or inviting her chaperone.

She found the man just a few blocks from where she had seen him earlier that day. His gait was slow and unsteady. Even though it was only mid October, the air was cold, the temperature near freezing. The man wore no coat, only a torn and ragged flannel shirt and denim pants. As Cherie got closer to him, she noticed that his shoes were full of holes. She stopped her car and tried to talk to him, but he appeared frightened and kept walking, so she got out of the car and approached him. "Mister," she called to him. He stopped briefly and looked up at Cherie, but then he continued to amble away. His fragile appearance gave her no reason to fear him. His facial complexion was ghastly pale. "I am sorry sir," Cherie apologized, "I don't mean to frighten you. You look as though you are ill. May I be of some assistance to you?" He was reluctant to open up to her at first, but with Cherie's gentle nature and persistence, he finally agreed to let her take him home for a meal.

When Cherie arrived home with her guest, she instructed Jeanie to prepare a hot meal for him. Jeanie's disapproval was evident by her attitude and facial expressions, but Cherie didn't care. Cherie felt they had plenty to eat, and believed she had an obligation to help this poor man who hadn't eaten is several days. Because he was so weak and sickly from his situation, no amount of disapproval from her highly paid maid servant would sway Cherie's decision.

Cherie sat with the man and conversed with him as he ate. He tried to be polite as he ate, but it was obvious that he was starved. He told her his name was Joey and described the heartbreaking story of how his wife and two children had died in a dreadful accident. He said he had become so distraught after their deaths that he neglected his job. "I just couldn't go on, I just didn't care anymore. They were my life," the man sobbed. Cherie could almost feel his pain as he continued with his story and described how his employers fired him for poor job performance instead of trying to help him. Joey went on to explain that he eventually he lost his home and everything else he owned. He had lived on the streets for several months, unable to obtain any assistance to get back on his feet. When he finished eating, Cherie packed up a few food items from the kitchen and gathered some of Josh's older clothes. She had persuaded Joey to let her take him to one of the small cabins for the night. Cherie had no idea how she was going to explain all of this to Josh, but felt in her heart that Josh would understand once she explained Joey's tragic circumstances.

Josh was becoming increasingly impatient for an explanation, and the sound of him intolerantly clearing his throat jolted Cherie out of her thoughts. He was demanding an explanation. "Yes, Josh," she replied meekly, "I did leave the house alone today. It's all true, but I can explain…"

Josh interrupted her attempts to explain her actions with a harsh demand. "I can't talk to you about this, I am too upset. You go upstairs and wait for me in our bedroom," he demanded. "I will be up in a few minutes and we will discuss this further! Right now, I need to calm down!" When Cherie opened her mouth to speak, he sternly pointed toward the stairs and commanded, "Go!"

A small tear trickled down her cheek as she slowly climbed the stairs. *Now I've blown it. He hates me just like mother did.* As she sat nervously on their bed awaiting her husband's arrival, she remembered the cruel beratings she would receive from her mother when she was angered. Cherie knew Josh wasn't finished scolding her yet, and she trembled at the thought of being yelled at and belittled once again. The memory of how her mother always took great pains in reminding her of her worthless existence turned fear to panic. Frantically she looked around the room for a place to hide as she heard Josh pacing downstairs. The thought of leaving crossed her mind. Perhaps if she could avoid this confrontation for a couple hours, Josh would calm down so that they could talk rationally about this.

Moments later Josh entered the room. He didn't say a word, but walked over and sat down beside Cherie on the edge of the bed. Before she could speak, Cherie found herself face down across his lap. His huge arm lay across her back and anchored around her small waist so that she couldn't move. Terrified, Cherie tried frantically to get up as she begged him to release her, but he only held tighter. All of a sudden, he began to spank her. His huge hand repeatedly crashed upon her bottom until she was so tender that she could not stop the tears. Cherie had never experienced such pain and embarrassment before. Josh continued in spite of her pleas for him to stop. "Why are you doing this to me," she cried out.

With his anger spent, Josh ceased the punishment and helped his young wife to stand. "Because you disobeyed me, little one," Josh reprimanded. Knowing his wife was traumatized by the punishment, he tried to pull her close to him and comfort her. But Cherie escaped his embrace and raced into the bathroom. Josh's heart was breaking for the pain he had inflicted upon his young wife. He knew he had hurt her deeply, but he had to impress upon her the importance of not going away from the house alone.

Cherie didn't feel any better alone in the bathroom. She was terribly sore, so she stood against the sink and tried desperately to regain control of herself. Her mind was spinning, and she felt so embarrassed. *How can I ever face him again ... how can I ever face Stephen and Jeanie again?* she thought to herself. But, Cherie knew she would have to leave the bathroom and face Josh again soon. She wanted to try to have some dignity when she went back into the bedroom. She felt so confused. No one had ever spanked her before. All of the abuse she had endured from her mother was normal at that time in her life. But, Josh had always been so loving and patient.

Cherie's attempts to calm herself appeared to be futile. She couldn't stop crying. She now wondered if marrying Josh had been a mistake. When she and Josh were dating, she knew he was a controlling person. For the first few months of her marriage, Josh had placed very few demands upon her, but then all of a sudden she was stripped of her freedom when Josh instructed her that she couldn't leave the house without himself or Stephen. He had refused to explain why he instituted the dictate. For the first time since the couple wed, Cherie considered returning home. She suddenly longed for the safety of her small apartment in Dryville, the one place where nobody could hurt her.

Josh waited patiently for Cherie for about twenty minutes, and then became concerned. He knew she was distressed that he punished her, but he had warned her in the past not to disobey him. Stephen had met Josh in the driveway when he returned from work earlier. Stephen had informed Josh that he should tell Cherie of the threatening letters so she would understand why it was so important for her to not leave the house alone. Josh insisted that Stephen tell him what prompted that conversation. Stephen was reluctant to tell his boss what Cherie had done because he knew that Josh would be enraged with her. But he also knew better than to hide the truth from his boss. Stephen had pleaded with Josh to at least give Cherie a chance to tell him about her day, but Josh's anger was in control of his actions.

Josh went to the bathroom door and called to Cherie. Not wishing to agitate him further, Cherie thought she must go out and face him. She still desperately wanted to salvage some semblance of dignity so, determined not to cry anymore, she splashed cold water on her face and patted it dry. When she opened the bathroom door she ran directly into Josh's six foot two inch frame. His dark eyes softened when he looked down at her. As soon as Cherie looked up at Josh, she lost all composure and began to sob again. Josh put his arms around Cherie and held her tight for a few minutes, then picked her up and carried her over to the sitting area of their suite. Josh sat down on the settee, and held Cherie on his lap. "Shh," he soothed. He held her close for a few minutes while she calmed then quietly told her, "We need to talk." Cherie felt like a small child at that moment, crying like a baby while he held her small body on his lap. He gently brushed through her hair with his fingers until she was able to stop crying.

"Cherie, we need to talk ... You need to tell me why you disobeyed me. I told you not to go off the grounds without Stephen or myself. And why would you endanger your own safety by having a stranger in your car alone and bringing him to our home?" His voice rose as he punctuated "alone," causing Cherie to tremble and weep again.

Not wanting to face him, Cherie tried to keep her face buried in his chest as she started to speak. However, Josh would not permit her avoidance. He cupped her chin in his hand, "Look at me when you tell me Cherie. I want you to look me in the eye. I need to know you are telling the truth."

"Josh, I have no reason to lie to you. I was going to tell you everything when you got home tonight. But, I can't face you right now," she whined, and began sobbing again. Josh held her and stroked her hair for a few seconds, giving her a chance to calm again.

Slowly Cherie began to recap the story of how she had seen Joey, and how he appeared to need help. Guarded, she explained that she thought Stephen would try to stop her, so she went without him. Fearful that the remainder of her story would provoke his anger again, Cherie stopped and looked up at him. "Josh, are you going to hurt me again when I tell you the rest? I don't think you are going to like what I have to say."

"No, little one. I will not punish you again for this. But I do want the truth."

Josh's jaw twitched with anger as Cherie described how she got out of the car and approached Joey, and how she drove him to their home. When she told him about feeding Joey a hot meal and how hungry the poor man was, Josh stopped her. Cherie knew his anger was re-escalating when he said, "Okay, Cherie. You can tell me the rest later. I think you and I have both had enough for now. Let's go down stairs and have some dinner."

"Please don't make me go down stairs tonight. I don't think I can face Stephen or Jeanie."

"It's alright. I sent them both on errands so we would be in the house alone. I was angry with you, but I would never humiliate you. Now come on, let's go to dinner." Before they left the room, Josh pulled Cherie close and hugged her tightly. "Cherie, I love you. You jeopardized your own safety today, and you disobeyed me. I couldn't let that go." He looked down at her red, puffy eyes and brushed his lips across her forehead.

"Yes, sir," Cherie whispered, trying desperately not to cry again. "I was hoping you would understand once I had a chance to talk to you about it. I didn't intend to hide it from you."

"I may not have been quite as angry if I had heard it initially from you, but you still disobeyed me, and I can't permit anyone to endanger you, not even you. Little one, I know this is hard for you to understand. You're hurt and embarrassed. I have already lost one wife, and I can't lose you."

"You are worried about losing me, so you abuse me?" she asked.

"I assure you little one, I will never be abusive to you. I won't scream at you or berate you the way your mother did. And, I will never criticize you or deprive you of anything you want or need. However, I will spank you if you disobey me. Especially when it involves you putting yourself at risk."

"I don't understand what has changed. You wanted me to go out alone and explore the grounds and get familiar with the area until a couple weeks ago, and then all of a sudden you took my freedom away from me. I feel like a prisoner in this house. It would help me if I understand what I did wrong," Cherie pleaded.

"You have done nothing wrong. You're just going to have to trust me on this because I can't tell you anymore at this time. And, you're not a prisoner. You are free to come and go as you please, but you must have me or Stephen accompany you. Now let's go and have some dinner. I sent Jeanie out for Porterhouse steaks for dinner. She'll be furious with both of us if we ruin her dinner after I made her make a special trip to town."

Josh and Cherie left the privacy of their suite and descended the stairs to the dining room. Cherie certainly didn't feel much like eating but thought it was better not to challenge Josh.

The couple ate in silence. Josh tried a couple times to make small talk by asking Cherie about her shopping spree but Cherie didn't feel up to conversation or eating. She picked at her dinner and ate just enough to keep from drawing Josh's attention to her plate. To add to Cherie's discomfort, she caught Jeanie's expression each time she entered the dining room, making Cherie suspect she knew what transpired upstairs in their bedroom. Cherie wanted to run upstairs and hide forever or flee the ranch.

There was still more to tell Josh, and Cherie didn't want to face another angry episode if he discovered Joey before she had a chance to tell him Joey was in one of the cabins. Because Joey couldn't travel very quickly and didn't have the strength to go very far, Cherie had decided to house him in the cabin closest to the house. That increased the risk of getting caught so she felt a strong need to tell Josh. When they had finished dinner, Cherie attempted to tell Josh the rest of her story. Josh was adamant that he had heard enough for one day, and sternly reminded her that he had already decided she had been through enough for today, "You may tell me the rest tomorrow. Now, come to the den with me," he instructed as he took her hand, "Let's watch a little television and relax before we go to bed."

Cherie pretended to watch television with Josh for a little while, and then excused herself to go prepare for bed. She hoped that she could be asleep before Josh came up to bed. While preparing a hot bath, Cherie entertained the idea of ending the marriage and returning to Dryville. Her life there was bland, but with Dean and Jeff out of the picture, she had no one to fear.

The hot water of the bath felt good on her aching body, and the privacy gave her the chance to sort out her thoughts. Some time later, Josh entered the bathroom. He had already removed his clothing. Even though she was upset with Josh for what he had done to her, she still could not resist admiring his tall muscular form. Josh's broad shoulders and huge biceps were accented by his rippling abs, narrow hips and tight bottom. He was perfect in every way. He looked over at Cherie with a concerned expression, "You okay?" he asked. Cherie didn't answer, but just nodded her head. Still not abandoning the hope of being asleep before he got into bed, Cherie promptly finished her bath and exited the bathroom while Josh showered. She donned a pair of white baby doll style pajamas and crawled into bed. Lying on her stomach, she intended to act as if she was asleep.

Moments later Josh entered their suite. He sat down on the bed next to Cherie and without speaking he began to gently message her back. Initially he rubbed over top of her pajama top, and then lifted it over her head and removed it. Cherie was still hoping to escape intimacy so she didn't move or respond to him. After he removed her pajama top, his message began to be a little more intense. He started at the base of her neck and slowly kneaded her skin and muscles with his fingers in a slow circular motion, gradually working down her back to her tender buttocks. Cherie wanted very much to remain angry at Josh, but she was not able to. She felt her body begin to relax. Exhausted, both mentally and physically, she felt herself fade into oblivion. The last thing she remembered was Josh's voice, soft and gentle, "I love you so much little one, I just can't bear the thought of losing you."

Josh had already left for work when Cherie awoke the next morning. She promptly felt an unyielding reminder of last night's punishment when she sat up on the edge of the bed. Panic struck her when she thought of Joey. She didn't get to tell Josh that she had put Joey up in the cabin closest to the house. *What if Joey attempts to leave and one of the groundskeepers or Stephen sees him before I have a chance to explain it all to Josh!* Cherie knew she had to get to Joey and tell him not to leave the cabin until she could talk to Josh. Going to the cabins alone was in defiance of Josh's order, but she had to take the chance and slip away. Either way she would be in trouble if caught, and Cherie didn't believe she could trust either Jeanie or Stephen. She was convinced that Josh wouldn't have been as angry with her if Stephen would have kept quiet and let her tell Josh in her own way. Cherie was not the type of person to be dishonest but she felt Stephen's conversation with Josh in the driveway last evening had precipitated his intense anger.

The tap on her bedroom door startled her. "Mrs. Tolsten, it's me, Jeanie. I came to see if you need me to straighten your room ma'am." Cherie's mind raced as she struggled to think.

"Oh no Jeanie. I'm not feeling well today. I think I am going to rest for most of the morning. Please see that I'm not disturbed until afternoon."

"Yes, ma'am. I'll check on you later." Jeanie hesitated and looked back at her, "Mrs. Tolsten, if I may ask. Are you still upset about last evening ma'am?"

"What do you know about last night," Cherie demanded.

"Well, ma'am, I could lose my job for this. But, Mr. Tolsten told me to go into town and buy some steaks. But after he went upstairs I remembered that I had just bought some earlier yesterday morning. His anger shocked me so that I didn't think about it. Then I heard, well, uh I thought it better not to interrupt. I'm so sorry ma'am. Is there anything I can do?"

Feeling mortified at Jeanie's confession that she was an audible witness to her husband punishing her the previous evening; she couldn't wait for Jeanie to leave, "No, Jeanie. Just provide me with some privacy today."

"Yes, ma'am. I'll check on you later," Jeanie promised.

"That won't be necessary Jeanie. I'll call for you or come downstairs if I need anything." Cherie felt Jeanie's gaze upon her as she exited the room. Suddenly she felt incredibly alone. She couldn't trust the help, their loyalty was to Josh.

Cherie knew if she showered the help would hear. She wanted them to think she was not feeling well and had remained in bed, so she dressed without showering or washing her hair. She wore a pair of older blue jeans and a heavy hooded sweatshirt. She tied her hair back the way she did when she worked at the diner. Then after donning her coat and gloves, Cherie slipped quietly down the front steps. Jeanie would be in the kitchen and Stephen should be in the security office or out on the grounds. Cherie had placed Joey in the east cabin, which was the closest to the main house. She silently prayed she wouldn't be seen by Stephen or any of the other help. The cold air almost made her regret that decision. To avoid being seen by the help, Cherie took the wooded pathways instead of the clearing. It took her nearly ten minutes to get to the cabin.

Before she entered the cabin, Cherie knocked on the door but no one answered. An intense feeling of dread crept through Cherie. Fearing her guest had left the grounds and was likely spotted by someone, Cherie tried the door. The door was unlocked, but still no answer when she called Joey's name. Continuing to call for him, Cherie slowly made her way through the small cabin to the bedroom. Cherie gasped as she looked at the still form lying in the bed. It was obvious that Joey had showered. He was cleaned up and was wearing Josh's pajamas. His face was ghost white and he was drenched with perspiration. His breathing was so loud and raspy that Cherie could hear it from across the room. Joey's eyes were open but she could tell he was struggling to breath. He didn't answer her when she spoke to him. Cherie saw the pleading for help in his eyes. "Hold on Joey," Cherie pleaded. "I'm going to go for help." Before she left him, Cherie went into the bathroom and moistened some washcloths with cool water. She gently wiped his face with one cool cloth then placed on his forehead and smoothed another across his lips. "I'll be back as soon as I can," Cherie gently assured.

~ CHAPTER 9 ~

BAD NEWS

Stephen was livid with Jeanie after she admitted she heard Cherie leave the house, but had no idea where Cherie was going. Stephen had grown curious when he didn't see her come down for breakfast with Josh, then didn't come down anytime later in the morning either. When he quizzed Jeanie about her whereabouts Jeanie was indifferent. "She told me she didn't feel well, and didn't want to be disturbed until afternoon. Then when I went up later to check on her she wasn't in her room. She told me she was still really upset about last night, so I left her alone," Jeanie said, her tone irritated.

"What do you mean–upset about last night?" Stephen implored.

"You mean you don't know what he did to her last night? I would be pretty upset too," Jeanie said smugly.

"How do you know about that?" Stephen insisted.

"I was here. I heard everything, him hitting her, her crying."

"When did you discover her missing Jeanie?" Stephen shouted impatiently.

Gosh, Stephen, relax. It was just about twenty minutes ago. In fact I heard the front door close. That's why I went to check on her."

"But you let her go, and you didn't bother to come and get me to alert me she was leaving!"

"What's that all about? Why would I come get you just because she left the house? You're not her keeper?" Jeanie replied, irritated.

"Nevermind, I am wasting too much time, I have to find her."

Jeanie smiled to herself as she walked away from the kitchen.

Stephen rushed to telephone Josh. Josh's secretary attempted to defer Stephen's call to voice mail because Josh was busy with a customer. However, Stephen persisted, "This is an emergency! I must speak with Josh."

Josh excused himself from his customer and took the call in his private office. "Damn!" he exclaimed, slamming his fist in the desk. "Why didn't you go with her? Why did you let her out alone? You're in charge of my security and you're supposed to keep her safe when I am away!"

"I didn't know she was going out Josh. She told Jeanie that she wasn't feeling well and asked not to be disturbed. Jeanie told me she's still pretty upset about what happened last night so she believed her."

"What are you talking about, last night? Josh demanded.

"Jeanie was in the house, she heard everything."

"What the … well we will deal with that later. Right now my wife is out there alone and her life is in danger. You get started and I will be home as soon as I can get there. We must find her!"

"Josh, do you want me get the rest of the staff together and have them help?"

"No, she's upset enough already. If she finds out you and Jeanie know what happened last night she'll be devastated. I promised her I sent you two away. So much for trusting my help to listen to me."

"I'm leaving now. I'll start searching closest to the house and gradually make my way farther out."

"Keep your cell phone on so we can communicate and when you find her, don't leave her alone again!" Josh commanded.

Josh slammed down the phone and shouted to his secretary that he had to leave to deal with an emergency as he dashed out the back door.

Defying all traffic laws, Josh arrived home in record time. He jumped from his truck and ran to the garage where the ATV awaited him. Before he could speed off he saw Stephen approaching him.

"I have searched the grounds around the house, the garage, the garden and the barn. She's not here close and nobody saw her leave. I'm going to start to search the cabins."

"Is her car still in the garage?" Josh asked impatiently.

"Yes, and her keys are hanging on the hook. She is on the grounds somewhere. No one has gone in or out of the gate," Stephen reassured his boss.

"That we know of. Since we don't know who wants to kill her, we don't know what we are up against. This person has been clever enough to sneak the letters onto the grounds and place them in my barn or on my front porch. We can't be too careful." Stephen heard the panic in his boss's voice.

Moments later Josh and Stephen saw Cherie running toward them. "Josh!" she exclaimed, "I was coming to the house to call you. I need your help! Some one is in trouble."

"Cherie, what are you doing out here alone!" Josh scolded.

"Please Josh, I know you're going to be upset with me. But right now, the homeless man I brought home last night is seriously ill. I am afraid he may die if we don't get help. Please help Josh. I'll tell you the rest later," Cherie pleaded.

The look in his young wife's eyes told him he should accommodate her request. Josh nodded and motioned her to climb into the ATV. "Where is he?"

Cherie explained that he was in the east cabin as she climbed on back. The three of them sped onward toward the cabin. They arrived at the cabin within moments. Cherie led Josh into the cabin and back to the bedroom where Joey lay, barely conscious. His breathing was labored and noisy, almost like the death rattle. Josh walked over close to Joey and pressed his hand across the side of Joey's face. Joey didn't speak, but Josh could see his pleading for help in his eyes. Josh's experience as a paramedic told him that this man didn't have long to live if he didn't receive medical attention immediately. "I'll be back in a few minutes. I'm going to call for help," he said then he quietly walked back outside.

"What is it Josh?" Cherie asked as she followed him outside. Josh was already dialing 911 on his cell phone. Cherie was surprised when she heard him ask for a helicopter. He then gave the phone to Stephen, asking him to provide directions for the chopper, and to make the arrangements with the rest of the staff to facilitate that its landing as close as possible to the cabin.

Josh then took Cherie's arm and said gently, "Cherie, your friend is critically ill. I'm not certain he will survive. I've asked for a chopper because I don't think there is enough time for a ground squad to get here."

"What do you think is wrong with him," Cherie asked.

"Well, I am certainly not a physician but it looks like he may have pneumonia.

Josh and Cherie arrived at the hospital about an hour and a half later. Initially the emergency room staff wouldn't provide them with any information about Joey's condition. Josh excused himself for a few minutes then returned with a physician. "Cherie, this is Dr. Shangar. He was the physician caring for Joey."

"*Was* caring for Joey? What do you mean was?" Cherie asked.

"Mrs. Tolsten. Joey passed away just a few minutes after he arrived here. He spoke of you before he passed on. He asked me to 'thank you for all you have done'."

Cherie felt terribly saddened and didn't know what to say at that moment. She had only known Joey for a little over one day, but her heart had gone out to him. "I'm so sorry. I wonder if I would have gotten to him sooner, if he would have survived."

"Mrs. Tolsten," the doctor reassured, "there's nothing you could have done for him. His body was so worn down from malnutrition and the abuse of living on the streets that he had no chance of fighting the pneumonia. Instead of beating yourself up for not doing enough, why don't you consider the fact that you gave him some comfort in his last days?"

"Yes, I guess you're right. He could have died alone and hungry in the streets. But, he still died alone."

"If it's any consolation, Mrs. Tolsten, the ER staff was with him when he died. Even though he had no loved ones with him, he was surrounded by caring people."

Cherie felt numb and saddened as she thanked the doctor and asked Josh to take her home.

When Cherie and Josh got into the truck, Cherie laid her head back against the seat and closed her eyes. There was so much to process from the past two days. Josh motioned her to sit next to him in the truck but she kept her eyes closed and pretended not to notice. Even with everything that had just happened, she knew she would have to face him when they got home for her last indiscretion. "Are you okay, Cherie?" Josh asked.

Cherie nodded silently in response, and hoped not to have to engage in further conversation.

They drove in silence for a few miles then Josh asked Cherie if she would like to stop for a late lunch. Cherie politely declined. She certainly didn't feel much like eating or being around people. "Cherie, I know you're upset. But my guess is that since you told Jeanie you were ill and didn't want disturbed, you haven't eaten anything today. And you didn't eat hardly anything last night."

With hot tears streaming down her face, Cherie insisted that she was not up to going into a restaurant. Josh noticed his wife's distress and turned the truck off the freeway. He pulled into an abandoned roadside rest area. Cherie shrunk back into the seat of the truck, fearful that she had angered him.

He pulled the truck off to the side and put the gearshift in park. "Cherie, you only knew this man for a couple days. How is it that this upsets you so?"

"Because Josh, no human being, or any living being should have to live that way!" she shouted. "I should've been able to do more to help him!" She was sobbing by then. Josh reached over and tried to pull her over next to him, but she pulled away. "I'm sorry, Josh. I know I disappointed you, and you are probably angry with me ..." She began to shiver as she recalled what happened the night before for disobeying him. She feared a repeat of the past evening.

Josh must have sensed Cherie's fear and once again reached for her. He wanted to consol and comfort her. Cherie panicked, afraid she was about to face the consequences of his anger again. She opened the door of the pickup and jumped out, then ran as fast as her legs would carry her. She had no idea where she was going to go, or what she was going to do. It didn't matter. Josh was immediately out of the truck and within a few sprints caught up with his wife.

Josh roughly picked her up off her feet and carried her back to the truck. Once safely back in the truck, he pulled her onto his lap and scolded, "Damn it, Cherie. Do you wanna get yourself killed?"

Cherie's struggled to be released from his iron grip but stopped suddenly when she realized what he had just said. "What did you say?" she sobbed.

"Why in the world are you trying to run from me?" Josh demanded.

"Because you're angry with me," she explained timidly.

"No, Cherie, I'm not angry with you. I realize I put you in an awkward position by not letting you finish telling me what happened. But, from now on if you have cause to leave, for any reason you must ask Stephen to accompany you. No exceptions! Do you understand?"

"Yes, sir, I understand. I'm a prisoner in my, I mean your home," Cherie said defiantly. And, I'd rather be stuck inside forever than to have to go with Stephen. He makes me so uncomfortable," Cherie complained.

"Why do you say that?" her husband's voice softened as he inquired.

"Because he makes it clear that he doesn't like me or approve of me."

"Cherie, it doesn't matter if he likes or approves of you. You have to learn to understand that he works for us. It's his responsibility to ensure your safety."

"What's the big deal about my safety? Why is that an issue all of a sudden? Why did you ask me if I want to get myself killed? What's going on?"

"I really would rather not get into that right now. You just need to trust me on this one," Josh responded. Cherie didn't reply. She was tired of being told repeatedly that her safety was at risk, but yet not trusted with the truth.

Josh took note of Cherie's silence and held her quietly for a little longer before he commented that she was still shaking. He did have a way of provoking her to say whatever was on her mind, so she admitted fear of being punished again. "Cherie," he said soothingly, "I never want you to be afraid of me. I have warned you in the past that it was not a wise idea to disobey me."

"So you will continue to treat me like a child?"

"I don't treat you like a child," Josh retorted.

"Well, then what do you call forbidding me to go out alone. And what do you call last night?"

"I think what happened last night had to do with you disobeying me, not you being a child."

"Yes, sir," she said, keeping her head down to avoid eye contact with him. Josh placed his hands upon her shoulders and pulled her close to his chest. For the first time, she allowed herself to relax against him. Inhaling deeply, she took in his masculine scent as her fingers toyed with the black curly hairs on his chest.

Josh thought about the trauma he was causing his wife. He had wanted to protect her from the fear and anxiety he was feeling, but maybe it wasn't such a good idea.

After several minutes, Josh spoke softly to her, "Cherie, I know you've had a rough couple of days. I didn't want to tell you this, but now I feel I must. I'm afraid my desire to protect you from worry is causing you more grief. Little one, I think you'll understand why I'm so concerned about your safety."

Already feeling emotionally drained, Cherie sat upright and looked into his eyes, questioning, "What is it Josh?"

Josh proceeded to explain the events of his first wife's death, that initially it was believed she died in the car accident. Evidence later proved that she had been murdered, but they were never able to identity her killer.. Pulling her closer to him, he went on to say he recently received anonymous letters threatening her life. In a consoling voice he added, "Cherie, I didn't want to have to tell you this. You have been through so much in your life. When I married you, I wanted to give you the life you deserve."

"Josh, you do give me a wonderful life. But how can you think that keeping this a secret from me is helping me? I wish you would have told me. I thought I had done something wrong, something to make you stop trusting me."

"No, little one, I have not stopped trusting you. We've only been married for a few months. I didn't want place a shadow over this time for you. It should be a happy time. Besides, you've had a lot to adjust too." Josh sighed and laid his head back, feeling remorse, "I had no idea someone had a vendetta against me or I wouldn't have brought you here. The letter indicated the person is angry with me. He said he killed my first wife to make me suffer, and he wants to kill you to further my suffering. I confided to Stephen and instructed him to heighten security on the ranch. That's why the gaits have been locked, and the new electrical fence on the grounds closest to the house."

"Is that why Stephen was in such a hurry to tell on me yesterday?" Cherie asked, still irritated.

"Actually, my love, Stephen tried to defend you. He knew he was obligated to tell me that you left unattended, but he wanted me to tell you the truth. I was so angry with you for disobeying me, that the truth wasn't an option last night."

"So what are we going to do?" Cherie inquired.

"I am going to do everything in my power to keep you safe until the police are able the catch this lunatic and lock him up. And that means a little cooperation from you little one," he exclaimed, punctuating it with a firm slap on her already tender behind. "I need you to listen to me and not get anymore ideas about going anywhere alone."

"I'm so sorry, Josh, and so afraid. I had no idea it was something like this. I won't go out alone anymore. But I still don't feel comfortable with Stephen."

Josh replied that Stephen was his oldest friend and most trusted, and that they had grown up together. "But, if you will not have him accompany you, then you will need to call me. If I can get away from the store I'll take you when you want to go. But never alone."

For the next couple weeks, Josh and Cherie did everything possible to make the best of a bad situation. The threatening letters continued to appear, at least one every other day. Some arrived by mail, but a couple were found on the ranch. One was left lying on the veranda, and another was found in the barn. According to the threat letters, the perpetrator's desire was to catch Cherie alone. Josh took time off from the store and they were together day and night. Cherie wasn't permitted to be alone for even a few minutes and was quite compliant with Josh. The more she learned of the situation, the more frightened she became. As the letters kept coming, the person behind the threats was getting more and more aggressive. A couple times the police thought they had a lead, but nothing ever materialized.

Two days later one of the newer ranch hands was found dead in the barn. He had been beaten to death with some sort of blunt object. His face and head were covered with massive bruises and blood. Police detectives swarmed about the ranch. They combed every inch of the ranch with the hope that the killer left clues to his identity. When the body was finally moved, a bloody note was discovered. The vulgarity in the note was beyond description. Cherie shook with terror as the detective read the killers words to them.

> *"This is just an example of what I am going to do to the bitch!!!!!*
> *She deserves everything that is coming to her!!!!*
> *And she is next!!!!!!!!!!"*

Josh tried to hide his panic as he kept his arm protectively around his trembling wife. The young ranch hand had caused no harm to anyone. He was friendly and kind, and had been an excellent worker. He certainly didn't deserve such a horrible fate. From that moment on, he decided he would not permit his young bride out of his sight. He would not be able to work in the store unless she was with him, so he would make arrangements for his assistant managers to run things until the killer was found.

The other ranch hands were questioned intensely. They all claimed that they really liked the new guy and were happy with his work. None of them could think of a reason that anyone would want to harm him. They also denied seeing anyone unusual in or around the barn, or on the grounds. Jed, one of the older men explained, "We were all goin' out to ride. Jessie started out with us then realized he forgot his water bottle. He thought it was odd because he said he remembered puttin' it in his saddle bag. He told us to go on and he'd catch up in a few minutes. So the rest of us went on, but we took it kinda slow, you know, to give him a chance to catch up. When he didn't come back, a couple of us decided to go back and make sure he was okay. You know, cuz he was ridin' the newest mare. She'd only been rode a couple times before. We thought maybe he was thrown or somethin'. We didn't find him on the path, so we came on back here, and this is what we found." He pointed over to the spot where Jessie's body was found, as he suppressed a sob.

Josh and Stephen decided that it would be best to keep Cherie off of the ranch as much as possible. They wanted to distract the killer by not keeping a regular schedule, so they made different plans each day. They also felt she would be safer in public places as opposed to the isolation on the ranch. Police officers were placed undercover on the ranch. They posed as ranch hands or security. The threatening letters continued, each seemed a little harsher than the previous one.

The first week Josh was off from the store, he took her sight seeing through out north western Montana. They used a different vehicle each day, and even borrowed Stephen and Jeanie's cars. Stephen was never far behind them during their outings. Josh was in constant contact with the local police department. The letters were dusted for fingerprints, but all of them came up clean. Whoever this person was, he was quite clever. Even though Cherie was included in the conversations with the police detective, she suspected that Josh was still not telling her everything. Finally, Cherie gathered up the courage to talk with Josh about her feelings. He surprisingly agreed and even permitted her to read the letters. Of course after reading the harsh verbiage in the letters, she almost wished she had let him continue to shelter her. The letters were graphically violent and displayed sheer hatred toward both Josh and Cherie. Hand written in black crayon, the latest letter read:

> *I have watched you two for long enough. I am tired of waiting and I plan to move soon. At first I was going to make it fast and painless, like it was with Leona, but I hate you even more. I know you have the police looking for me and that really pisses me off. You will suffer great pain before I finally have enough mercy to let you die. And you will see death as your only option when I'm finished with you. I promise you will not have that pretty little face or that cute little body when I am done with you. What I have in store for you is far worse than that nosey Jessie got. The nosey little snit. He should have minded his own business!"*

Jessie must have stumbled onto the killer when he returned to the barn, so he was beaten to death. Josh shuddered at the thought, knowing his wife was in danger of facing an even more horrible death. He knew he had to do everything within his power to protect her. At that point he decided it was no longer possible to keep her safe on the ranch. He and Stephen talked quietly and decided that Josh and Cherie would take an unannounced vacation. The hired help, other than Stephen, would not be told of their employer's departure until after the couple arrived safely in Ohio.

Josh quietly confided his plans to take Cherie to back to her apartment in Ohio. Cherie was surprised to learn that Josh had continued to keep the lease up on her old apartment. "I was afraid you would get out here with me and decide you were unhappy. So I kept your apartment for you. I planned to keep it for a year. That way if you decided you wanted to return home, you'd have a home to return to," he explained.

"I don't know what to say. You have done so much for me, it still overwhelms me."

The couple decided they would leave for Ohio by the following morning. The only person, other than Stephen who knew in advance of their departure was the police detective in charge of the investigation. Stephen could manage the ranch and any problems at the store while they were away. Josh and Cherie planned to carry no luggage. They did not want to alert anyone of their plans. As far as the help would be concerned, they were going on one of their daily outings.

~ CHAPTER 10 ~

REVENGE

Almost since her arrival on the ranch, Cherie had been asking Jeanie to teach her how to cook. She felt that she could never repay a man who has everything for all the kindness and love he had shown her, so she wanted to prepare him a romantic dinner. She thought that way she could at least show some of her gratitude. Because during her childhood there was barely enough to eat, learning to cook and prepare a meal was not an option. After she got out on her own money was tight, so Cherie didn't have the funds to purchase foods to practice cooking. Consequently, she lacked greatly in cooking skills. She barely knew the basics. Jeanie always had a logical excuse as to why she couldn't help Cherie.

Then, out of the blue Jeanie announced while serving breakfast that she was going to prepare a special lunch for the couple. She invited Cherie to join her in the kitchen. Josh and Cherie were to leave for Ohio later that day. Josh thought it would be a nice distraction while he made the final preparations and nodded to Cherie in approval. Cherie could barely conceal her excitement, "Yes, Jeanie, I would love to help you make lunch," she said.

As the couple finished their breakfast they were interrupted by one of the younger ranch hands. Dwayne came bursting into the dining room and breathlessly told Josh that one of his prize mares had fallen lame. Because Josh had been a paramedic and had worked in his father's veterinary clinic he was called upon to examine the horse and determine what further action needed to be taken. He instructed Dwayne to remain in the house with Cherie and Jeanie while he went to the barn. Josh kissed Cherie and told her he would only be a few minutes. Cherie helped Jeanie clear the breakfast dishes and then joined her in the kitchen. Jeanie seemed preoccupied as she found other menial tasks to do instead of beginning to prepare lunch. Dwayne puttered about in the dining room. He was obviously restless and uneasy. Jeanie's mood was suddenly different, dark and disinterested. All at once, without warning, Jeanie pulled a gun out of one of the kitchen drawers. "Miss Cherie," she said, her voice filled with contempt, "you are coming with us."

"Jeanie, what's wrong? Why are you doing this?"

"Well, Miss Cherie, you're not going to get a cooking lesson, but you are going to get a lesson. And 'little-one'," she said with sheer hatred in her voice, "I have to thank you for the idea. I wasn't sure how I was going to pull this off, but you gave me the idea, a way to get you alone," Jeanie spouted. "Josh has not let you out of his sight for weeks. So your hounding me to learn to cook gave me the ability to get you away from him for a few minutes. Good job, little one."

"What are you talking about, why do you have the gun?" Cherie asked.

"Shut up," Jeanie ordered. "You're coming with us, NOW!"

"I can't leave with you, Jeanie. I can only leave with Josh or Stephen because of the, well you know someone has threatened … my … life … Oh … my … it's you," Cherie concluded, her entire body suddenly shaking in terror as she faced the person who had sent the letters, the person who had been threatening her life. Cherie looked around, searching for Dwayne. He was standing quietly in the archway between the dining room and the kitchen, grinning sadistically.

"No wonder your husband beat you, you little bitch! You just don't know how to listen and do what you are told!" Jeanie yelled, and then Cherie's head felt like an atomic bomb exploded inside. It took her a few moments to realize that she had been struck across the face with the gun. She felt herself begin to sway as the room faded around her.

Minutes later Cherie awoke to cold water splashing across her face and upper body. When she opened her eyes she saw Jeanie standing over her with a water pitcher. "Get up!" she demanded. "There isn't time for a nap now. I have to get you out of here before your husband or that nosy Stephen comes back to the house. MOVE!"she shouted.

Cherie managed to get up onto her feet and stumbled as Jeanie pushed her forward, jabbing the gun firmly into her back. "What's happening? Where's Josh?" Cherie questioned, "What's that smell!"

"Shut up, little one," Jeanie shouted then she slapped Cherie on the right cheek with her free hand, "Now, straight to my car, and act like you are going of your own free will," Jeanie instructed. As they exited the back door of the house, Jeanie paused, and instructed Dwayne to go back into the house and get her purse. When he went back toward the pantry, Jeanie bent down and picked up a bottle lying on the corner of the patio floor. She removed the cap then lit a match and held it to the top of the bottle, then turned abruptly and threw it through the kitchen window. All of a sudden the kitchen went up inflames. "Hurry!" she instructed. "Get to the car." Jeanie had her car hidden close to the main gate so they had to run in the cold. That is, Jeanie ran, while pushing Cherie in front of her. She kept as close to the wooded area as possible until they passed the horse coral, all the while, Cherie could felt the presence of Jeanie's cold hard gun pressed into the middle of her back.

Cherie's clothes were soaking wet from the ice bath that Jeanie had given her in the house and her body was shaking violently. Once in the car, Jeanie sped out of the driveway not pausing to look back to see if they were followed. "We're going for a long drive. Your precious husband will never see you again. And, L I T T L E O N E," she said, punctuating every letter, "you already know you're going to die. But, if you try anything stupid your beloved husband will die a horrible death too!" Cherie sat quietly as she listened, and wondered, *how this could be happening to me*? She continued to shiver, in part from being in the cold with her clothes soaked with cold water, and in part from the utter terror she was feeling.

"Why Jeanie? Why are you doing this to me? Have I done something to hurt you? I don't understand," Cherie pleaded.

"Shut up little one!" Jeanie screamed. Then she reached over and struck Cherie in the face with her hand, causing her nose to bleed. "If I have to tell you again, I'll shoot you now and be done with it. I've loved him since we were teenagers, but I was never good enough for him. I did away with his first wife, that two timing witch. He was too good for her, her and her cheating ways. Couldn't he see that I was in love with him? He wouldn't even look my way. I have loved him since we were kids. I thought after she was out of the picture, but instead, he brought you home!" she shouted, her thoughts fragmented and repetitive. "I'm through giving him chances. This time I'm really going to make him suffer for ignoring me. And I'm going to make you suffer for taking away my last chance of happiness with him. After I think you've suffered enough, I'm going to kill you and bury your body so no one will ever find you. If he never finds your body, he can never collect off of your life insurance, like he did Leona's! He got so rich over her life insurance. And I did him the favor. Do you think he bothered to thank me for helping him get all that money!! No, the selfish bastard. He kept it all to himself. Do you know he has a huge policy on you too? But guess what bitch!!! He will never see a penny of it. There has to be a body first. I told all of the other help that he beat you up, so they would all think that is why you left. Maybe no one will even bother to look for you!"

Jeanie drove the rest of the day. Cherie didn't speak anymore. But her mind whirled with everything that was happening. *Did Josh only marry me to take out an insurance policy on me; is he going to profit from my death? Are him and Jeanie in on this together? Did she really kill Leona to help Josh?* Tears spilled as she thought, *I thought he really loved me. Could it be true? Is this why he wanted to marry me so fast? Is that how he got so rich?* Her thoughts raced with panic and despair. *If Josh doesn't love me, it doesn't matter what she does to me.*

The bleeding from her nose continued to flow so profusely that she had to use her sleeve to contain the blood. "Jeanie," she asked meekly, "Do you have a tissue or something?"

"Shut up Bitch!" Jeanie responded as she reached over and struck Cherie again in the face. The blow caused her nose to bleed even harder. Cherie had no way to control or contain the blood. She held her arm up against her face and nose but the blood soaked her clothing.

They continued to drive for hours. When Jeanie finally stopped for a bathroom break, she chose an older service station with the bathroom in the back of the building. "I can't take a chance on anyone seeing you, little one," she told Cherie. "And don't try anything stupid or I'll kill you now, and then go back for your precious Josh!" Before she permitted Cherie to get out of the car she struck her again in the face, a blow with such force that it cause the bleeding to start again.

While in the restroom, Cherie attempted to clean her face and clothes with some paper towels but Jeanie became impatient, "Come on, little one," she mocked as she grabbed Cherie's hair, "We don't have time for you to try to make yourself beautiful. You will never be beautiful again, I promise you that." She struck her hard in the mouth with the handle of her gun before she drug her out of the restroom and pushed her into the back seat of the car, "There, now I don't have to look at you, you whimpering little pansy. But don't even try to get out of the car, because I'll run you over if you do."

They drove into the night and didn't stop until they crossed the state line into South Dakota. On the other side of the state line Jeanie pulled into a small motel. As she stopped the motor to the car she ordered, "You let me do all of the talking. I'm already going to fry if I get caught, so it means nothing to me to kill you now. And don't even think about trying to run off. I've never missed a target. You won't be the first."

Obediently, Cherie walked beside Jeanie as they went in to register for a room. The elderly man at the registration desk gazed at the dried blood and bruises on Cherie's face and clothing. Cherie could see the question in his eyes but he didn't ask. Jeanie noticed his curiosity but offered him no explanation. "Nosy old man," she remarked after they left the building.

Jeanie pulled a thick rope out of her suitcase. "Go ahead and shower and use the john. Once I tie you up for the night you won't get untied until morning."

Cherie went obediently to the shower. She took her time in the shower, hoping for some idea or clue how to get help, but thoughts of despair and isolation reminded her that it didn't matter if she got help. If Josh didn't love her, there was no use fighting for her life. The pain in her head and face was so severe that it was hard to think. Just the light water running on her face caused excruciating pain.

When she got out of the shower, she looked in the mirror. Her reflection was frightening. She thought she looked like a monster with her face so swollen and bruised. She felt like crying. *Will Josh still love me now that I look like a freak?* She cried to herself. *If only I could tell Josh where I am.* Feeling sorry for herself, she started to cry for the first time since being abducted, but the salty tears caused her open wounds to hurt worse than they already did. *Kidnapped,* she thought, *I've just been kidnapped. And now I am going to lose my life. I shouldn't have married Josh. I truly wasn't good enough for him.* Cherie squeezed her eyes closed, trying to make it all go away. *Maybe this is my punishment for thinking I deserved someone like him, maybe he really did only marry me to collect off my life insurance. Maybe he is in on this with Jeanie.* When Cherie opened her eyes, she saw the reflection of Jeanie standing behind her, "Hurry it up little one," she mocked.

Embarrassed to have Jeanie look at her while she was not dressed, Cherie promptly wrapped in the huge white towel provided by the motel. Jeanie tossed one of Cherie's nightgowns at her and ordered her to put it on. When Jeanie saw Cherie's expression of recognition, she smirked, "Yes, I packed some of your things before we left. I knew you and Josh were planning to leave without any luggage. They'll never know. The house and everything in it was destroyed by the fire. I made certain the fire and explosion would be severe enough to completely gut the house."

Jeanie roughly tied Cherie's wrists and feet together, and then tied the ropes to the head and footboards. Cherie couldn't move. "There," she said. "Now I can get some sleep without worrying about you trying something stupid," she hissed while patting her gun. "Oh, and by the way, don't even think about screaming. I have already killed three people. That nosy new ranch boy, he should have minded his own business. And the last one, well I just didn't want any excess baggage to deal with." Jeanie turned to walk away, then abruptly turned back and slapped Cherie several times on her face, "There LITTLE ONE that is for thinking you might be able to get away."

Cherie's mind raced. *Jeanie said she had already killed. Dwayne, she must have killed Dwayne. The smell, it was gasoline. That must have been what Dwayne was doing when he allegedly went back for Jeanie's purse.* Cherie knew she was in grave danger. Jeanie had calculated and planned this for a long time. It seemed she had all bases covered. Was she setting Cherie up to believe that Josh didn't love her, or was it true?

I have to try, I have to believe that he loves me. I have to believe, I just have to believe.

Jeanie woke Cherie at 5:30 am the following morning. She was already up and dressed. She untied Cherie's hands and feet and ordered her to get up and get dressed quickly. It didn't seem to concern her that Cherie's extremities were completely numb from being bound so tightly all night or that her arms were stiff from being bound and tied above her head. She laughed when Cherie nearly fell as she got up to go into the bathroom. In the bathroom, Cherie noticed Jeanie had left her makeup case on the counter. There were several lipsticks inside the case, so with the hope she wouldn't notice one missing, Cherie took one and carefully hid it in her jeans.

"I'm ready Jeanie," Cherie said quietly. Jeanie ordered Cherie to grab the suitcase and again, reminded her not to try anything foolish. When they were both in the car, Cherie doubled over and cried out on pain.

"What's the matter with you?" Jeanie asked.

"Jeanie, I need to use the restroom again before we go," Cherie pleaded.

"You already had your chance!"

"My stomach gets upset when I get nervous, please Jeanie, just a few minutes please," Cherie pleaded.

Jeanie finally relented and permitted Cherie to go back into the room, "If you're not back in five minutes, I'm coming after you and it is not going to be pretty."

After Cherie closed and locked the bathroom door, she took out the lipstick and wrote 'HELP' in large letters on the mirror then beneath it wrote the license number of Jeanie's car. Reluctantly she removed the gold watch Josh had bought her before they were married and left it on the sink. Josh had it engraved before he gave it to her, so if it was found Josh would know without a doubt that Cherie was the one who left the message. Cherie locked the bathroom door from the inside before she closed it in case Jeanie came back in to inspect. She was surprised to see that Jeanie was still waiting in the car. Before she locked the door to the motel room she tossed the room key inside. One more attempt to prevent Jeanie from seeing her note.

When she stepped outside of the motel room, Cherie noticed Jeanie was still in the car and appeared to be looking straight ahead. She took a big chance and ran into the registration office. Almost as though Jeanie read her thoughts, she got out of the car and screamed, "Don't do it!"

Once inside the office, Cherie was fully aware that Jeanie was coming behind her. She flipped the lock on the door as she shouted breathlessly. "Mr, Mr. Please help me, that woman has kidnapped me and is going to kill me. She has a gun and she's going to kill me. Please call the police. Hurry!" The old man understood the panic in her voice because he immediately picked up the phone and dialed 911. Jeanie was furious when she found the door locked. She used the butt end of her gun to break the glass then reached in and unlocked the door.

When she entered the building she was quite the actress. She draped her arm around Cherie's shoulders and cooed, "Oh, there you are sis. You frightened me. I thought I had lost you. Come on now, we have to get going if we are going to make it home before nighttime." Then she looked at the old man and mocked, "Sir, please excuse my little sister. She has some problems," then pointed to Cherie's head and added, "If you know what I mean."

The old man continued to hold the phone and wait for the police to answer his call. Jeanie insisted, "Sir, you really don't need to do that." But the old man ignored her plea and began to explain the situation to the police officer on the other end of the phone line. Jeanie rushed behind the counter after the man and grabbed the phone from his hand. After she pulled the cord out of the wall jack and threw it, she began to beat the man in the face and head with the butt end of her gun. She slammed him over and over until the old man crumpled to the floor. Blood was gushing out of his nose and mouth and from several huge gashes on his head.

Cherie tried to run while Jeanie was beating the old man but as quickly as she ran out the door, Jeanie grabbed hold of her arm. She practically dragged her to the car and pushed her inside. Inside the car, she yelled, "You stupid little bitch!" then began to strike Cherie in the face and head with the same blood covered weapon she had beaten the old man with. She finally stopped beating Cherie when she lost consciousness.

Jeanie grumbled and complained to herself as she drove. She took back county roads as much as possible to avoid being caught. "Now thanks to you, bitch, they'll know what way we are going and what we're driving. She pounded the steering wheel in anger. "I have to think, I have to do something," she said, half to herself and half aloud. As she neared the next town, she noticed a small used car lot. She looked over at her unconscious prisoner. *Um*, she thought, *if I can just keep her unconscious for another hour or two, I can make this work.*

Jeanine turned off the main road and parked the car in a small wooded alcove. She quietly got out of the car and went to the trunk. She pulled out the ropes she had used to tie Cherie the night before and tied her hands and feet together. As she turned to leave, she paused then turned abruptly and struck Cherie in the back of her head. *There, that ought to keep her out for a little while longer.* She then covered Cherie with a blanket and locked the car.

The next few days were completely a blur to Cherie. The beatings Jeanie had given her had left her in a stuperous state. She barely remembered being tied up and then pulled out of the car and shoved into another one. She would wake up for a few minutes. When she tried to look around she couldn't see because everything was fuzzy. Then, that same excruciating pain would return and everything would go black again.

~ CHAPTER 11 ~

PAINFUL AWAKENING

Cherie had no idea how much time had passed or where she was when she awoke. She was lying on a sofa in a strange room. Her hands were tied together and secured to something above her head and her feet were tied together so she couldn't move. Disoriented, she tried to look around but her vision was still cloudy. The room was filled with a dreadful stench. When she sniffed the air she suddenly felt ill. The air reeked with the smell of human urine and feces. Cherie tried to take a deep breath but couldn't, and the pain in her chest was growing more intense with each attempt to breath. Every part of her body hurt. Her face and head throbbed. And she was bound so tightly that she could barely feel her hands and feet.

As her vision began to clear, Cherie recognized the fireplace in the farmhouse where she and Josh picnicked the day she accepted his proposal. *Funny*, she thought, *this is where my marriage plans began, and this is where my life will end*. She wanted to cry but was too weak. Her eyes stung and burned, partly from the sadness she was feeling and partly from the odor.

Cherie was trying to wiggle around and get some circulation back into her hands and feet when the realization hit her. *The horrible odor is coming from me*. Her clothes were wet with urine and she had soiled herself sometime in her oblivion. Cherie was mortified. At that very moment she wanted to give up and die, and then she feared that if she did give into death she would be found in that awful condition. *I must hold on, at least until I can get into some clean clothes*, she told herself.

When Cherie turned her head she saw Jeanie sitting in a chair across the room. "I see you are finally awake. You slept the entire trip. How are you feeling?"

Appalled that Jeanie could pretend to be so sweet, Cherie couldn't think of a word to say in return. The room was suddenly very hot, and it was getting more and more difficult to breath. She tried to sit up but the ropes kept her restrained. "Please Jeanie," her voice barely above a whisper, "can I go to the restroom and get cleaned up?"

Jeanie untied the ropes and helped Cherie to stand. Her hands and feet were still numb and she was unbelievably weak and shaky. It was hard to put her arms down to her sides. They were stiff and almost frozen over her head. The room spun around and Cherie had to sit back down. Jeanie smirked, "I don't think I have to worry about you trying to run off again. We're in the middle of nowhere and you are much too weak." Cherie had no choice but to accept Jeanie's help to get up the stairs to the bathroom. It was so difficult to breathe that she had to stop every couple steps to catch her breath. Jeanie offered no patience for Cherie's condition. She became more irritated and impatient each time Cherie needed to stop and catch her breath, "Come on bitch, I don't have all day!" she shouted as she pulled and tugged on Cherie's sore arms.

The warm bath felt incredibly good on her battered body. The exhaustion and the soothing feeling of the bath resulted in Cherie falling asleep in the bathtub. Cherie was not sure how much time passed by when she awoke to find Jeanie tugging on her arm, "Come on, get out of here," she said cruelly. "You've been in here long enough and I have stuff to do."

Reluctantly Cherie climbed out of the bathtub and dried off. The clean clothing Jeanie handed her was from her home in Montana. It reminded Cherie of how she missed Josh. Cherie silently prayed to God that she would live to see him again.

"What are you doing," Jeanie demanded.

"Praying," Cherie replied meekly.

Agitated, Jeanie informed her, "There's no need to pray because not even God can help you now." To Jeanie's dismay, God did hear Cherie's prayer. Within moments after she told Cherie it would do her no good to pray, the two women heard male voices in the kitchen. Cherie felt a glimmer of hope. *This may be the first time in my life that I will be glad to see Dean and Jeff.* The surprised look on Jeanie's face told Cherie that there was no way the guys were a part of Jeanie's plan.

Cherie thought, *Jeanie had no idea that anyone lived here.* She could only hope they would not take this opportunity to inflict more pain upon her. After all, her husband did force them to live here.

"Where did all of this stuff come from?" Cherie heard one of them say. Jeanie heard them too. She rushed down the steps ahead of Cherie and dashed to her purse for the gun. She then went into the kitchen she pointed the gun at the two men. Cherie slowly made her way down the stairs and to the kitchen. From behind Jeanie, Cherie saw her former tormenters with their hands in the air staring down the barrel of Jeanie's gun. Dean was in front, closest to

Jeanie. Jeff glanced up and saw Cherie weaving unsteadily behind Jeanie. "Cherie," he gasped. At that point, Jeff turned abruptly and dashed out the back door.

Jeanie moved closer to Dean and grabbed his arm. She pushed him toward the basement door and ordered him down the stairs. With a gun pointed to the back of his head he had little choice but to comply. She locked the basement door then turned to Cherie and ordered her back onto the soiled sofa. Jeanie then quickly tied the ropes around her hands and feet. Jeanie instructed Cherie, "Do not try to move, little one," then struck her several times in the face before she left the house. Cherie assumed Jeanie was going to find Jeff. A few moments later Jeanie returned to the house. She was furious that she had left her keys in her car and now her car was gone.

Angrily, she slapped Cherie in the face. It was already difficult for Cherie to breathe so the added blow that caused her nose to bleed again made it even worse. She gasped for air as Jeanie struck her several times in the chest with the butt end of her gun. "Damn you bitch!" she shouted. "You knew they were here. They recognized you. I may have to kill you sooner than I had planned you little bitch! But you will suffer first! You will pay for all of the suffering you've caused me. And, if I'm going to go to jail for you, I'm going to make it worth my while!" The continued blows to her face, chest and abdomen caused Cherie to lose consciousness again.

Outside several federal agents and the local sheriff silently surrounded the house. Jeff had led them into the farm by a small back lane that was barely visible to those unfamiliar with the land. Two ambulance units sat in the back, beyond the trees and out of sight. The agents had been ordered to maintain their positions and silence until further orders, unless they heard shots fired. If an anytime shots were fired, they were to obtain immediate entrance to the house. The plan was to try to steal quietly into an unused side door and take Jeanie by surprise.

In the house, Jeanie paced and ranted at Cherie even though she was still unconscious, "This is all your fault, bitch, all your fault. You knew there were people living her and you didn't bother to say a word to me about them. Well, I know I am going to fry, but I will not let you live through this!" she shouted as her agitation escalated. At the moment Jeanie turned and aimed to fire the gun at Cherie, Dean burst through the basement door. Jeanie, already in the process of firing the gun turned abruptly toward Dean as the gun went off. The bullet hit Dean in the abdomen and he collapsed to the floor. Jeanie, disgusted that she missed her original target, turned to finish the job she had started when a shot fired from outside the living room window struck her in the back.

~ CHAPTER 12 ~

DAYS OF ANGUISH

Tears streamed down Josh's face as he stared at the hot ashy remains of his home, still engulfed in flames. "Cherie!" he cried out. He felt lost and grief-stricken. Cherie and Jeanie were in the kitchen. Jeanie was supposed to be giving Cherie a cooking lesson when he left the house for just a couple minutes to check on one of the horses that had fallen lame. For the sake of pretenses, Josh and Cherie decided for Cherie to go ahead with the long coveted cooking lesson. The plan was for them to leave the ranch in the early afternoon. Cherie had been asking Jeanie to teach her to cook for months. Today she announced at breakfast that she was making a special lunch, and asked Cherie if she would like to assist.

During breakfast, one of the ranch hands rushed into the dining room and interrupted their breakfast to announce that one of the prize mares had fallen ill. With Josh's medical background it was necessary that he go and check on the horse. He reassured Cherie that she should be okay with Jeanie for just a few minutes while he assessed the mare and instructed Dwayne to remain in the house with the ladies until he returned.

It happened only moments after Josh left the house. Josh and Stephen heard the thundering explosion and raced back to the house, only to find it completely consumed by the blaze. The heat emitted from the fire was so intense that it was impossible for anyone to get near the house. It left no hope for anyone in the house to be alive. Immediately the ranch hands went to work to try to contain the blaze.

The fire department was summoned, but it seemed like hours before they finally arrived. Huge orange flames shot from the center of the house as the roof and walls collapsed. Josh was oblivious to the crews of firemen and police officers who swarmed around him. He could only think that his wife was in the house when the explosion took place. Stephen put his hand on his boss's shoulder, "Josh, come with me. The police need a statement. You're not going to do her any good here. Let's go." Numbingly, Josh followed his friend.

The police detective introduced himself as Detective Gray. He questioned Josh and Stephen, as well as the hired help, about any recent unusual events. Josh didn't speak, so Stephen brought the detective up to date about the letters they had been receiving for the past two months. The hate letters that threatened Cherie's life. Stephen told the detective he should speak with Detective Browning, the detective handling the case.

Josh bent forward, buried his face in his hands and sobbed. The detective placed his hand on Josh's shoulder, "We will find whoever did this, Mr. Tolsten. I promise you that," Detective Gray said, trying to reassure Josh.

Josh's voice exploded like a roaring train, "What the hell are you talking about, you people told me that after my first wife was killed, and you still haven't had a lead! This son of a bitch has something against me. Why can't he take it out on me! Cherie has never hurt anyone in her life. I was supposed to be protecting her and I left her alone. Now she has lost her life. Now she is gone, because I left her alone," his voice trailed of despondently.

"Mr. Tolsten, I know this is a bad time for you. I don't mean to be insensitive, but I must ask some more questions to get an investigation going," the detective pleaded.

"Yes, I know. If you think you can find him, I'll cooperate. But before you take him in, I want my time with him."

"Yes, sir. I understand your wife brought a vagrant home with her a few weeks ago. Do you think there could be any connection?"

"No," Josh responded. "The homeless person was quite ill. He stayed overnight in the one of the cabins. When Cherie went to check on him the next morning he was nearly dead. We sent him to the hospital by air squad and he passed away within minutes of his arrival there. Cherie had a heart of gold. She couldn't bear to see him suffering, so she took him in. She never hurt anyone. Why would someone want to hurt her?"

"You said the perp has something against you. Do you know of anyone who is angry with you?" Detective Gray asked.

"No, that's the problem. I can't think of who it could be."

"Sir, you own the Western Store in town, is that correct?" Detective Gray asked.

"Yes, what does that have to do with this?" Josh demanded.

"Any disgruntled employees? You know, have you fired or reprimanded anyone?"

"No, no, no," Josh swore, "My employees are loyal. I don't ever recall reprimanding or firing anyone."

After the detective finished questioning Josh and Stephen, he excused himself and began to question the other residents and employees of the ranch. Josh and Stephen overheard Detective Gray's assistant question as they walked away, "Isn't it odd that this is the second wife this man has mysteriously lost. Have you ever looked into his possible motives?"

Josh was too grief stricken to respond to the comment but Stephen was irate. "Excuse me," he said as he caught up to the two detectives, "Would you mind telling me why you had to say that where Josh could hear you? Can't you see that he's devastated?"

"Well," the second detective said, "It is strange. And he wouldn't be the first husband to kill his wife to collect the insurance moneys."

"Okay," Stephen responded, "Why don't you check out the amount of life insurance Josh collected from Leona's death. Then why don't you keep this in mind. If the police department had done their job and caught Leona's killer, then Cherie wouldn't be dead right now." Stephen was furious that anyone could even consider the idea that Josh could be a murderer. His anger continued to grow as he chastised the detectives, "Your people put him through so much by looking at him as a suspect! And so much wasted time!"

Detective Gray gave his partner an irritated glance then apologized profusely, "Sir, please accept my apologies for my partner's over vigilance. Please be assured that Mr. Tolsten is not a suspect in this case at this time."

Stephen, too angry to respond, turned abruptly and walked back to his friend's side.

The detectives interviewed each member of the ranch team, only to discover nothing more than they already knew. No one saw, or admitted to seeing anything unusual or any strange person on the ranch in the past few days.

Two days later, after the fire marshal and police investigators combed the remains of the house, Detectives Browning and Gray requested a meeting with Josh and Stephen. Josh and Stephen were temporally residing in the west cabin, the only cabin with two bedrooms.

"Mr. Tolsten," Detective Gray started. "I have some news that may offer you a little hope. However, please understand, this is only a preliminary result. This may change with further investigation."

"What is it?" Josh demanded impatiently. Josh's mood had been dark and ugly since the fire. He was in no mood to have some young kid patronize him.

"Mr. Tolsten, Stephen, our preliminary findings show no trace of you wife or your maid within the remains of the house. We did however find remains of a male body. "

Josh suddenly came to life and sprang from his chair, "What the hell are you talking about Gray! Are you telling me she's not dead? Where is she if she wasn't in the house?" Josh asked.

"I don't know where she is, but at this time it appears neither she nor your maid were in the house at the time of the explosion. Did your maid have a car on the premises, Mr. Tolsten?"

"Yes, she did have a car, but I thought she had taken it in for servicing." Josh paced in distress, his clenched fists white with stress.

Stephen attempted to calm his boss, "Josh, calm down man. You have to think. Where could she be? We searched the entire grounds when we were looking for the perp."

"You need to get another search together, and cover every inch if this ranch. I want you there leading the search. We have no idea what we are looking for, but look for something! Some clue!" Josh demanded.

"Yes, sir, I'm on it," Stephen replied.

"Stephen, she was afraid of you. Be careful if, I mean when you find her," Josh instructed.

"Josh, afraid of me? Why on earth?" Stephen quizzed, looking puzzled.

"I'll explain another time, just find my wife. If she's missing and Jeanie's missing, then where are they?"

All three men stopped short and stared open mouthed at each other.

"Oh shit! Right here under our noses all this time!" Josh exclaimed.

Detective Gray was already on the radio to put out an APB on Jeanie and Cherie.

Josh heard him describing Jeanie and his wife, "consider the taller one armed and dangerous ... No, we don't have a clue of their destination." Gray paused briefly to ask Josh to describe Jeanie's car.

Stephen and Josh both questioned the loyalty of the rest of the staff before organizing a second search. "Did Jeanie have any of the other staff helping her?" Josh instructed him to take a couple of the ranch hands, but to be sure that he supervised all activities. "And Stephen, watch your back." Detective Browning stopped Stephen and instructed him to await police back up. The detective called the precinct and asked for every available officer to participate in the search. There was little doubt that Jeanie and Cherie were long gone, but they were hoping for some sort of clue as to Jeanie's plans.

~ CHAPTER 13 ~

NEW HOPE

Detective Gray's voice beamed with hope as he spoke with Josh over the telephone. "Josh, we have a lead!" he exclaimed.

"What is it, Gray? Come on, don't keep me in suspense. This is my wife you know!" Josh shouted impatiently. The more time went on without news of Cherie's whereabouts, the more difficult he became to deal with. Impatience was Josh's best quality over the past few days. He raged, paced and yelled at the smallest provocation. Most of the time Detective Gray chose to speak with Stephen. But this time, he felt strongly that Josh should hear the news first.

"They found the word *help*, and a Montana license plate number written in lipstick in a slum motel, just on the other side of the South Dakota line. The license plate is registered to your former housekeeper. Josh, we also found something else we need you to see."

"What?"

"A gold watch was left on the sink in the bathroom where the note was written. I need you to identify the watch," Detective Gray added.

Josh felt dread rise in his throat. He wanted to scream. "Gray, do you think that means Jeanie has harmed her? Cherie loved that watch. She would never leave it behind deliberately."

"Oh, on the contrary Josh. Your wife is one smart little lady. My guess is she was well aware of what she was doing, and planted the watch to help us locate her. She locked the bathroom door behind her, and locked the key in the room. She thought it out quite well." Detective Gray praised Cherie's efforts to aid in her own rescue. "But Josh, there is one more thing you need to know about."

"What is it," Josh asked impatiently.

"The clerk in the registration office was severely wounded. He was struck several times in the face and head with a blunt object. He had called for help, but Jeanie beat him senseless. He's still unconscious, and he's not expected to live," Gray added. Josh could hear the sound of peril in Gray's voice.

"Stephan and I will catch the next flight out. We should be there in just a couple hours," Josh said hurriedly. He promptly summoned Stephen to aid with the preparations for their flight. He instructed Stephen to assign Doug, the senior ranch hand to be in charge of the ranch and security until their return.

Josh and Stephen were able to secure a flight to South Dakota within the hour to view the motel room and identify the watch. Josh was positive the watch was the one he had given Cherie as a gift just a few short months ago.

Detective's Gray and Browning, as well as the local sheriff met Josh and Stephen in the motel room. Detective Browning reassured Josh that at least now they knew what direction the two women were traveling. Gray called the positive ID on the watch into his precinct and requested an update on the APB. They were then advised that the elderly man had passed away because of the injuries from Jeanie beating him.

When there was nothing more for Josh and Stephen to do in South Dakota, they left the small motel with the intent to fly back to Montana. In route to the airport Josh suddenly exclaimed, "Oh, MY! They're headed to Ohio! Stephen, we have to get to southern Ohio, and we have to go now. You call the airport and get us a flight to as close to the Ohio River as possible. There's a small airport in Cadiz, Ohio. It is just about fourth-five minutes from the farm. We can fly into the Cleveland Airport, and then take a small commuter flight into Cadiz. You arrange for the plane and I'll arrange to have a car waiting for us," Josh's speech was manic as he spouted off orders to Stephen.

"Josh, what on earth are you talking about?" Stephen demanded of his boss.

"Just move!" he ordered. "I'll explain on the plane. There isn't much time. I'll call Detective Gray and let him know."

Josh was angry while talking to Detective Gray. "Yes, yes I know this is now a federal case. But I want you there too. We have to move now. I know where she is. At Jeanie's request, I bought her aging uncle's farm. He was ill and needed the money for his health care. Or so she said. Jeanie thinks the farm is uninhabited. It would be the prefect hide out. We are going to fly into a small airport in Cadiz, Ohio. It is only a short drive from there."

"Josh, wait a minute. Let's organize this a little better. I'll arrange the flights and get us there. You can fly with us. That way we can work together on this. I need to make some calls. Because it is federal jurisdiction, I have to let them in on what we are doing," Detective Gray insisted.

Josh agreed, but requested they can do that once they were in the air. He said a silent prayer thanking God for this chance to find her, and prayed that Cherie was still alive and unharmed. *How can I ever make this up to her*, he thought to himself. He had placed her in harms way by leaving her alone, and now he could only hope and pray that she was alive.

The two detectives boarded the flight with Josh and Stephen. The detectives had gotten an emergency warrant from the court that mandated an immediate flight. They were to land at the Akron-Canton Airport, which was significantly closer than Cleveland. The FBI was in charge of securing a commuter flight from the airport to Cadiz, where FBI agents and the local sheriff's department would await their arrival.

While they were in the air, Detective Browning received a call from a federal agent who he had been working with. He spoke quietly, not wanting to alarm any of his companions or the other passengers, but his facial expressions did alert the others of cause for concern. When the call was discontinued, he quietly asked Josh to accompany him to the men's restroom.

The two men walked to the back of the plane to the men's room. Inside the men's room, Detective Browning warned, "Josh, I brought you back here because I don't want you to make a scene. I understand how upset you are, and I'd be beside myself too. But, we don't want to alert the rest of the passengers to what is going on." Detective Browning knew from Josh's expression that he had better not push any farther. "That call was from the feds. They are awaiting our arrival in Cadiz. A young man named Jeff rushed into the local police station and reported dangerous and suspicious activities on the farm. He described Jeanie, and recognized your wife. He called her by name. He said Jeanie has a gun and Cherie looks pretty battered. Apparently Jeanie was not aware that someone was residing at the farm. When she discovered the two young men she pulled her gun on them. Jeff said he was behind his buddy, Dean and took the chance of running for help. He's not sure of what happened to his friend."

Josh felt a dark shadow of doom. Impatiently he asked, "What if Jeanie was angered by Jeff escaping and decided to kill them both. How do we know if she's still alive? What if she's not?" Josh kept firing questions about his wife's condition much too rapidly for the detective to answer. "What did he mean by battered? What did she do to my wife?" Josh's anguish continued to mount.

The detective hesitated, "Josh, when Jeff called, he said she was alive, but didn't look good. But," he reinforced, "We know she was alive and alert. You have to hold on to that thought and have faith. When we land, we are going to have a crew of paramedics waiting to accompany us to the farm." Detective Browning, being nearly the same size as Josh took him by the shoulders and said firmly, "Keep your faith man. We've come this far. We are going to get her back. You just need to follow our lead now, and let us do our job. The feds are on their way too. And remember, the feds are well equipped to handle kidnappings."

"I know. And I know I haven't been that easy to deal with. I lost one wife, and for the past few days, I've thought I had lost Cherie. And to top it off, it's all my fault. I should have never left her alone, I failed her, I couldn't protect her..." Josh said apologetically.

"Josh, it's not your fault. Your former housekeeper is obviously a very sick and malicious woman. You had no way of knowing." The two men left the men's room and returned to their seats. Detective Gray and Stephen looked at them with puzzled expressions. Josh quietly informed them of the latest news.

The four men were silent for the remainder of the flight. Josh's mind took him back several months in time, to the day he met Cherie for the first time. He remembered her innocence and sincerity, and how she became so flustered when he was kind to her. He knew at that moment there was something incredibly special about her. "You know," he said, breaking the silence, "Cherie's an incredible young woman. There is no other like her. When I met several months ago, I fell in love with her immediately. There's not a lot of people in this world today with a character and value system like hers. We met in a small diner. Even in her waitress uniform and her hair pinned up she was the most beautiful young woman I'd ever seen. Not the kind of beauty that is painted on, but pure and simple beauty, inside and out. I wanted to take her and protect her, and give her the life she deserved." Tears were streaming down Josh's face as he said hopelessly, "But, because of my stupidity she is worse off than ever before." Josh leaned forward in the seat and buried his face in his hands.

Stephen placed his hand on his bosses shoulder. "Josh, look man, she knows you love her. You couldn't have known that Jeanie was the culprit. None of us could have known. She gave no clues."

Josh pulled himself together as the plane landed. A chopper was waiting for them to transport the four men to the small Cadiz airport. "Remember

Josh," Detective Browning instructed, "When we arrive at the farm, you must stay back and let the feds do their job." Josh nodded in understanding. Detective Browning knew only too well that Josh would want to burst into the farm house and attempt to subdue Jeanie, gun or no gun.

The small Cadiz airport was essentially deserted when the chopper landed. There was one federal agent in an unmarked car waiting for the four men. The agent explained that because of Jeff's description of Jeanie's behavior, and Cherie's battered appearance, the swat team went on to the farm. Jeff knew the grounds well and could show them a way in to prevent Jeanie's knowledge of them being there. They were planning to take Jeanie by surprise for fear that if she saw them she would harm her two hostages.

~ CHAPTER 14 ~

IS IT OVER?

Two paramedics were wheeling a cart to their ambulance unit when Josh and the others arrived at the farm. Josh's heart raced in panic, *Oh God, please let her be alive*, He silently prayed. He jumped out of the car before it stopped moving, nearly causing himself injury. Ignoring the fact that he stumbled out of the moving vehicle, he ran over to the medic unit. Relieved to see that it was Dean on the cart, Josh took a breath for the first time. Dean was barely conscious and gasping or breath. Josh looked helplessly at the medics. "Where's my wife," he asked meekly. "Is she still alive? Please, tell me she's alive?"

One medic responded, "She's still in the house. There are two other medics with her. We must get this man to the hospital. He's been shot and is bleeding out." Josh didn't hear anything else; he was already running toward the house.

Cherie was sitting on a chair in the kitchen when Josh burst into the back door. He didn't have a clear view of his wife because she was being examined by the medics. "Cherie," Josh exclaimed, his voice barely a whisper. The two men caring for her looked up at Josh when they heard his voice. As they stepped back from Cherie, Josh gasped in shock at the sight if his young wife. Her face was battered with cuts and bruises, almost beyond recognition. Her nose was swollen severely and appeared broken and deformed. Both eyes and the surrounding areas were deep purple in discoloration. Her right eye was open only a small slit from the swelling. Her face and clothes were soiled with blood.

Cherie attempted to stand and meet her husband's embrace but her legs wouldn't support her. She collapsed into his arms. "Josh," she said weakly with broken speech, "I ... didn't ... think ... I'd ever ... see ... you again."

Josh picked her up and held her close to him. When he felt how weak and frail she was, he sat down on the chair and held her on his lap. "I'm here now, baby girl," he said soothingly while he tried to suppress his own sobs. He wanted to caress her, to brush away her pain but he didn't know where to touch her. "My God, what has she done to you?"

Cherie was much thinner than a week ago when she was accosted from their burning home, and severely dehydrated. She sat quietly in her husband's arms, struggling to breath, but taking comfort that he was there. Josh could hear the rattling and wheezing from his wife's lungs as he held her. He gently brushed his hand across her forehead. "Baby girl, we have to get you to a hospital. You're burning up."

"Josh ... please ... don't ... leave me. Let ... me stay ... with you ... please," Cherie pleaded with gasping breaths.

"I won't leave you. I promise, I'll be right beside you. But we have to let the medics get you to the hospital," he said softly. The medics brought the cart over and Josh gently laid his wife down. Once she was lying on the cart, Cherie lost consciousness. One paramedic told Josh the oxygen in her blood was dangerously low as he carefully placed an oxygen mask on her battered face. The medics lifted the head of the cart to try and ease her breathing.

"Sir, we need you to ride in the front of the ambulance," one of the medics said to Josh, as he attempted to direct Josh to the front cab of the unit.

"Absolutely not. I promised her I would be right by her side, and that's where I'll stay," Josh demanded.

Detective Gray overheard the argument and ran to Josh's defense, "Look guys, put yourself in his place. His wife was accosted from their home and is barely alive when he finds her."

The older medic nodded to his partner then shouted, "Okay, okay let's go. We have to get this lady to the hospital!"

Josh rode in the back of the unit and held Cherie's hand. He quietly reassured her that he was there each time she stirred, as she faded in and out of consciousness "I won't leave you," he said over and over. Several times while she was unconscious, Josh heard Cherie mumble something that sounded like, "life insurance."

The emergency room staff swarmed around his wife. Several times the nursing staff asked Josh to leave while they worked with Cherie, but he adamantly refused. Finally, one of the nurses spoke up, "Look, the man has nearly lost his wife. Let him be with her." Josh silently thanked the woman when their eyes met.

The nurses and the doctors fired question after question at Josh about his wife's medical history and the events of the past week. Unfortunately, he wasn't able to help them with any history of what had happened in the past week, other than she was kidnapped and severely beaten.

The x ray report revealed that Cherie had pneumonia in both lungs and there was internal bleeding within her chest wall. Cardiac tests showed her heart was badly bruised from being struck repeatedly in the chest with a blunt object. Intravenous fluids were being given because she was so dehydrated. The doctor said she must not have been given anything to eat or drink during the entire past week, and the way her lab test looked, it was a miracle that she was alive. Cherie's condition was described as critical.

After the emergency room staff worked for hours to try and stabilize her, Cherie was admitted to the surgical intensive care unit. They were uncertain if her internal chest injuries were going to require surgical repair. The physician's were concerned that she could not survive surgery in her weakened condition.

Before she was transferred to the ICU, the emergency room physician, Dr. Blakesmit discussed the possibility that Cherie may need to be transferred up north to a trauma center. "But we are afraid she won't survive the trip right now." He cautioned Josh that the next twenty-four to forty-eight hours were critical for Cherie's survival. "Her body had been brutally battered which as caused severe damage to her internal chest wall and heart. She has advanced pneumonia in all lobes of her lungs. And, besides the malnutrition and dehydration, she has lost a tremendous amount of blood. We are pumping it into her as quickly as we can."

Hours later, Stephen and the two detectives arrived at the hospital. Jeff was with them. Josh stepped just outside of Cherie's small cubicle, but wouldn't leave sight of her. Stephen spoke quietly, "Jeanie is dead. Apparently she decided it was time to kill Cherie. But when she aimed the gun at her, Dean, who had been locked in the basement miraculously managed to break through the door. They were still unable to determine exactly what happened after that because Dean took the shot. He has been unconscious since then. The federal agents heard the gun shot and entered the home through the back door. Jeanie aimed at them but they fired first. Jeanie was shot and pronounced dead at the scene.

Josh sighed with relief. "Well, at least we don't have to worry about her coming back again." "

After a few moments of silence Josh managed to ask, "How is Dean?"

"Well," Detective Gray interrupted, "He was shot in the abdomen and is currently in surgery. That's all we know. But he saved your wife's life."

"If she lives," Josh said sadly, "If she lives."

Stephen interrupted, "Josh, don't think like that man. You need to believe she will be okay."

The men exchanged a few other words about the details of the rescue before Josh excused himself to return to his wife's side. As he turned to go he looked at Jeff, "I don't know how I can ever thank you and your friend enough for saving her life."

The first day after Cherie was rescued was touch and go. The doctors remained uncertain that she would survive. Her vital signs were unstable and her temperature didn't drop below 104 degrees. Josh refused to leave her side. Around midnight that night, the alarm went off on her heart monitor. Her heart was racing dangerously fast – beating over one hundred and seventy times a minute. The doctors and nurses worked for over an hour to stabilize her. They were satisfied when they finally got her heart rate to drop down to one hundred beats per minute.

Dr. Black, Cherie's cardiologist, told Josh that the episode may have been precipitated by pain. "Even though she's unconscious, she is still acutely aware of pain. Her internal injuries are actually more severe than those injuries you can see. We are going to keep her medicated and somewhat sedated for the next day or so." Dr. Black continued on, explaining that the tubes they had placed in her chest to drain the blood were necessary, but contributing to Cherie's discomfort.

The next three days were equally unstable. It was difficult to keep her intravenous therapy going because Cherie had periods of restlessness. During those episodes she kept raising her arms above her head and murmuring the words 'life insurance'. When Josh or the nurses tried to put her arms back to her sides, Cherie would moan and thrash about in the bed. No one could offer an explanation to her bizarre behavior. The nurses attempted to place soft wrist restraints on Cherie's wrists to keep her arms tied down at her sides, but Josh became lived. "Don't you understand, she is in this condition because she was kidnapped and held captive? I absolutely forbid you to apply any sort of restraints to my wife."

One nurse, bold enough to argue with Josh informed him, "Sir, don't you understand that we are trying to help your wife. We are doing this for her own good."

Josh was in no mood for argument but he understood that they were doing everything possible to help his wife, "I promise, I will sit here and hold her hand."

The nurse was forced to relent, "As long as we can keep her IV running."

Josh refused to leave her side except for short periods to shower or eat a small amount of food. He was only able to do that at Stephen's insistence. Stephen promised not to take his eyes off of Cherie in Josh's absence. By the fourth day of Cherie's hospitalization, her temperature was down and her vital signs began to stabilize. She opened her eyes for the first time since she was taken from the farm.

Josh and Stephen were both at her bedside when she awoke. Cherie opened her eyes and looked into Josh's coal black eyes. She smiled up at him as he bent down and kissed her brow. "You finally decided to wake up," he said. "How are you feeling?"

"Like I have been hit by a train or something," she said weakly.

Cherie's expression changed when she saw Stephen stand up behind Josh. "Stephen," she said, "I'm so sorry, I thought it was you."

"Miss Cherie," Stephen replied gently, "I'm just glad you're going to be okay."

The heart monitor began to alarm as Cherie's heart rate raced. She was becoming very anxious at the sight of Stephen. Josh motioned for his assistant to leave the room. Knowing his wife, he bent down and slipped his arm under her shoulder and held her close to him. "SHH, calm down," he soothed. "I'm not going to let anyone hurt you, ever again." Cherie relaxed against her husband and the alarm ceased just as the nurse entered the room. "Just give us a few minutes," he said to the nurse.

Cherie was still distraught by Stephen's appearance at her bedside. "I treated him so poorly … I thought he was the one … writing the letters," she whispered feebly.

"Cherie, you have done nothing wrong. Stop worrying about others for a little while and worry about getting you better." Josh held her next to his broad chest and stroked her hair until she relaxed and fell back to sleep. The nurse came back into the room to check on Cherie. "She's okay now," Josh explained. "She got anxious when she saw my assistant. She was convinced before this all happened that he was the one who wanted to hurt her."

"Mr. Tolsten," the nurse instructed. "Your wife's heart was badly bruised. It's imperative that she doesn't get upset. If your assistant's presence upsets her, perhaps it better if he doesn't come in until her condition is stronger."

"Yes, ma'am, I'll take care of that," Josh responded.

Josh watched his wife sleep peacefully for a few minutes then kissed her battered face. The bruises were fading from the deep purple to a dark greenish color, and the swelling in her nose and eyes was almost gone. The doctor's didn't think the damage to her nose would require surgical repair. They felt the deformity was mostly due to the swelling.

Josh stepped just outside Cherie's cubicle where he could talk quietly with Stephen and keep view of Cherie. He explained to Stephen that since Cherie must be kept calm, the nurse didn't want him in the room for a while. "We can settle this after she's well. Cherie feels guilty because she thinks she mistreated you. That's just the kind of person she is. You're just going to have to let her apologize and tell her you forgive her. She can't accept that she has been unkind to another person."

"Josh, I understand. But are you certain you want me to leave?"

"Yeah, you need to go back to Montana and oversee the ranch and the stores. I know we have a huge mess to clean up. Doug can manage the day to day stuff, but not the clean up. And, he knows nothing about the stores.

"Are you sure you are going to be okay here alone? You will have no one here to help you or even run errands for you," Stephen questioned. He knew his friend had been traumatized by the near loss of his wife and was concerned for his well being too.

"I'll be fine, but thank you for your concern. I really do need you to take care of things at home. Then I can focus all of my energy on Cherie and feel comfortable that the ranch and the stores are being taken care of. There is something I would like you to do for me before you go," Josh asked.

Stephen said, "What's that?"

"I would like for you to phone Pastor Mark before you leave. I think it would be good for Cherie if he would visit her," Josh requested, "I think Cherie will take some comfort in seeing a familiar face." Josh gave Stephen the numbers to Pastor Mark's home and the church. "And also, see if you can get in touch with Mongo and Katie. They were the ones who looked after her when her mother died."

Josh remained at Cherie's bedside day and night for the next three days. Cherie would be awake for only short periods of time. Her physical condition was so weakened from the pneumonia and her internal injuries that speaking a few words would exhaust her. Josh refused to permit the nursing staff to attend to Cherie's personal needs. Each morning and evening he would bath her and apply fresh linens to her bed, then gently brush her long auburn hair. As Josh gently caressed Cherie's thin body with a warm wash cloth, he allowed his mind to drift back to the first time he met her. *She was so beautiful,* he recalled, not realizing that he had spoken aloud.

Josh was so absorbed in his thoughts about his young wife that he didn't realize that one of Cherie's IV pump was alarming. Nurse Kerri had heard the alarm and entered the room to correct the problem when she heard Josh thinking aloud, "Mr. Tolsten, she is still beautiful. The swelling and the bruises will heal within a few weeks, I promise."

"Oh, Kerri," Josh replied with a start, "I didn't see you there. I was just remembering the first time I met Cherie."

"She must be very special, Mr. Tolsten."

"Oh yes, Kerri, she's the most wonderful person I have ever met. I have been truly blessed to have her as my wife. She is so caring and loving, the kind of person who would save the world if she could. She will put her own needs aside to help others and never think twice about it," Josh boasted.

"Well, Mr. Tolsten, Cherie will get better. She has already shown an improvement. You just have to be patient. She was in pretty bad shape when she came in here, classified as critical condition. The doctors upgraded her condition to guarded today."

Josh's face lit up. For the first time in days he felt a ray of hope, "Really, you mean her condition is improving?"

"Yes, but don't get too excited yet. She is coming along, but very slowly. She needs you to keep your faith."

"I know Kerry, but it's really hard. I have prayed over and over for God to spare her and heal her wounds. I just don't know what I'll do if she doesn't get well," he said, nearly sobbing.

"You know, Mr. Tolsten, if you don't take care of yourself, you won't be any good to Cherie. You really should get some rest," Nurse Kerri coaxed.

"No, Kerri, I can't leave her. I knew she was in danger, and I left her alone for just fifteen minutes, and look what happened. I'm to blame for her condition, I should never have left her alone," Josh's voice trailed off as he sunk into sorrow.

"Mr. Tolsten," Kerri attempted to reassure, "I know you're blaming yourself, and I don't know exactly what happened to Cherie, But, I do know that she loves you and you love her very much. Please stop blaming yourself. If I understand correctly, the person who hurt Cherie is dead. She can't harm your wife any more."

"That's true Kerri, but I don't want my wife waking up alone. She's been through too much, and I'm not going to take any chances."

"I understand," Kerri offered sympathetically. "I'm off work in half an hour. If you would like to leave for just a little while, maybe to get a shower and some decent food, I'll sit with Cherie. She knows me since I have been caring for her for the past three days. Will you at least do that?" Kerri inquired.

A hot shower and a change of clothes would be nice, he decided, so he agreed to Kerri's suggestion, "but I will not leave the hospital."

Kerri left the small cubicle, and then returned a few minutes later with a fresh pillow and blanket. "Here Mr. Tolsten, at least tonight I can try to make you a little more comfortable." As she turned to leave the room, "I'll be back as soon as I finish my shift."

Cherie awoke soon after Nurse Kerri left the room. She was able to sit up in the bed for a few minutes and asked Josh for a cold drink. Josh was thrilled to see this glimmer of life back in his wife. *I can't possibly leave her side now. Nurse Kerri will have to understand.*

Cherie was still awake when Nurse Kerri returned half an hour later. Josh hadn't spoken to Cherie about the plans for him to take a short break. "Ah, Cherie, you're awake. How are you feeling?"

"Weak and sore, but otherwise, I think I'm okay," Cherie responded softly.

"Do you think you feel like eating a little something?" Kerri asked her patient.

"Maybe some Jello or soup? Something light." Cherie surprised herself that the thought of food made her realize she was hungry.

Nurse Kerri returned a little later with soup and Jello for Cherie, and a burger and fries for Josh. She looked at Josh and said, I understand you don't want to leave now, but you still have to take care of yourself so I grabbed a burger for you." Turning to Cherie she said, "I hope you don't mind Cherie, but your husband hasn't left your side for days. And he hasn't eaten anything on my shift for three days. I told him he needs to take care of himself so he won't be sick when you get to feeling better,"

Cherie looked at her husband, confused, "If I wouldn't have woke up, you would have left?" she questioned.

"Well, little one, not exactly. Nurse Kerri offered to sit with you so I could go shower and change clothes. I didn't want you left alone," Josh explained.

"You can go, Josh. I'll be okay for a little while," Cherie reassured.

"I would rather be here with you, little one," Josh replied.

Realizing what Josh meant, she attempted to reach for his hand, "Josh, I think I'll be awake for a while. If Nurse Kerri sits with me, maybe she can talk to me a little about what it's like to be a nurse. And maybe you could buy me a chocolate shake while you're out.

Josh reluctantly agreed to leave the cubicle for just half an hour and Kerri promised not to leave Cherie's side until he returned. It felt good to walk around and stretch his aching muscles but he couldn't stop worrying about his wife. Before Stephen left he had rented a car for Josh and purchased some spare clothing. Josh went to the car to retrieve the clothing and then went to a nearby hamburger stand to purchase Cherie's milkshake. The hospital staff had given him permission to shower in the employee lounge, so he headed back to the hospital. *I'll take Cherie her milkshake, that way I can check on her before I go and shower*, Josh thought. He wanted to trust Kerri, but it was difficult after his own hired help had betrayed him in such a viscous way.

When he returned to the intensive care unit Kerri was talking to Cherie about her nursing career. Josh stood back and watched his wife's face as she listened intently. Even in her weakened condition, he could see the light in her eyes as she listened to Kerri's stories. Josh understood how Kerri felt. He had worked as a paramedic for many years while he was in college. He had always enjoyed being able to help others. His current occupation didn't allow time for him to work as a medic and at times he missed it greatly.

Cherie noticed the twinkle in her husband's coal black eyes when he came around the corner to her cubicle. She smiled up at him and thanked him for the opportunity to talk with Kerri. "Well," he said, "I haven't made it to the shower yet. I wanted to get your milkshake for you first. So, if you two don't mind, I'll go now."

Kerri smiled and nodded. "It's okay, Mr. Tolsten. Cherie and I were having a wonderful conversation, or I should say, I was talking and she was listening." Josh bent down to kiss Cherie then promised to return shortly.

~ CHAPTER 15 ~

RECOVERY

Cherie's condition had improved enough by the next morning that she was transferred to an intensive care step-down unit. She had been awake for several hours during the night and was permitted solid food for breakfast. The doctors explained to Josh that the antibiotics were working and the pneumonia was improving. However, she was still at risk with her internal injuries so she would need to remain on a heart monitor. They were, however, able to remove the tubes in her chest.

Cherie was permitted to get out of bed to sit in a chair or to walk only a few feet with help of Josh or the nurses. Dr. Engles made it clear that due to the chest trauma, her heart was very weak. She would have to be up a little at a time and build up her tolerance gradually; he did not want her heart to be overly stressed. Because she still tired very easily, it wasn't difficult for her to comply with his instructions.

Cherie gasped in shock at her own appearance the first time she looked into the mirror. Even though the bruises had faded to green with yellow circles around them, and the swelling of her eyes and nose had decreased significantly, her face still looked disfigured. Dr. Engles and Josh both attempted to comfort her by the reminding her that there was no need for surgical repair of her broken nose and it would heal on its own. In addition to the disfigurement from her facial injuries, Cherie had continued to lose weight; her weight under ninety pounds.

The hospital staff on the step-down unit was not as patient with Josh's constant presence. They were determined to persuade him to leave his wife's side. The first night after Cherie was transferred, two of the nurses attempted to force him to leave and went to the extent of calling security to try and remove him. The disagreement ended with Josh telephoning the hospital administrator. By the third night, the same nursing staff had grown increasingly impatient. The same two nurses who had previously given Josh a hard time were adamant that Josh was going to leave, to the point that Cherie felt the need to intervene. She attempted to calm the situation by asking Josh to go buy her a burger and fries at a local fast food restaurant. She thought if she could get him away from the hospital for just a few minutes she could talk to the nurses and give Josh a chance to calm down. "Are you sure that's what you want little one?" Josh asked. When Cherie persisted, Josh finally agreed to leave her alone long enough to get her the food.

While Josh was gone, Cherie overheard the two nurses talking about her and Josh in the hallway. She heard the first nurse say to the other, "I'm absolutely certain he abuses her. He's so possessive. He will not leave her alone for one minute. The day shift nurse said he won't even let the nurse's assistant help her bathe."

The second nurse responded, "And did you see the way she cringes when he calls her 'little one'?"

The conversation went on as the two nurses discussed their plan to keep Josh away from Cherie so they could save her from his abusive ways. Cherie couldn't tolerate listening to them any longer. She knew she wasn't able or permitted to walk more than a few feet, but she had to put an end to that conversation. Slowly she climbed out of bed, taking care not to dislodge the IV line in her left forearm. As she stood up and took a couple steps away from the bed a sudden wave of dizziness came over her that caused her to lose her balance. She stumbled and fell backwards. At first she caught herself with the foot of the bed, but she was too weak and fell hard to the floor. She landed on her buttocks and left arm, then her left leg slid under the foot board. Blood gushed from her left arm. The intravenous catheter had been torn from her arm, and she had sliced her leg on the footboard.

The conversation between the two nurses in the hallway came to a sudden halt when they heard a loud "THUD" come from Cherie's room. Both nurses looked quickly at each other then dashed into Cherie's hospital room. The first nurse, Janie, gasped in horror when she saw her patient lying on the floor with blood coloring her gown and the floor around her. "Cherie, oh my goodness, what happened honey?" she asked as she knelt down to assess her patient.

Angered, Cherie responded sarcastically, "I guess it looks like I fell."

"Why were you getting out of bed with out help? You know you're not supposed to be up alone," the second nurse lectured, her voice curt and unfeeling.

Even though Cherie was furious with the two nurses, she was too weak to argue further with them. She sat silently while they cleaned up the floor around her, and then permitted them to assist her back into bed. Josh returned moments after Janie and the elder nurse left the room to obtain some bandages for Cherie's arm. He knew at first glance that something was very wrong with his young wife. "Cherie, he exclaimed as he tossed the fast food bag onto a chair and rushed to her side, "Oh God, what happened? You're bleeding!"

"Josh, please don't yell at me too," she pleaded.

"I'm not going to yell at you, but what happened?" he demanded.

"Well, I was trying to get out of bed. I wanted to go and talk to the two nurses out in the hallway, and I got dizzy and fell. Please don't yell at me. The nurses already did," she pleaded again with her husband.

"Cherie, I'm not angry with you, but I think you need to start from the beginning and tell me everything," he said as he stroked her brow tenderly.

Cherie knew her husband's temper only too well and hesitated to tell Josh about the conversation she had just overheard. Josh was becoming more and more impatient with the two nurses on this shift. Everyone else had been kind and accommodating. As she thought again about what happened, she decided he needed to know. *Why should I protect them*, she told herself. Slowly she began to recap the things she heard them saying about her husband. "Josh, I know I'm not supposed to get up alone. But I couldn't stand to listen to them anymore. If they had to talk like that, why did they have to do it right outside of my room?" Cherie tensed as she saw the set of her husband's jaw and the bulging of his neck veins. She turned away in shame, fearing he was angry with her.

Gently he asked, "Did you get hurt anywhere beside your arm?"

"I'm not sure Josh. I landed on my left arm and my left hip. And I cut my leg. It does kind of hurt a little. I tried to catch myself but I was too weak. I'm sorry."

Josh bent down and kissed her lightly. Its okay, hon. Did the nurses check you over?"

"No, they just looked at my arm."

"Why don't you let me take a look?" Josh helped her to roll to her right side so he could examine her left hip. "You're covered with blood little one. It looks like you cut you hip here too. I'm going to go get some towels and washcloths and get you cleaned up. Then I'll dress these wounds."

"That was one of the things they were complaining about."

"What do you mean," Josh asked.

"They were complaining that you won't let them do anything for me, that you have to do everything. And that you won't leave me alone. They think you are an abuser and they need to get you away from me so they can save me from you," Cherie confided.

"Is that so?" Josh replied. "They think I am an abuser, but they let my wife get hurt, and they don't bother to take care of her. After I get you cleaned up and comfortable, I'll deal with them. Right now, I need to take care of you."

Janie walked into the room with bandages and a new IV kit in her hand as Josh finished looking at Cherie's hip. "Hi, Mr. Tolsten. I was just coming in to bandage Cherie's arm. She tried to get out of bed by herself and fell. My supervisor said I'll have to put a restraint on her so she can't get up alone. We can't permit her to injure herself again."

In a rage of fury, Josh slammed his fist against the table. "Lady, you are walking on thin ice right now. First you cause my wife to get hurt, and then you say you want to tie her down! I want you to get Dr. Engles and your supervisor in here, NOW!!!!"

"Sir, the doctor won't be in until morning. But I'll be happy to get my supervisor."

"Young lady, you either call Dr. Engles right now, or I will. And if I have my way, you won't have a job when I get done with you"

Nurse Janie left the room to summons her supervisor. In her absence, Josh went and got the washcloths and towels and began to help Cherie get washed up. Josh could feel his wife's body tremble as he gently bathed her. "Relax my sweet. I'm not going to do anything to crazy. But they need to know they can't treat people this way. And I will not let them speak that way to you again."

Cherie's voice quivered, "They want to tie me up." Memories of being tied on the sofa at the farmhouse flooded her mind. Her thoughts raced with fear and dread.

"That won't happen little one, I promise you. And you won't have to listen to that sort of talk anymore. We'll put a stop to this once and for all," Josh promised.

Josh finished bathing Cherie and helped her into a clean nightgown. He cleansed the laceration on her leg and hip, "Cherie, I know you're not going to like this, but this cut will need a few sutures. It's pretty deep." He taped a gauze bandage over it to protect it until Dr. Engles arrived. The wound on her left hip was superficial and Josh was able to get the bleeding to stop, and then cover it with a clean bandage. "There, almost as good as new," he teased.

Janie and the nursing supervisor knocked on the door. Josh looked up and bid the two to enter. "We need to have a little talk, the four of us."

"Mr. Tolsten," the supervisor attempted to present an intimidating demeanor with her arms folded and a stern expression, "I know you're angry that your wife fell, but we all know she was told not to get out of bed with out help."

Josh took a deep breath in attempt to control his anger, "I think you need to hear what my wife has to say before you use that as your defense. Cherie, will you please tell the ladies what you heard?"

"Josh, if it's okay with you, I'd rather wait until Dr. Engles gets here, then I will only have to say it once."

"Okay, you heard my wife. She doesn't want to talk until her doctor arrives. I will ask that the two you return then."

"Mr. Tolsten, we have many other patients to care for. We can't just stop caring for our patients…"

Her voice trailed off as Josh stood up. "Ladies, you will come back when Dr. Engles arrives, and we will have our conversation then. So I suggest you work on making arrangements for your other patients to be cared for while we have our little conference. Now you may leave until Cherie's doctor arrives."

"Mr. Tolsten, I really need to assess Cherie's wounds and restart her intravenous," Janie insisted.

"I have already cared for her wounds. The laceration on her leg will require several stitches. I have dressed them both with gauze bandages. That'll do until Dr. Engles gets here. Did he give you an estimate of how long it will take for him to get here?" Josh asked.

"No. I haven't called him; doctors just don't come in the middle of the night. He will probably tell us to send her down to the emergency room for the sutures, if the wound does need sutured," the supervisor responded.

Barely raising his voice, but with a blood curdling tone, Josh replied, "Haven't the two of you figured out that you're in a lot of hot water right now? I'll telephone the doctor myself." The two nurses left the room while Josh dialed the phone. He spoke briefly with the doctor and explained that there had been some trouble and Cherie had been injured. "I'll be there within the half hour," the doctor promised. Josh informed the doctor that upon his arrival, he wanted the two nurses in the room too, that his wife was too tired and weak to have to share her story repeatedly.

In the nurses' station the two nurses looked at each other, "Now do you believe me when I tell you he's an abuser," Janie asked. "He has one hot temper. I'm telling you, that man makes me nervous. I just hate the thought of sending that poor girl home with him."

"Yes, I see what you mean. We definitely need to talk with Dr. Engles when he gets here. And I'm going to notify social services. In fact, I'm going to leave them a voice message right now so they'll know about this first thing in the morning," the nursing supervisor replied.

Dr. Engles arrived at the hospital within fifteen minutes. He immediately summoned the two nurses, who denied any responsibility for Mr. Tolsten's anger. Both nurses knew without a doubt that Dr. Engles was quite disturbed about being called into the hospital so late in the evening. "Tell me what happened before I go in and see Mr. and Mrs. Tolsten. Tell me why I'm called by a family member to tend to a patient's injuries!"

"Dr. Engles," Nurse Janie began, "I'm so sorry that they called you. We told them we would take care of her and you would be here in the morning. But Mr. Tolsten was too angry to listen. That man has a terrible temper. He's not easy to deal with. And to top it off, he never leaves her side."

"Well, what happened that made him so angry?" demanded the doctor.

"Mrs. Tolsten fell. She got up out of bed without assistance, in spite of our instructions. She became dizzy and fell. When Mr. Tolsten returned he was furious and blamed us for her noncompliance," the nursing supervisor added.

"Very well ladies, let's go in and talk with the Tolsten's, and see what we can do to calm this situation. Mr. Tolsten told me his wife was injured. What do you know about that?" asked the doctor.

"Well, we heard the loud thud then went into her room immediately. She was lying on the floor with her gown soaked in blood. There was blood on the floor, but she had pulled out her IV and you know how they bleed. She also cut her arm a little and I guess she cut her leg too, but I didn't see that," Janie responded.

"Why didn't you see if there were any more injuries?"

"Well, when I helped her back into bed I only saw the laceration on her arm. I guess I should have assessed her better. I was just so upset with her right then, for trying to get out of bed alone. I needed to get out of that room and calm down so I could take care of her without upsetting her. She's so timid you know. And I am afraid she takes enough abuse from him, I didn't want to upset her too." Janie confided to Dr. Engles.

"What do you mean he abuses her?" asked Dr. Engles.

"Dr. Engles," the nursing supervisor interrupted, "That couple has all of the classic characteristics of an abusive relationship. And look at her! She is such a tiny little thing. How could a man as big as he is pick on a little thing like that?"

Dr. Engles's impatience was mounting with the two nurses. "I'm going to talk with the Tolsten's right now. You ladies give me about ten minutes then you come in the room."

The nursing supervisor winked at Janie, "Now see, I knew he would support us."

Dr. Engles had wanted to speak with Josh privately, to give him and Cherie an opportunity to speak freely and without intimidation before the two nurses came in to meet with them. Josh rose as he entered the room. The two men shook hands then Dr. Engles looked over to Cherie. "She was exhausted after her ordeal. She's fallen asleep, but I promised I would wake her as soon as you arrived," Josh explained.

Josh gently woke his sleeping wife, "Cherie, your doctor is here."

"Hi Dr. Engles. I'm sorry you had to come back to the hospital this late."

"Cherie, why don't you tell us what happened. Something obviously had you very upset."

"Yes, sir, that's true. I had asked my husband to go get me a burger and fries. Before that, the nurses were fighting with him that he couldn't stay here with me. You said he could, but they said you didn't write an order. I tried to explain to them that I wasn't ready to be alone yet. Well, anyways, after Josh left to get me a burger, I overheard Janie and the supervisor talking outside my room. They were close enough and loud enough that I could hear every word. What they were saying was upsetting me and I finally had enough and wanted to set them straight. So I got out of bed…"

"Cherie," doctor interrupted, "What were they saying that was so upsetting to you?"

"They were saying that my husband was abusive, and they were trying to get him away from me, so they could save me from him. They were complaining that he's too possessive, and that he won't let them help me with my care."

"You have a right to be upset about that Cherie," the doctor said with obvious irritation in his voice. "Go on."

"Well, I wanted to set them straight, so I decided to try to walk out to the doorway and get their attention. When I got up, I was okay at first, and then after I took a couple steps I got dizzy and lost my balance. I was too weak to catch myself and I fell. I'm sorry." Cherie said softly.

"Cherie, you don't have to apologize," Dr. Engles said sympathetically,

"I'm sorry you had to hear that kind of talk."

When the two nurses entered Cherie's room, Dr. Engles looked crossly at them, "Ladies, I was just having a conversation with Mrs. Tolsten, and it seems you failed to tell me what prompted her to attempt to get out of bed unassisted." The nurses started to protest but Dr. Engles ignored them and continued, "It appears that Mrs. Tolsten's primary caregiver was in the hallway outside her room having a conversation with her supervisor; a conversation that was quite upsetting to Mrs. Tolsten."

"Oh!" both nurses exclaimed simultaneously. "We had no idea you could hear us," the supervisor added.

Janie spoke up, "We have every reason to believe there is a possible abuse situation going on here. He never gives her an opportunity to be alone with the staff, and he insists upon doing all of her care. That in combination with all of the bruises would give anyone reason for suspicion."

The nursing supervisor added sarcastically, "And if you would see the way she winces every time he calls her 'little one' you'd know what we mean. Why, you can tell it upsets the poor little thing. And she is less than half his size. You should be ashamed of your self!" she added, pointing at Josh.

"And," Janie added, "One of the ICU nurses told me that while she was still delirious, she kept mumbling something about life insurance. What's up with that anyway?"

Dr. Engles suddenly lost all control. "Have you bothered to read this young lady's medical record? Are you aware of all that she has been through in the past two weeks! Do you even know what you are talking about?"

"No, we haven't read her chart." Janie replied. She has been here along time. No one would have time to a chart that thick."

"Yes, but you have time to stand outside my patient's room and talk about her. Now where is the sense in that?" Dr. Engles shouted.

"Dr. Engles," Cherie interrupted, "they said they want to tie me in bed. I can't stand the thought of being tied up again. Please don't let them do that to me, please!!" Cherie begged.

The memories of being tied on the soiled sofa with her arms tied above her head crept back into Cherie's consciousness. Her heart rate began to escalate beyond the safe limits. The alarm on her heart monitor sounded. Josh placed his hand on his wife's brow and rubbed soothingly, "Cherie. It's alright. No one will ever tie you up. I promise I will not leave your side again. I'm not going to let any one hurt you." He kept rubbing her brow until she relaxed and her heart rate began to ease down to normal limits.

"Can you please just get them out of here? They're lying and I don't want to see them again," Cherie pleaded with Josh. Josh's heart broke as he gently brushed the tears from his wife's battered face. She had already been through so much because of his negligence, and now this.

"You heard the lady," Josh said to the two nurses, "you may leave now. And, I would suggest that neither of you enter this room again while my wife is a patient here."

Dr. Engles was furious when he discovered the extent of Cherie's wounds that the two nurses didn't assess and treat. He gave his word that both women would face disciplinary action as a result of their unprofessional actions. At Cherie's request, he called to the intensive care unit and asked for Kerri's assistance to suture her wounds. Kerri had been off work for a couple of days, but was called at home and agreed to come and be Cherie's nurse for the night. With Kerri's assistance, Dr. Engles sutured the laceration. It took a total of twenty stitches to close the wound.

Josh sat in quiet agony while Dr. Engles and Kerri took care of Cherie's wounds, his face buried in his hands. *How could have I let this happen to her*, he berated himself over and over? *I should have known Jeanie was up to something. Why on the day we were planning to leave did she suddenly decide to help Cherie learn to cook? Why didn't I see it? Why was I so stupid to leave her alone? I can never forgive myself for letting this happen her. How can I ever make it up to her? Well, no one, absolutely no one will ever hurt her again.*

While Dr. Engles was talking with Cherie, Kerri looked over and noticed Josh's grief. She walked over to him and placed her hand gently on his shoulder, "Mr. Tolsten, are you still blaming yourself for this," she asked quietly. "Please stop doing that. The two nurses you have had problems with have had a bad attitude for years. You are the first to have the courage to stand up to them. Most patients are intimidated by them."

"Yeah, Kerri," he said, his voice almost a whisper so his wife couldn't hear him, "But if it wasn't for my stupidity, my wife wouldn't be in this hospital and wouldn't be going through all of this, it's all because I left her alone."

"You couldn't have known, you can't blame yourself," Kerri said.

"I should have seen it. If I would have looked at the obvious, right under my nose. Right in my own home. I put her in jeopardy and look at her now because of me!"

"I'm sorry Cherie, I'm sorry that your stay here on this unit has been an unpleasant one," Dr. Engles stated.

"Everyone else except those two has been very kind to me and Josh." Cherie responded.

As Cherie and Dr. Engles concluded their conversation, Cherie looked over and saw Kerri and her husband talking quietly in the corner of the room.

She could see the expression on Josh's face, "Hey, you okay?" she asked. Then trying to lighten the moment, "I thought you didn't get sick at the sight of blood?"

Later that evening, when the couple was finally alone in the room, Cherie took Josh's hand, "I think I know what you were talking to Kerri about."

"Yeah, the sight of blood, right?"

"Josh, I don't blame you for what happened to me. Please don't blame yourself. I was so afraid, while I was gone, that I wouldn't live to see you again, or if I didn't listen and do what she told me to do, that she would hurt you too. She was evil, Josh, evil."

Josh bent down and gently kissed his wife. "I love you so. I was terrified that I had lost you forever too. I don't know what I would have done." The two fell silent and took comfort in being close to one another. Josh gently stroked her brow until Cherie fell asleep.

The unit director visited Cherie the following morning. "Mr. and Mrs. Tolsten, my name is Clara. I'm the director of this unit. I'd like to touch base with you and discuss what happened with two of my nurses last evening. Would you like to tell me what happened?"

"Well," Cherie began, "We did discuss it with Dr. Engles already."

"Yes, Mrs. Tolsten, I understand. But I need to do an investigation of all the events in order to decide what, if any further action is needed."

Josh interrupted, "This whole thing has been upsetting to my wife, Clara. So I'll tell you about it. As you well know by Cherie's history, she's already been through a severe trauma. Your two nurses last evening had not read Cherie's medical record, and decided among themselves that my protectiveness of my wife was an indication that I was abusive to her. Cherie overheard them having such a discussion just outside of this room. Even though she was ordered restricted activity, she was upset by the conversation and tried to get out of bed alone. She wanted to stop them from the things they were saying. Consequently, she fell and was injured. To top it off, the nurses were not only unkind to her, but the failed to assess her for injury, then threatened to apply restraints."

"Oh, Mr. and Mrs. Tolsten, I'm so sorry that had to happen. I didn't get quite the same version from the nurses, but Dr. Engles had been quite upset also. Normally, I would not discuss a staff members behavior with a patient or family member when I respond to a complaint, but let me assure you, this hospital nor this unit will in no way endorse such behavior," Clara attempted to reassure the Tolstens.

"Clara," Cherie added, "Apparently there were other members of the nursing staff who discussed suspicions of my husband. The two last night were complaining that the day staff told them Josh helps me with my bath and stuff."

"Actually, Mrs. Tolsten, I did hear a comment to that effect, but it wasn't meant in a derogatory manner. What the day nurse reported was the staff didn't have to do anything for you other than medically related tasks because Mr. Tolsten does your care. The day nurses were merely reporting, they were not complaining. Most nurses are appreciative when a family member helps. It takes some of the load off of them."

"Look," Josh said, "I don't know or really even care what you do with those two, but I certainly do not want them to be a part of my wife's care. And I would appreciate it if you would communicate to all of your staff that I will not be leaving my wife's side."

"I don't think they understand, I'm not ready to be alone yet," Cherie added.

"It's okay Mrs. Tolsten. There actually is an order on you record from Dr. Engles that says your husband may be with you at all times. I don't know where my nurses got the idea there was no order." Clara exited the room after reassuring Josh and Cherie that there should be no further problems with her staff. "And if you have any more problems, day or night, please call the hospital operator and have me paged."

Later that same morning the social worker visited Cherie. "Mrs. Tolsten, good morning. My name is Lisa. I am the social worker for this unit. Cherie greeted the woman with a confused smile. "Would it be okay if I have a few minutes to speak with you alone?"

"Is this by some chance related to what happened last evening," Josh asked.

Appearing to ignore him, the social worked continued to speak directly to Cherie. Cherie responded, "You can talk in front of my husband. I have nothing to hide from him."

"Mrs. Tolsten, it is customary when I do my assessments to speak with the patient alone."

"Why do you need to do an assessment for my wife?" Josh demanded. We have no need for social services at this time."

Lisa, still ignoring Josh, proceeded to insist she speak with Cherie alone.

Dr. Engles entered the room and overheard Lisa speaking with the Tolstens. "Good Morning Lisa. I don't recall ordering a social services consult for Mrs. Tolsten."

"Good Morning Dr. Engles. You didn't. The nurse on the afternoon shift made the referral. Based on the concern she express, she didn't require a physician's order."

"Yes, yes, I know what her concern was. Your services will not be needed in this room."

"Dr. Engles, could I please see you outside?" Lisa asked.

"Dr. Engles, when there is an abuse report made, I am obligated by law to perform an assessment," Lisa argued.

"Well, Lisa, there nothing you can do at this time for this couple. The person who abused Mrs. Tolsten is dead. Now, need I say anymore? And, if you had read her chart before coming in here, you would understand"

"No, sir, I understand, I think." Lisa responded.

Dr. Engles re-entered Cherie's room, "Good morning Cherie, Josh. I'm sorry. It appears this situation is never ending.

Cherie was released from the hospital a couple days later. Because of Josh's experience as a paramedic, Dr. Engles felt it would be safe for Cherie to recuperate at home, under Josh's supervision. The only stipulation was she was not permitted to travel for at least two weeks, and she would see Dr. Engles every three days. Josh was provided a long list of instructions for his wife's care.

Josh found Cherie to be quiet and withdrawn her first couple days home. The couple temporarily resided in Cherie's old apartment. Josh's hope was that Cherie would find some comfort and peace in the apartment. Because she would not talk about the kidnapping ordeal or the hospital episode, Josh was at a loss for ideas to help her. As she gradually became physically stronger, she became increasingly irritable when Josh attempted to enforce Dr. Engles restrictions.

Josh was concerned that other than the brief encounter with the nurses in the hospital, Cherie had not spoken a word about her ordeal. He knew her emotional health was at risk if she didn't ventilate some of her feelings. Then one day Cherie exploded. She had wanted to leave the apartment and go out for lunch at Mongo's diner. Josh was agreeable to visiting the diner, but refused to permit her to walk up and down the steps of their second floor apartment, "I'll carry you," he insisted, "You can't overly exert yourself."

Disgusted with his constant mothering, Cherie lost her temper for the first time since they had been married. She began to pace and yell at her husband. "I'm tired of being treated like an invalid," her husband heard her say. She continued to rant as Josh stared at his young wife in astonishment. With his jaw wide open in disbelief, he heard Cherie yell, "always have to do what you say…" and then "Been told what to do for the past two weeks … Even told when I can go to the bathroom!" Suddenly Cherie became physically and emotionally exhausted and collapsed on the sofa.

Josh rushed to her side, "Cherie," he gasped, "I've never seen you like this." Still fearful to touch his enraged wife, he maintained some distance between them. "Cherie, you haven't spoken one word about your ordeal. Baby, you need to talk…" He hesitated for a couple seconds then added, "To someone."

Cherie leaned back into the corner of the sofa and tucked her knees under her chin. Slowly she began to reiterate the day she was kidnapped. She carefully watched Josh's expressions as she recalled Jeanie and her in the kitchen with the gun to her head. All of a sudden she remembered why she came down with pneumonia. Josh's jaw was set firmly as she described in detail the events of that morning.

Josh remained quiet while Cherie spoke. He was afraid if he interrupted her she would stop talking. As painful as it was for him to hear the graphic details, he needed to know what had happened to his young bride, and he knew she needed to talk about it. Cherie recapped her attempt to escape or be rescued at the motel. At that point Josh interrupted briefly to tell her that was when he and Stephen speculated that Jeanie was taking Cherie to Ohio. He praised her creative efforts at the motel.

Cherie suddenly became quiet. "What is it Cherie? Please go on."

Tears welled up in Cherie's eyes as she thought about the elderly man in the motel, and that she had caused his death. "The man in the motel …

because of me, he's dead. If I wouldn't have tried to be stupid..." Cherie mumbled.

Josh stopped Cherie, "You did not cause his death ... Jeanie did. You can't take responsibility for anything she did."

"But, he wouldn't be dead if I hadn't gone in there and asked for help. Jeanie warned me not to try anything stupid. And I did!" she sobbed.

"No, little one, Please, you can't blame yourself for any of Jeanie's actions. "What happened after you left the motel?" Josh asked, attempting to prompt Cherie to continue with her story.

"I'm not really sure. When we got into the car she started hitting me in the face. I don't remember anything after that until I woke up in the farm house. Even that is a blur. I was so sick." I don't even know how long I was in the house before I woke up. Cherie couldn't bear the humiliation of telling Josh what her condition was like just before Dean and Jeff discovered her there. She was grateful that she had been able to bathe and change into clean clothing before they had seen her. "You know she'll come back for me," Cherie fretted.

"Oh, baby, I'm so sorry. I didn't realize you didn't know. Jeanie's dead. When she went to shoot you, Dean managed to break open the basement door and Jeanie shot him." Josh reached for Cherie and held her tight. "Jeanie was shot and killed by a federal agent." She had enough for the time being and lay quietly in his arms until she fell fast asleep. Josh's heart ached for his wife as he held her frail body in his lap and stroked her auburn locks while she slept.

Cherie awoke to the sound of someone knocking on the apartment door. Gently, Josh lifted his tiny wife up and rose to answer the door. Josh opened the door to see the concerned expression on Pastor Mark's face. "Josh, I just got back from vacation and heard your message. Is Cherie okay? May I see her?"

"Pastor Mark, hello. Yes, you may see her, please come on in. She'll be happy you're here." Pastor Mark gasped at the sight of Cherie's emaciated body and bruised face. "Cherie, my goodness, what happened? Are you okay?"

Josh interrupted before Cherie had a chance to respond to Pastor Mark's question. "What exactly did Stephen's message say?" he questioned.

"The message on my answering machine, both at home and at the church said Cherie had been injured and was in the hospital," Pastor Mark replied.

Josh turned to Cherie, hoping this was an opportunity for her to talk about her ordeal, "Cherie, would you like to talk with Pastor Mark alone? We haven't had lunch yet. I could go and pick up a pizza and some salads. Would that be alright?"

"Yeah, that's okay," Cherie responded, then turned to Pastor Mark, "if that's okay with you. Can you stay for lunch?"

Pastor Mark sensed that there was a need for Cherie to talk with him in private and agreed to remain with Cherie while Josh was gone. After Josh left the apartment, Pastor Mark turned back to Cherie with a concerned expression and asked, "Cherie, I'm very worried about you. I wasn't expecting anything like this. You look like you've been badly beaten and you've lost a ton of weight."

Cherie confirmed both of his observations. Pastor Mark continued to question Cherie, "And why did Josh find an excuse to leave here as soon as I arrived?"

Pastor Mark, please, if I may start from the beginning, you'll understand. Josh has been trying to get me to talk about my ordeal, but I find it very hard to talk to him about it. He knows that, and was hoping I'd talk to you."

"Of course, Cherie. You can talk to me. I'm here for you."

Cherie began be telling Mark about the threatening letters and then told him about the events in the kitchen on that dreaded day. "She held a gun to me, and told me she was going to make me suffer, and then when things were so bad that death looked like the only way out, she would kill me. And she told me if I did anything stupid, she would make Josh suffer and kill him too." Cherie went on to express concern for their home in Montana, "I know she started a fire, but I have no idea how much damage the fire caused."

"So," Pastor Mark questioned, "You still have so many unanswered questions that you're worried about, but you're not asking your husband for the answers. Why are you afraid to talk to him about all of this?"

"Pastor Mark, if you would've seen him while I was in the hospital. He went through so much. I saw the pain and the worry in his face. I just did not, and I still don't want to worry him or upset him anymore."

"Cherie," Pastor Mark lectured sternly, "Do you remember when I counseled the two you before you were married? What did I tell you was the most important thing in a marriage?"

"You said honesty and communication," Cherie confessed."

"You and Josh both have this habit of wanting to protect each other, but you end up causing each other undue stress and worry. You need to open up to him and let him know what happened while you were gone, and ask him for the answers to the questions you have. And you need to let him ask you questions too. You will both feel a lot better. Trust me." Pastor Mark lectured.

Cherie and Pastor Mark continued to talk until Josh returned with lunch. The three of them enjoyed lunch together, and then Pastor Mark decided it was time for him to leave. He gently hugged Cherie and whispered "Talk to you husband," before he left.

Josh walked Pastor Mark to his car. "I don't want to ask you what she said, I just want to know if she talked about it to you," Josh pried.

"Yeah, Josh, she talked to me. And now the two of you need to talk. I'm going to give you the same advice I gave her. Both of you have a habit of withholding information from one another, each trying to protect the other. You need to be more open and trusting of each others abilities to deal with stresses. You're both placing undue stress on one another."

"You know, you're right. When I met Cherie, I wanted to take her away and give her the perfect life. I wanted to make it up to her for the miserable life she had before we met. So, I have always tried to protect her."

Pastor Mark assured, "Josh, yes Cherie's life was not the ideal life. But it wasn't lousy. Your wife is a strong woman, with a strong value system. Even thought she didn't have a good childhood, she did have a wonderful relationship with God. And, she made a decent life for herself after her mother passed away. So man, give her a little credit. She's not a china doll."

"Yeah, I guess you are right. Thank you Pastor Mark for coming by. I think we both needed to talk with you. "I had my assistant leave a message for Mongo and Katie too, but they haven't responded." Josh added.

"They are in Niagra Falls, have been for several days. So, I guess you haven't visited the diner yet?"

"Not yet. Because of the severity of Cherie's internal injuries, she is to have limited activity. Going up and down the steps is a little too much stress on her heart just yet. She's not happy about me enforcing that part, but I am obeying doctor's orders. I will not give in there. I almost lost her once. I'm not taking any chances," Josh said firmly.

"You two are so much in love. It is refreshing to see the kind of commitment you two have with each other. Before he left Pastor asked Josh is he wanted him to update Mongo and Katie.

"Please do. We actually had a bit of a disagreement earlier today because Cherie wanted to go to the diner. I reminded her that she couldn't be walking up and down them steps and doing too much until she sees the doctor tomorrow. She wasn't very happy with me," Josh responded.

"Well, maybe she will feel better if she gets a couple visitors. She does look pretty frail now. And she has lost a lot of weight," Mark said with concern in his voice.

"Did she talk to you at all about her injuries?" Josh asked.

"No," Pastor Mark replied. "No, she did not."

"Well, she wasn't given any food or water for the entire week she was gone. And her face was beaten severely with the butt end of the maid's gun. But worse than that, the maid beat her repeatedly in the chest with a blunt object. We are guessing it was the gun too. Her heart was severely bruised. She has managed to avoid surgical repair, only because her physical condition was too weakened to withstand the surgery. I'm not certain Cherie realizes how critical her condition has been. She was unconscious for over three days. Oh, and I almost forgot, she is also recovering from pneumonia, both lungs. You see pastor, not only was my wife kidnapped by my former maid, she was nearly killed."

"I'm not sure Cherie knows all of that either Josh. There are a lot of holes in her memory of the past two weeks. I think she may have questions for you too, but she's afraid to ask you. Please be patient with her. As she heals, parts of her memory may return, in bits and pieces. And she may begin to have nightmares. She has a lot of mental healing to do too."

The two men said their goodbyes. Josh invited Pastor Mark to visit again, and invited him and his family for a vacation out to Montana. Then, he promptly excused himself, "I've left her alone too long. I need to get back up there."

Josh returned to the apartment to find that Cherie had cleaned up the lunch dishes and was fast asleep on the sofa. He sat down beside her and gently stroked her hair as he watched her sleep. Nothing else seemed to matter to him as long as she was with him. *My life is complete with you,* he thought.

Later that evening when Cherie awoke, Josh gently approached the subject of her unanswered questions. Josh became agitated as they talked. He was being faced with the full reality of what his young wife went through. "Why didn't you talk to me about this sooner? You have been holding this in and carrying this burden alone for nearly a week now."

"Josh, you've been through so much. I could see that this was all wearing you down. You didn't sleep much at all, and you kept worrying so about me. I couldn't bear to give you something else to deal with."

There were no more words for Josh to say. He was speechless and overwhelmed. With all that she had been through, and his young wife was more worried about him than she was herself. He stopped pacing and sat down on the edge of the sofa then buried his face in his hands. As he sat there overwhelmed by his grief, Cherie moved to her husband's side in attempts to comfort him. She put her arms around him and held him close to her. She stroked his black curls and kissed the top of his head as he relaxed against her, "Josh, I'm so sorry. This past two weeks has been so hard on you." Josh sat upright and pulled his young bride onto his lap.

"You never cease to amaze me, little one. After everything you have been through and you are worried about me." Josh felt his wife's body tense and become rigid, "What is it Cherie? Am I hurting you?"

"Well, yes, in a way you are," she replied.

"Tell me, little one, what is it?" Josh prodded.

"That's it, Josh, when you call me little one. Please don't call me that anymore," Cherie begged.

"Okay, but do you wanna tell me why?"

"Josh, every time Jeanie called me that, she hit me. The entire time I was with her, if she called me that, I knew I was going to get hit with that gun."

Josh hugged his wife close to him and stroked her hair. "I promise, I'll never say that to you again. I'm so sorry I failed to protect you, I'm so sorry," his voice trailed off.

"It is not your fault, Josh. Please don't blame yourself. I'm the one who asked her to teach me how to make a meal for you. I didn't have any idea that it could be her."

The next two days were filled with activity for the young couple. Cherie had her follow up doctor visit. Her wounds were healing slowly, and her cardiac EKG was normal. She was given permission to gradually increase her activities. Dr. Engles gave her permission to travel home in one week. The physician told her he had located a cardiologist for her to follow up with in Montana, and he would send copies of her medical records to him. "You must follow up Cherie. You are not completely out of the woods yet. Your injuries were severe. They are only healing slowly. You could have a heart attack or even die if you don't care for yourself properly," Dr. Engles lectured. He advised her and Josh that he wanted to see her one more time before they flew home to Montana. "Cherie, before you go," he added, "I understand you have been a little impatient with your husband enforcing my restrictions."

Cherie gave a husband a shocked look, "You told on me?"

"Cherie, I," Josh began, but Dr. Engles interrupted.

"Look Cherie. Your husband is right by telling me. I don't think you realize just how critically ill you were. By the values of your lab results and you chest x-rays, you should not be alive right now. It is by pure miracle that you survived."

"Oh, I guess I didn't realize..."

"I'm certain that you didn't. You were unconscious for several days. I would appreciate it if you would make every attempt to comply with my instructions," the doctor lectured sternly." We are trying to keep you alive."

Cherie put her head down in shame. "I'm sorry."

~ CHAPTER 16 ~

HOMECOMING

Even with all she had been through, nothing prepared Cherie for how she would feel when confronted with the sight of the charred remains of their home. Josh had described it to her in detail, hoping it wouldn't be a complete shock when they arrived at the ranch. But no amount of talking in the world could have prevented the grim reality that Cherie was faced with.

As Josh's SUV drove into what was once their driveway, Cherie saw only an empty plot of land. Stephen had the area cleaned of all the burned debris and had the basement filled in. There wasn't even a blade of grass growing in the charred area, just bare dirt. The only evidence that their home had ever existed was a plot of bare land. Words could not describe the intensity of emotions Cherie felt at that very moment. She had wanted to be brave, to show her husband that she was not an emotional cripple and that she could handle this. She wanted to believe she was finally starting to heal. Visions of Jeanie holding the gun to her head and forcing her into Jeanie's car as she threw the lit gasoline bomb into her home passed through Cherie's head over and over in slow motion. Until that minute, Cherie had tried to avoid thinking about the moment of her abduction, but with the sight of the empty plot, the memories came flashing back into her conscious memory with a vengeance.

Cherie tried to remain outwardly calm, to maintain a brave façade in front of her husband, *I can't cry, he has to be getting tired of me blubbering all of the time*, she told herself. But Josh knew his wife well enough. He could clearly see that she was getting upset, and he had expected as much, recalling how he felt the days after the fire.

For the first two days after the fire, Josh, still believing his wife had perished in the blaze, trampled around the remains for hours looking for something of Cherie's, some sign of her. He had cried for days, calling out her name. Others had difficulty dealing with him. He was agitated and at times hateful. The police detectives had chosen to talk with Stephen because they couldn't deal with Josh's agitation. Even though they understood his feelings, interactions with him were, at best, unproductive.

Josh stopped the SUV and reached across the seat for his young bride.

"Cherie, are you okay? You're ghost white?" he said as he placed his arm on her shoulders.

Cherie couldn't answer him. She knew if she tried to speak she'd lose control. Josh parked the SUV and walked around to open her car door. He wrapped his arms around Cherie and then he pulled her out of the car and held her tight against his broad chest. All attempts to be strong were crushed. Cherie crumbled in his arms. He held her in his arms for a few minutes then took her face in his hands. "Cherie, I know this is hard, but you have to see this. You have to face the reality of everything that has happened. If you don't, you won't be able to heal." He paused for a few seconds then added, "I know it is going to be painful and frightening, but I'll be right here with you."

Cherie suddenly felt full of rage; her anger directed at him. Still sobbing, she backed away from her husband and shouted, "Why do you have to be so perfect! Why is it that nothing bothers you and I look like a blubbering idiot?" She stopped abruptly, immediately feeling sorry for yelling at him. She wanted to shrink away and hide.

Josh remained calm and understanding. "Baby girl, I haven't been so calm through all of this. But the last thing you need is for me to be upset around you." He stopped for a couple minutes, his voice cracking. "I was scared to death. I thought I had lost you. At first I thought you and Jeanie were still in the house. The fire was so powerful that no one could get close to the house, so there was no chance of saving either of you. The only thing I could do was watch my home burn to the ground with my beloved wife inside. I just stood there and cried." Josh reached for Cherie and pulled her back close to him, then guided her to a tree log where he pulled her onto his lap. Continuing, "Then one of the detectives called me with the fire marshal's conclusion that the only person who perished in the fire was one male. I knew you were still alive, but had no idea where you were. I was more afraid then than I was when I thought you were dead." Josh paused, his voice cracking again.

"Why would you say that" Weren't you happy that I was alive?" she demanded, still annoyed as she recalled Jeanie's comments about life insurance.

"Of course I was ecstatic that you were alive! But I had no idea where you were or what you were going through. I was in agony. All I could think of was: were you being hurt, would you be okay. I still didn't know if I would ever see you again. Many people who are kidnapped never return home alive. And then, when we did find you, you were beaten so badly that we didn't know if you would be able to recover."

"I'm sorry for yelling at you like that Josh. I know you've been through a lot too. But, I do feel like all I do is cry."

"I think that is the best thing for you. You have to let the feelings out and deal with them, or else they will haunt you forever."

"Jeanie informed me she told the rest of the staff that I left because you beat me. She said no one would look for me. They would believe I left because I was angry and afraid of you," Cherie added, "I just kept praying that I'd live to see you again."

"She didn't tell anyone that. I had Stephen talk with the rest of the staff. They were all genuinely concerned about you." Josh paused and there was a couple moments of silence between the two before he continued. "Cherie, you led us in the right direction when you left that note and your watch at the motel in South Dakota." At that moment Josh reached into his pocket and pulled out the watch. "I was waiting for the right moment to give this back to you. We were called to that little motel room where you left this – to identify it. It wasn't long before we figured out where Jeanie was taking you. Stephen and I were going to Ohio when we got a call from the feds. Our tenant, Jeff had seen you there and eluded Jeanie's capture. He took Jeanie's car and drove into town to call for help. Dean had been locked up in the basement, but Jeff was far enough away that he was able to elude capture."

"Do you know what happened in the house Josh?" Cherie asked. Her memory of being there was cloudy at best. She remembered waking up soiled from not being permitted to use the restroom from the time they had left that motel in South Dakota. With all of her heart she hoped and prayed that Josh didn't know about that.

Josh responded gently, "The feds and the medics were already there when I arrived. It appears that Dean had managed to break through the basement door as Jeanie decided to shoot you. Dean took the shot."

"Is he alright?" she asked, fearing the worst.

"Well, he wasn't doing well when we left to come home. Stephen has been following his progress. He was shot in the abdomen. Several of his internal organs were torn up," Josh stopped abruptly.

"All of this is my fault. Two people have been hurt badly, and three people are dead because of me," she said quietly.

"Why, Cherie, why would you think this is your fault?"

Feeling sorry for herself, Cherie started to sob again. Josh held her close until she was able to speak. "Because Josh, if I wouldn't have married you and come out here to live, Jeanie wouldn't have been so angry with you."

"Is that what she told you Cherie?"

"Yes," she sobbed. "And now, look how many people have been hurt…"

Josh stopped her. "Cherie, it's not your fault. You were the victim here. You nearly lost your life. Please baby, don't ever blame yourself, please."

"She told me she was in love with you, and when you married me you ruined everything. Josh," she hesitated. She knew she had to tell him about Leona, but how would he feel?

"What is it Cherie, go on."

"Josh, did you know that it was Jeanie who killed your first wife?"

Josh's face paled, "It was Jeanie. All these years and until this happened, I had no idea."

"Yes, Josh, It was her. She was angry that Leona was two-timing you, and she was angry that she had been in love with you since high school. She said you never gave her a second look. She said she hoped after she killed Leona, you would turn to her; all you did was collect off of her life insurance. She was angry coz you didn't share it with her, after she helped you. Jeanie said she always believed you thought you were too good for her because she grew up in a poor family, so when you brought home poor white trash like me she became furious, and, well, you know the rest. She was angry because she helped make you a rich man,"

"Cherie, my staff was never informed of your 'social status,' they would have no way of knowing. The only thing I told them is that we met when I was in Ohio purchasing her uncle's farm."

"She knew Josh, she knew I was just poor white trash."

"Ah Cherie, I am so sorry, so very sorry. I had no idea. And I left you alone with her. I made it possible for her to kidnap you." Holding her tight, he kept apologizing over and over again.

"Josh, there were times I thought she wanted to be my friend."

"Cherie, I think we need to clear up this thing about the life insurance. Do you believe her?"

"Well, I don't believe that you had your first wife killed, if that is what you mean, why do you ask?"

"Because," Josh began, "while you were unconscious, you kept mumbling about life insurance. None of us knew what you were talking about. The nurses at the hospital also heard you."

"I'm sorry, Josh. Jeanie kept telling me that you wanted me dead so you could collect my life insurance, but she would see to it that no one ever found my body."

"My God, I'm so sorry for what you have had to go through. I guess I never had cause to tell you, but there was no life insurance for Leona, and there is none for you. I didn't get richer off of my first wife's death, nor do I have anything to gain if something happens to you."

"Why, why wouldn't you have life insurance on us?" Cherie asked.

"I carry it on myself, so you will be taken care of if I should leave this world. But I have enough money; I don't need to carry insurance of that sort on you. Besides, you would have to sign for it if I did get a policy."

Cherie began to sob uncontrollably. Josh held her tight and stroked her hair. "What is it baby?"

"I'm sooo sorry that I doubted you. I thought she was telling the truth. I thought you didn't want me anymore, that maybe you spent too much money on me and needed to make it up."

"That's called brainwashing, hon. She had you in a vulnerable position and she probably wanted to make you feel hopeless so you wouldn't try to escape." After a long pause, he added, "It's not uncommon when a spouse is killed, that the surviving spouse is investigated. I was questioned when Leona was killed. Especially due to the fact that she was killed with another man, then it was established that she had been having an affair. The police records prove I had no policy and collected no money as a result of her death."

The couple sat there in silence for the next hour or more, each of them trying to manage their own grief and comfort the other. Cherie thought for a while that talking about all of the things they had been trying so hard not to say lifted a tremendous weight off of both their shoulders. As they sat there Cherie's fingers kept tracing around the inscription of the watch.

"Josh," she said quietly, breaking the silence.

"Hmm."

"I'm sorry for the awful things I said to you earlier," she said, feeling horrible for saying being unkind to him. He was always so calm and patient with her.

"It is okay, baby. But maybe I will collect on that apology later."

She felt the cold hard gun against her right temple. The abrupt onset of excruciating pain in her head and face blinded her as she felt her body being dragged away. "Please, please," she begged, "I'll do whatever you want. Please don't take me away again."

"Shut up," a gruff voice ordered, and then everything went black.

When she awoke, everything around was black. She couldn't tell where she was. Her hands were tied above her head and her feet were tied together, just like the last time, and there was the awful stench. She felt something biting at her toes. Horrified, she tried to scream for help, but her voice was paralyzed. "Cherie, Cherie," she heard a male voice calling. He was holding both of her hands so she couldn't get away; he just kept pulling on her, "Cherie," the voice called again.

"Cherie, wake up." This time she realized it was Josh. Something cold was brushing across her face. Cherie opened her eyes to see her husband's concerned expression. "You were having a nightmare. "It's okay now," he reassured, hugging her close. Cherie's pajamas and the sheets were soaked with perspiration. Josh had a cold cloth and was wiping her face. Furious, she grabbed the cloth from his hand and threw it across the room.

"I thought that was a gun when I felt that cold against my face!" she shouted at him.

"I'm sorry, baby; I was just trying to wake you. You were crying and screaming. You were all over the bed."

Cherie pulled away from Josh's grip and got out of bed. She was shaking violently, so much that her knees where like rubber. She nearly fell and had to grab the nightstand for support. Josh reached out to steady her but she pulled away from him. "Can't you just leave me alone," she shouted.

In the privacy of the shower her tears fell freely. She hid there for nearly an hour. She didn't feel up to dealing with Josh, and she was terrified to return to sleep. Cherie hoped the memory of what happened would wash down the drain with the water and her tears. She hoped the longer she stayed in there, the more of it would be washed away.

When Cherie finally returned to the small cabin bedroom, Josh had replaced the soaked bed linens with fresh ones and prepared a small snack of cheese and crackers for her. "I thought this might make you feel a little better."

He just didn't seem to understand. "No, Josh, no! Food will not make it all better!" she shouted at her husband. "Could you please just leave me alone for awhile?" There was no mistaking the hurt expression on her husband's face. He quietly picked up his pillow and left the bedroom.

Even though Josh understood what Cherie was going through, he was still human, and her behavior hurt him deeply. He didn't sleep at all the remainder of the night. He decided perhaps it was best if Cherie had some time away from him. Concerned that she would have another nightmare, he remained in the cabin until the sun came up. Then he summoned Stephen, who was temporarily residing in the east cabin. He asked Stephen to remain with Cherie until he returned later that evening, then he dressed and left the cabin quietly.

Cherie awoke to find Stephen sitting in the cabin living room. It was the first time she had seen him since the incident. "Good morning, Miss Cherie," he greeted.

Gasping in shock, Cherie didn't know what to say. From the time Cherie came to Montana with Josh she had not trusted Stephen. Then when she became aware of the threats upon her life, she truly believed Stephen had a hand in them. "Uh, good morning Stephen." The moment was strained, neither of them knowing what to say next. Finally, Cherie spoke, "Stephen, I am so sorry. I thought it was you. I am so sorry. I wouldn't blame you for hating me."

"Miss Cherie, I don't hate you. None of us knew it was Jeanie. Josh and I have known her since high school. I would've never guessed that she could have been so evil and malicious."

Stephen's reassurance didn't help Cherie's feelings of guilt. "I'm just sorry I didn't trust you. Josh told me you really worked hard trying to help him find me."

"Yes, Miss Cherie. So did the other staff. Everyone was very worried about you."

"I thought you hated me," she said.

"I'm sorry that you had that impression."

"Where is Josh?" she asked.

Stephen explained that Josh felt she needed some time to away from him, so he went to work at the store for a few hours. He said Josh told him she wasn't ready to be alone yet and asked him to stay with her.

Cherie was instantly angry, "Stephen, I don't need a babysitter. You don't have to stay with me. Actually, I would rather you not stay with me."

"Very well, Miss Cherie. I have set up a two – way radio, as a means for the two of you to communicate with me. It's on the kitchen counter. I'll be out with the horses. If you need me, all you have to do is press the talk button and I'll hear you."

"Fine, Stephen. And stop calling me Miss Cherie. My name is Cherie."

"Yes, ma'am," he said, nodding his head as he left.

Fuming, Cherie threw the radio out the back door of the cabin. The radio struck a rock and shattered.

When Josh returned to the apartment, Cherie's mood was no different. She remained cold and distant with him. Josh tried a few times to make initiate a conversation with her, but she would only respond with curt one word answers. Josh believed in his heart that Cherie blamed him for what happened. He did not ask nor realize that she was angry with him for leaving her alone with Stephen.

The nightmare repeated itself every night for the next two weeks. Josh would wake her up and change the bed linens while she showered. When she returned from the shower, he pretended to be fast asleep. Cherie's mood was so labile that she often exploded without provocation. She and Josh rarely spoke. Any conversation they did have was superficial. As Josh became more withdrawn Cherie's anger grew more intense. She was not released to return to work, and her physical activity was still restricted. There was nothing for her to do each day but think and remember.

Finally she couldn't take it anymore and exploded. The couple was having breakfast in the small kitchenette with total silence. Even though deep down Cherie knew that Josh's silence was directly related to her temperament, she superficially wanted to blame him for her terrible feelings. She tried a couple times to make small talk with him and received only one or two word answers. As her anger grew she became so frustrated that she threw her breakfast dish, filled with cereal and milk across the room. As it smashed against the wall she shouted, "How long are you going to stay mad at me! How long are you going to keep punishing me?"

Exasperated, her husband put his food down and stood up. "For one thing, I will not tolerate you throwing things in our home any more, and for another thing, I have never been angry with you."

"Then why won't you talk to me," she sobbed.

"Because, Cherie, I don't know what to do with you. If I try to talk to you, you explode. So, I'm just trying to give you what you want. Why don't you tell me what it is you want?"

Crying, she stuttered, "I, I don' don't k-know. I j- just w-want it all t-t-to go away."

Josh walked around the table and picked her up. He held her in his arms for the first time in over two weeks. "Cherie, I can't make it go away. I wish I could. I can be here for you and help you if you will let me. But you have to talk to me. I don't mean yell and scream. You have to let me in and let me know what is going on. Talk to me baby."

She climbed off his lap and paced. "Josh, do you have any idea what it's like to be stripped of your entire identity. To be told you have no rights and to be treated worse than a caged animal?" Josh remained silent, His coal black eyes glistening with tears. "For over a week I was nothing. Not once was I permitted anything to eat or drink. After I tried to escape in South Dakota, I wasn't even permitted to use the restroom. It seemed like every time I woke up, she beat me in the face and head until I passed out again. And, have you ever had to go to the bathroom so bad that it hurt and not be allowed to go. She would not untie me, not even for a couple minutes. I even thought my hands and feet might fall off. When I did wake up in that old farmhouse, you can imagine what I looked and smelled like. I was mortified. At that time, I didn't even want to be found alive. I would have rather been dead than to have anyone see me like that. But then I was afraid that if I let go and died, that the whole world would see me like that."

Cherie paused for a few minutes, trying to regain enough composure to speak again. Josh still remained silent. Cherie thought, *he must be thinking the worst of me now*.

It was almost like Josh just read her mind. "Cherie, no one would have blamed you. You had no control."

"That's just it Josh. I had no control. And I am sorry for saying this, but since I have been married to you, I have had no control over my life. You tell me what I can and can't do; you even tell me when to eat! You tell me that I need to gain weight. You tell me I have to have a chaperone when I leave our home. And then you send Stephen to babysit me when you go to work. I have no control!" she shouted.

Tears were streaming down Josh's face. "I'm so sorry Cherie. I didn't know you felt that way."

Cherie looked at her husband's tear soaked face, "Josh, I didn't want to hurt you. This didn't bother me so much before, but after being tied up for a week, well I'm sorry. Maybe it is best if I don't talk about this anymore."

"No, Cherie, You need to get this out. If you're unhappy, we need to work together to make things better. We are in this together. Now, go on."

"Before I married you, I had made a life for myself. I didn't have much, but what I had was mine. I didn't have to answer to anyone but God and I always lived my life knowing that I answered to God. So, the one thing I had that no one could take from me was my integrity."

"Cherie, you still have your integrity. You are a woman of high moral standards and the kindest humanitarian I have ever met."

"Do you have any idea how it feels to be told that the people who tormented you most of your life were the two that saved you? The two people who did everything in their power to strip me of my integrity! And they saw me in the horrible mess I was in?"

"Cherie, you were cleaned up when we all got to you. The guys didn't see you when you were soiled."

Cherie wanted to feel relieved, but questioned Josh how could he be so sure of that. She remembered being forced back onto the soiled sofa when Jeanie left to look for Jeff. "Cherie, your clothes were a little wet, but Dean and Jeff never got close enough to you to know that. Jeff was never permitted to return to the house. He led the feds into the farm, and then was kept in one of the cruisers for his own protection. Dean was shot the minute he burst through the basement door."

They both fell silent for a few minutes; the Josh spoke, "Cherie, I love you. I love you so much that it hurts. I feel helpless. What can I do to help you? I hate seeing you like this. I want my wife back."

"Josh, I love you to. You are the first person to ever love me. But, I need to be allowed to be myself, not your puppet."

"Baby, I'll admit that I want to take care of you. And now, even more than before, because of all you have been through. But I would never stand in the way of you being the person you are."

"But you do Josh. You have questioned everything I have wanted to do since we met, and you haven't respected any of my opinions! You told me that I'm not allowed to leave the house without you or Stephen, you…"

The expression on my husbands face stopped her from speaking further. That statement was unfair and she knew it. She had hurt him deeply. Josh was trying to protect her and felt guilty enough that he hadn't been able to. "I need to think right now," he said after moments of silence. "I am torn between wanting to hold you and try and make all of your pain go away, and wanting to put you over my knee and spanking you for the way you have been behaving." He stopped for a couple minutes while they both sat in silence. "And no, I'm not angry with you, and I don't want you to get the idea that I won't listen to you, or don't want you to talk to me. But right now, I need some time to think. I'm going to the barn for a while. Perhaps while I'm gone, you can clean up your mess," he said, pointing to the dish with cereal that she had thrown against the wall. He bent down and kissed her softly on the lips and told her he would be back to continue their conversation by lunch time.

"But understand this. I love you and I'm willing to do anything to help you through this time. I'm aware that you have been traumatized. But, I will not tolerate you breaking things in your fits or rage anymore. That radio you broke cost thousands dollars. If you do it again, you won't like what happens afterward."

Josh walked out of the cabin and left her standing there with her mouth open. *How could he even consider threatening me like that after all I've been through*? Cherie immediately felt a pit in her stomach. Emptiness filled the room. *What am I going to do? Damn Jeanie for ruining my happiness*, she thought as she flopped down on the hard dining room chair to sulk. Mother's famous words kept running through her head. She slammed her fist on the table and stood up. *No one is going to ruin my life again*, she decided. *Not my mother and not Jeanie. They're both dead and I need to bury the memories and move on*. The anger raged uncontrollably again. Cherie picked up a glass vase from the end stand and threw it against the television set. Not only did the vase shatter, but it left a huge dent in the side of the television.

Panic suddenly filled her. *What have I done*? Josh will be furious and has every right to be. She paced frantically, running her fingers through her hair. The memory of the last time she angered Josh flooded her mind.

After several minutes she decided it was time to stop sulking and try to make amends with her husband. He had repeatedly proven his love for her and it was time she accepted it and returned it tenfold. *Since we met I have done nothing but challenge his love.*

Cherie began to pick up the broken glass from the vase and the dish she had broken earlier. Cherie would have never dreamt of behaving so poorly a few weeks ago. She went into the kitchen and moistened a cloth to wipe off the wall and the floor where the cereal and milk had started to dry. The carpet was stained and would need to be cleaned professionally. Cherie couldn't blame Josh for being angry with her.

After she cleaned up the broken glass and food mess, Cherie retreated to the bedroom to shower and dress for the day. For the first time since they had returned home, Cherie decided to fix her hair and try to look presentable for Josh. Clothing choices were limited since she only owned the few pieces they bought back in Ohio. All of her other clothes were burned in the fire. She dressed in a pair of denim jeans and a pink sweater.

Because Josh was trying so hard to appease and comfort her, he didn't get to finish his breakfast. He would be hungry when he came back into the house. Cherie went into the kitchen to try and prepare lunch for him. The thought of cooking raised her anxiety, but she decided she must get past it and not let the old ghosts keep haunting her. Josh came back into the cabin just as she was scraping the burnt remains of the hamburgers into the garbage disposal.

"Oh, what is that smell?" he questioned, sniffing the burned air as he entered the smoke filled kitchen.

Cherie walked over to her husband and embraced him. "Josh, I'm so sorry for the horrible things I said to you. I was trying to make lunch, to make up to you, but as you can see, my cooking skills haven't improved much."

Josh gently kissed her. "You look nice," he said, then he told her he would be ready in fifteen minutes and would take her out to lunch and maybe shopping if she was up to it. Josh headed for the bedroom to shower and change when he stopped short in front of the television. "What happened here," he asked, the softness in his voice turned to anger.

"I happened, Josh." Cherie said softly. "I lost it again after you left. I'm sorry. I don't blame you for being angry with me. I'm angry with me too."

"Cherie, we are going to go into town and see your doctor. If he can't give me an explanation for your behavior, I am going to put you across my lap and spank you when we get home. I warned you before I left the cabin this morning that I would not tolerate that anymore, and you did it again. The only thing that is holding me back right now is I don't know if you are physically strong enough yet." With that he did an about face and went into the bedroom.

"I've been thinking," Josh said as they drove into town. "You're right. I do treat you more like a child that a wife. I've always seen you as fragile and helpless. So it's time for me to stop treating you that way, and start seeing you as an equal partner." Cherie tried to interrupt Josh to tell him that she was not really unhappy with the way he treated her, but he insisted on finishing his speech. "No, hear me out. It still stands that you are to respect my wishes if I tell you to do or not to do something, but for the most part, I would like your input in how we manage our lives. Would that be agreeable to you?"

Shocked, she answered, "I guess so. I don't know anything about running a ranch or managing employees."

"Well, you're going to learn. The first thing we need to do is decide on a plan for rebuilding our home. Tomorrow we have an appointment with a contractor. It is time to get started with rebuilding. I don't think I can tolerate living in that small cabin for much longer."

"What do I know about building a house Josh? That's something best done by you."

Josh insisted that she participate. "You're correct, Cherie. I gave you no control in your life. You are going to have to work with me here, because I've always managed all of the financial and business affairs. It's going to be an adjustment for me too. But a worthwhile adjustment if it'll make you feel better."

"So you are giving into me because I threw a tantrum?"

"No, I'm not giving in to you because you had a tantrum, but because you had a valid point. I would not suggest anymore tantrums though. I realize that I can't begin to understand what you've been through, but I will do anything in my power to help you. You can talk to me and tell me how you are feeling. When you are a little stronger you can work out and jog or something to work off excess stress. But for now, you and I are going to work on curbing that little temper of yours.

Cherie felt relieved when the lecture ended and Josh changed the subject. She felt embarrassed enough about her behavior with out him scolding her over and over for it too. Josh diverted the subject back to the rebuilding of the house. "Do we have to rebuild in the same spot?" Cherie asked. Josh agreed that they could look into other parts of the ranch to build on. There was plenty of clearing in the center and the northern sections. Every time Cherie went past the empty lot where their home had been, the memories flooded back into her mind, resurfacing all of the feelings of anger, guilt, and fear that she was trying so hard to get past. "I'm afraid if I have to look at that sight everyday, I'll go completely crazy," she added.

"Tomorrow, we'll go out and pick out a sight before the contractor arrives," Josh promised.

At the doctor's office, Josh and Dr. Jones discussed Cherie's behavior as if she were not even in the room. Irritated, she got up off the exam table and began to pace in her hospital gown. "What is it, Cherie," Dr. Jones asked.

"What is it! What is it?" she shouted. "You two talk about me as if I'm on another planet or something and I'm supposed to sit here in this damn gown and listen! Who's the patient here, and where the hell did you get your manners?!"

Josh cleared his throat and gave his wife a chilling look. "Cherie," he said harshly. He firmly took her arm and helped her back up onto the examination table. The look in Josh's coal black eyes offered he clear warning not to push her luck any further.

"Mr. Tolsten, would you please wait in the waiting room while I examine your wife."

"You must be quiet a brave man to be alone in this room with her. She's been pretty volatile here lately," Josh said in a condescending tone.

After Josh left the room, Dr. Jones turned to Cherie. He began asking her dozens of questions while he ignored her belligerent behavior. Cherie felt worse than if he would have lectured or scolded her. At least then she wouldn't have felt so guilty. Instead he remained calm and unmoved by her slurs of verbal abuse. Eventually, Cherie realized that she was pouring her heart out to this stranger she had only seen a couple times before. She talked to him told him about her mom and about Jeanie and how she was held captive. They discussed the memories, and the nightmares, and she even told him about being left to urinate and defecate in her clothes.

Dr. Jones listened to Cherie rant and rave for over an hour. When she was finished he politely asked her if he could listen to her heart and lungs, and perform an EKG test on her heart. The doctor did not sugar coat anything with Cherie. He told her that usually he would have his nurse do the EKG, but because of her agitated mood he would do it.

After the exam was complete, he asked her if he could bring Josh back in. "I would like to talk with the two of you together if that's okay with you, Mrs. Tolsten."

Irritated at his apparent insensitivity about her attire, she demanded, "Well, would you mind letting me get dressed first. I'm not exactly comfortable in this thing!" she said, flipping the lower hem of the hospital gown.

While Cherie was changing clothes, Dr. Jones took the opportunity to speak privately with Josh. "How are the two of you doing?" he asked. "You have both been through such a terrific trauma."

"We are just surviving," Josh replied sadly. "I am at a point where I just don't know what to do with her. If I try to talk to her she gets angry, and if I don't talk she gets angry. She throws and breaks things ... I, uh I just don't know what to do to help her."

"Mr. Tolsten, your wife is suffering from post traumatic stress disorder. She really needs a lot of time and patience. She has been through a terrible ordeal. Has she been having flashbacks or nightmares?"

"Yes, terrible nightmares. But she is always angry with me when she wakes up. I feel so helpless. I am to the point where I avoid her because I don't know what else to do."

"Maybe she's not ready to be alone yet?"

"I don't know," Josh said. "I am willing to try anything."

Moments later Cherie joined Josh in Dr. Jones office. Dr. Jones sat across from the couple, behind his huge Mahogany desk. He stared silently at the papers he had lying in front of him for what seemed like eternity. Finally he cleared his throat and spoke softly, "Mrs. Tolsten, you have a clean bill of health. Your heart is strong and there are no abnormal rhythms detectable on the EKG. You can return to normal activity. I want you to start an exercise program to gradually increase your strength and endurance."

"That's wonderful news, Dr. Jones, but what about Cherie's awful mood swings? She is so explosive. I don't know what to do with her," Josh demanded.

"Mrs. Tolsten, your husband and I have already had this conversation. You are suffering from Post Traumatic Stress Syndrome. You have been through a terrible ordeal and have been emotionally and psychologically traumatized."

"Like I need you to tell me I have been through an ordeal. You couldn't possibly begin to know!" Cherie exclaimed, obviously irritated.

Unaffected by her sarcasm he went on, "Mrs. Tolsten, you may want to consider counseling. I can give you the name of an excellent psychologist, if you would like."

"I don't want to go to no psychologist!" she said angrily.

Dr. Jones concluded that some physical activity may be helpful as well, but gave her and Josh the business card of the psychologist he was recommending. "Mr. Tolsten, I would like you to have one of these cards too. You may find it necessary to have someone to talk to yourself. The two of you have both been through a horrible nightmare. You need to take care of yourselves."

The rest of the afternoon went relatively smooth. Josh and Cherie had lunch and shopped to replenish their wardrobes. They actually enjoyed one another's company. Before they concluded their outing, the couple visited Josh's western store. Cherie purchased two new pair of boots, one for riding and one for causal wear, and a pair of jeans. She was happy to talk with some of the other sales clerks. "Are you coming back to work," one of the girls asked.

Cherie just smiled and nodded. "I just got my release from the doctor, so maybe someday soon I'll be able to work a couple days a week."

When they arrived home that evening, Cherie was thoroughly exhausted. After they finished putting away their purchases, Josh ordered Cherie into the shower. "We have a little matter of unfinished business to deal with," he said. Cherie knew what she was in for and there was no use trying to talk her way out of it. She went in and showered then dressed for bed. She had bought a white satin night gown with spaghetti straps and a high bodice. She donned the gown, then brushed her hair and pinned it up neatly and applied lightly scented perfume. When she returned from the bathroom Josh smiled and kissed her brow. "You look wonderful," he said, then disappeared into the bathroom.

When Josh returned from his shower, Cherie was in the kitchen preparing a light snack. "Come here, Cherie," he ordered. When she tried to delay he called a little louder, "Come here now, Cherie."

Slowly she walked into the bedroom. Her body trembled and she felt like she was walking her last mile. Josh walked over and met her at the doorway then took her by the hand.

He saw the expression on his wife's face and noticed her trembling body. She had been through so much pain, and now he had threatened her and caused her even more anxiety. "Sit down here with me Cherie. I need to talk to you," he said tenderly.

"Yes, sir."

Josh wrapped his arm around her shoulders, "Look," he said, "I know you know that I'm a man of my word. When I say I am going to do something, I follow through. This morning I threatened to spank you. And up until this very moment, I intended to do exactly that. But Hon, when I saw the expression on your face just now, I realized that I could not inflict any more pain on you." He paused for a few minutes, realizing that his own behavior over the past two weeks had only served to increase her suffering. Cherie remained silent, tears streaming down her face. Josh continued, "I haven't done right by you since we've been home. The truth is, the night you kicked me out of the bedroom you hurt my pride. I have consciously chosen to avoid you, rather than deal with you. I was at a loss. I didn't know what to say or do, so I stayed away as much as possible."

Cherie finally felt safe to speak, "Josh, I don't blame you. I haven't been very nice to you."

"No, you haven't. And I have felt like you were blaming me for what happened to you, as much as I've been blaming myself."

"I don't blame you, I love you. I am mad, but not mad at you. I'm just mad. I can't explain it, but it never seems to go away. And I don't know what to do about it," Cherie sobbed.

"Well, that is where I think I fell short with you. I have left you alone here everyday since we moved into this cabin. So here you were, alone in this cabin with nothing to keep you company but the memories. I am so sorry for that babe."

"I understand you have to work, Josh," Cherie answered between sobs.

"But the truth is, I really don't have to work every day. I have plenty of staff to do what needs to be done. I was hiding from everything. Starting tomorrow I'm on vacation. I'm not leaving you alone until you're feeling better. And no matter how nasty you get, you won't drive me away," he chided.

"You mean you don't hate me? I was afraid you were going to tell me to go away for good."

"Cherie, baby, you still don't understand the meaning of love. When you really love someone, you love them for everything they are, not just the good. Yes, I was upset with you so I avoided you. That was my stupid pride. I always have to be in control of everything and I couldn't control you. But I have never, and will never stop loving you. You are my life, young lady. You are everything to me," Josh promised.

"I love you too, Josh, so much that it hurts. I didn't want to live when Jeanie told me you only married me to do away with me and collect my life insurance. I felt like nothing mattered if you didn't love me. And this past two weeks, I thought you hated me."

Josh and Cherie made love that night, for the first time since she had been abducted. Cherie's body responded to him with a fire that was almost insatiable. His strong hands rubbed and caressed her body in all the right places, causing her skin to tingle like it was the first time he had ever touched her. He explored every inch of her body with his lips and tongue. When he reached her most private part, she screamed with delight, an orgasm so intense that she shivered for several minutes after. Cherie wanted so desperately to give back. She climbed on top of him and let her tongue explore his body, tasting every inch. She began with his earlobes and gently licked and suckled as she slowly worked her way down every inch of his body. Then Josh lifted her to straddle his hips and entered her. They rocked together and loved one another until they both collapsed, mentally and physically exhausted.

Josh lay next to his lovely wife, holding her and caressing her until she fell asleep. As he held her close and caressed her back and ran his fingers through her hair, Cherie felt a strange sense of relief. Josh loved her and would stay by her side in spite of her anger. She slept that night without any nightmares; the first good night's sleep she had since they returned home.

Josh felt the same sense of relief. They had opened the lines of communication and renewed their love for one another. He slept that night, knowing he was getting his wife back; the loving and gentle woman he knew and fell in love with would be back.

~ CHAPTER 17 ~

AN UNEXPECTED CHRISTMAS GIFT

Cherie awoke Christmas morning to find her husband had already gotten up and left their small cabin. She smiled to herself as she recalled the events of the holiday season. Josh was certainly a generous man, and his generosity extended to each and every one of his employees. Because their new home was not yet completed, and the cabin afforded little space for entertaining, Josh had the barn cleaned and decorated for the local employees Christmas party last evening. The party ran for most of the day and into the evening to accommodate all employees and their families. Each person who worked either on the ranch on in Josh's store received a notable Christmas bonus in addition to door prizes and tons of food. There were also small gifts for the employee's spouses and children.

For the two weeks prior to Christmas, Josh and Cherie had traveled to Utah and New Mexico, to his branch stores to provide Christmas parties for the employees there. Cherie had been astounded by Josh's generosity. "Your employees are your business," Josh told her. "If you keep your employees happy, they'll make a profit for you. I like for them to think of their job as more than just a job. I want them to think of their work as an investment. Each employee is given a bonus of one percent of the company profit at the end of the year. Managers receive two percent. For the employees that I don't see routinely, and for my local employees, I know they will work hard for me and take care of my business because they know I appreciate them, and they know they will gain from a good year."

Josh's generosity was well spent on Cherie over the past months of their marriage. Not only had he provided her with an excellent place in which to live, but all of the clothing her heart desired and a new car. If she even looked at something while they were shopping, it was purchased for her. Because Josh was constantly showering her with gifts, and because her past experience with Christmas, Cherie didn't expect any gifts on this blessed day. She considered herself grateful for Josh and that was enough for her.

Cherie showered and dressed, then went out in to the small living room to find dozens of wrapped packages beneath and around their beautifully decorated Christmas tree. Her heart fluttered as she thought, *this must be what a small child feels like who has waited all night for Santa to come.* Then she felt a small tinge of guilt. She had only bought a gold watch and a small Devotional Bible for Josh.

Cherie walked outside to see that her husband was no where in sight. Shivering against the cold, she went back inside to retrieve her coat and boots. The snow was deep but the staff had cleared a path to the barn. At the barn, Cherie watched as her husband skillfully mastered the young black mare she had befriended a few months ago. At that time, the mare was much too young to break and train to ride. Josh looked over to see Cherie standing near the fence of the coral and rode over to her. "Merry Christmas, Mrs. Tolsten."

Cherie smiled and returned the greeting. "I'm surprised to see you riding her!" she exclaimed. Josh promptly dismounted from the mare and handed the reins across the fence to Cherie.

"Merry Christmas, my love."

Cherie gasped. "Josh, are you saying…"

"Yep, she's yours."

"But how did you get her ready so soon. You rode her with such ease."

"Well, young 'en, for you all things are possible. We've been working day and night to have her ready for you. Come on, how about a ride." Josh swiftly lifted Cherie over the fence and helped her on the horse. He smiled to himself at how beautiful she looked atop the black mare. Cherie bent down and kissed her husband then kicked the horse gently. Josh watched with pride as his wife rode the beautiful mare. It looked as though the two of them were made for one another.

Cherie had forgotten about the abundance of Christmas gifts that await her beneath the Christmas tree until Josh called her in from riding. "Come on Mrs. Tolsten, there are many more presents for you to enjoy today." Regretfully Cherie dismounted her new treasure and hugged her husband tightly. "Thank you Mr. Tolsten, I love her and I love you." The couple walked arm and arm back to the cabin.

To say she was showered with gifts was an understatement. She was correct in her original estimation. There were dozens of packages for her. He gave her a beautiful diamond teardrop necklace with a matching bracelet and earrings, and another sapphire and diamond necklace and matching ring. There was a new coat – parka style for the cold wet winters in Montana. Josh had also bought several new sweaters and a beautiful evening gown with matching accessories. "That is for our New Year's Eve celebration," he advised her. Cherie was delighted with each new gift she opened. "I feel like a little kid, Josh. You shouldn't have bought so much."

"I told you that your holidays with me would be much different than anything you have ever known. Now do you believe me?"

Cherie smiled and got up to give her husband his gifts from her. "I feel a little embarrassed Josh. This in no way compares to what you have just given me." Josh opened the watch first and examined it closely. "I love it, and I really needed a new one. I lost my other one last week." When he opened the Devotional Bible and Cherie thought she saw the glimmer of a tear in his eye. "I have never had a Devotional Bible. I will always cherish this. But you have given me something far more valuable than any amount of money could buy."

"What's that?" she asked.

"You gave me my wife back. Than sweet loving lady I fell in love with." The couple embraced in a passionate kiss when they heard the sound of a strange vehicle approaching the cabin. Josh grumbled about the help not securing the ranch good enough, and then shouted with joy as he saw his parents step out of the car.

"Cherie, Cherie, come quickly. It's my mom and dad." He grabbed Cherie by the hand and nearly dragged her out the front door to greet the parents he hadn't seen in over a year. Both parents hugged their son with great pleasure and warmth. Then Mrs. Tolsten stepped back and looked Cherie over, "Josh, who is this?" Mary Tolsten inquired.

"Mama, Dad, this is my wife, Cherie. Cherie these are my parents, Don and Mary. The tension mounted within Cherie. Her thoughts racing, *Oh my, what must they be thinking, they are probably thinking that I …*

Cherie's thoughts were interrupted when Mrs. Tolsten grabbed her in a full embrace, "Cherie, I'm so happy to meet you. Shocked, but still happy. After Leona's death, I never thought my Josh would marry again."

Mr. Tolsten hugged Cherie, a little more gently, "Yes, we are happy to meet you. Our son looks well. You must be making him happy."

"She does make me happy, happier than you'll ever know," Josh said as he directed his family to continue their emotional reunion in the cabin.

"Mr. and Mrs. Tolsten are you hungry; can we get you something to eat, or maybe some coffee?" Cherie asked. It wasn't until then that Josh smelled the aroma of the turkey cooking in the oven.

"Oh yes, we have Christmas dinner cooking in the oven. Mama, Dad, would you like to freshen up in the spare bedroom while I help Cherie finish dinner? Then we can all sit down and eat together. We have a lot of catching up to do."

"You're right about that son, like what on earth happened to your beautiful home, and why are you two living here?" Mr. Tolsten asked.

"Well, Dad, I'll update you on everything, just as Cherie and I want to hear all about your mission trip. But, right now we need to see to that turkey or you will have a burned dinner."

When the couple was alone in the kitchen, Cherie looked pleadingly at her husband, "What are you going to tell them Josh. I really don't want to talk about all of that today. It is Christmas, and it's supposed to be a happy day. And I don't want that to be their first impression of me."

"Relax love. With my parents, it is best to tell them the truth. I know it brings up unhappy memories for you, but it is best to say it and get it over with. Trust me; my parents will not judge you for what happened."

"But what if they blame me for the loss of your house!" Cherie exclaimed, almost crying.

Josh wrapped his arms around he, "Baby girl, don't do that to yourself. I have done all that I can to show you love and to try to make up to you for what happened. But I can't stop you from beating yourself up. Look, I'm a product of my parents and I'm not so bad, am I?"

"No, I guess not, I kind of like you," Cherie replied. Josh hugged his small wife then with a gentle swat told her they must hurry with dinner.

Josh, well aware of his wife's poor cooking abilities prepared the remainder of the dinner while Cherie prepared a small vegetable tray and performed other small tasks that kept her safely away from the stove.

Dinner proved to be relaxing and enjoyable. To Cherie's delight, Josh's parents kept the conversation focused on the mission trip they had been on for the past fourteen months. They talked about South Africa and the poor living conditions the people were forced to live in, as well as, the starvation and extreme hunger experienced by the population. Mr. Tolsten, a retired Veterinarian, explained that in addition to their primary duties, he provided care for the ailing animals. He taught the residents how to care for their animals and how to get them to work more effectively. They also participated in building better housing and assisting with food supplies. "We did what ever they needed us to do," Mr. Tolsten added. "There's nothing so heartbreaking as to see another human being starving to death, or a small child crying of hunger."

"Cherie has an interest similar to the two of you, Mama and Dad. I have seen her put herself at risk to help a homeless person."

Mary. Tolsten smiled softly at Cherie. Cherie knew instantly where Josh got his gentle nature and his smile. "Tell me about it Cherie, I would love to hear."

"Well," Cherie began shyly, "there really isn't much to tell. I just saw a man walking one day. He looked sick and hungry, so I went back after him and brought him home. I couldn't bear the thought that I was well fed and dressed in warm clothes, and the poor man was in rags and deathly thin."

"You know, Cherie," Mary began, "the Tolsten family has been blessed with great wealth. But I do not believe for one minute that God intended for us to keep our good fortune to ourselves. I think you did a fine thing there. You have to be careful, because being a woman of wealth leaves you wide open to all kinds of scams and well, you know."

Cherie felt her heart sink to her feet when Josh added, "She scared me to death, Mama. All I could think of were the dreadful things that could've happened to her. But it turned out that the man she brought home didn't have long to live. He died at County Hospital the very next day."

"I'm happy to hear that you are willing to reach out to a person in need," Mary Tolsten praised her daughter-in-law.

"Well, someday, I hope to be able to do more for the lesser fortunate. I don't mean just feeding them, but helping them find a way back, you know, retraining and such," Cherie added.

The group had finished their dinner. Cherie was afraid Josh would embarrass her by telling his parents more about the day she brought Joey home, and excused herself to obtain the deserts. Josh excused himself and followed Cherie into the kitchen, "Hey, you doing alright? Why'd you run out like that?"

"I, I j-just w-wanted to get the d-deserts," Cherie answered nervously.

"Ah, you were afraid I'd tell too much." Josh hugged his wife. "Cherie, how many times do I have to tell you, I'll never deliberately humiliate you. Now, just relax and enjoy yourself."

"Your parents are so warm and loving."

"Yes, and they are going to love you. I can already tell you have met their seal of approval. Just be yourself. That's how you won me over, you know."

"But I wasn't trying to win you over, Josh."

"Exactly. Now let's get these pies in there before they come looking for us." Cherie cut and served each of them a piece of pie while Josh provided them each with a fresh cup of coffee.

When the group finished their desert, Josh's father excused himself to go outdoors and smoke his pipe and asked Josh to join him. Once they were safely away from the cabin, Mr. Tolsten confronted his son, "Okay Josh, I got the feeling you didn't want to talk about the house in front of your wife, so tell me now."

"You're right Dad. Not today, I didn't want to put a blemish on our first Christmas together." Josh went on to recap the events that led to the destruction of his home and the capture of his wife. "So you see Dad, this is a very sensitive area. It took Cherie a long time to get over being kept in bondage for several days. She still gets upset easily, and understandably so. She was terrified at the thought of having to talk about it to you and Mama."

Josh's father turned and hugged his son, his heart heavy for what his son had endured his absence, "I am so sorry son. I had no idea that you were going through so much. I'm sorry we weren't here to be with you."

"It's okay Dad. As much as I wished you were here at the time, I wouldn't have been much company to you. I never left her side once we found her. Stephen managed everything, the stores and the ranch."

"I'll have to thank him for helping you. Please tell your lovely wife not to be uncomfortable with us."

"It would mean more coming from you and Mama. She's afraid the two of you will blame her for the loss of the house."

"I would like to talk to her and spend some time getting to know her. We can do that tomorrow. I understand not wanting to bring up old ghosts on Christmas Day."

The two men returned to the cabin to find Cherie and Mary Tolsten together in the small kitchenette, laughing and talking comfortably. Josh felt a sense of relief. With all that Cherie had been through with her mother, he had been uncertain how she would respond to his mother's doting ways. *At least they're getting off to a good start*, he mused as he remembered how Leona had resented his parents' visits to the extent that it made all of them uncomfortable.

His parents had responded to Leona's resentments by staying away. He had always been close to his parents, but to keep Leona happy, his parents stayed away, and Josh suffered silently.

Cherie excused herself to the restroom. Mary Tolsten walked over and warmly hugged her only son. "She's quite a young lady; are you happy son?"

"Yes, Mama, we are quite happy. We have had some rough times, but we stuck together. I believe we will be okay now."

"Are you going to at least tell me what happened to your beautiful home?" Mary prodded.

"Mama, I know you are curious and concerned, but I don't want to discuss it around my wife today, not on Christmas day. The memories are too painful for her and I don't want to ruin today for her. Tomorrow we will sit and talk and do all the catching up we need to do, I promise," Josh responded.

"It's okay, Josh, you can tell them today. They have a right to know," Cherie said as she re-entered the room. With that, Cherie turned to her in-laws, "Mr. and Mrs. Tolsten, it's because of me that the house burned to the ground. I'm so sorry. I only hope that you don't hate me for it. Now, if you will excuse me, I'd like to go to rest now." She then returned to the safety of her bedroom.

The older couple exchanged concerned glances. Don Tolsten was already aware of the trauma his daughter-in-law had been through, and had hoped to be able to tell his wife in the privacy of their room later that night, but it was too late. He nodded to his wife, and then Mary added, "I've pushed too hard. I'm sorry Josh. We can talk more tomorrow. Right now, we are going to go and find a motel room for the night."

"Absolutely not," Josh protested. "We have a spare bedroom here. There's no need for you to battle this weather and go back into town this late."

"Josh," his mother countered, "Thanks to me, you and your wife need to have some time alone. It's obvious that she's upset. You should go and be with her, and we'll see you tomorrow."

Josh took his mother by the hand and led her into the small kitchenette. "No, Mama, you don't understand. If you leave now, Cherie will be convinced that you're angry with her. I promise, after you get to know her better, you'll understand."

Knowing her son well, Mary saw the pleading in her son's eyes. *Something is dreadfully wrong here*, she thought to herself. Don Tolsten nodded to his wife then quietly went to retrieve their suitcases.

"No, No, please stop!" Cherie cried out in pain as the butt end of the gun smashed into her face. She suddenly felt cold, chilled deeply as though someone poured ice water over her. She was soaking wet, it was freezing and her nose was bleeding, where did all of that blood come from? Why wouldn't it stop? It was getting harder to breath. "You'll never see your precious Josh again. And if you don't behave yourself, I will kill him, kill him … kill … Cherie cried out again. She couldn't move. Her hands were being tied, and the pain, that awful pain in her head …

Cherie thrashed back and forth in the bed so fiercely that she had herself tied and restrained within the blankets. The bed linens were soaking wet. "Cherie," she heard Josh's voice, Josh, maybe she would see him, and maybe Jeanie didn't kill him yet.

"Baby, it's me, please wake up. You're dreaming." When Cherie opened her eyes, Josh saw the horrified expression on her face. She was ghost white and looked like a small animal, cornered and about to die.

Neither of them spoke. Josh quietly helped her from the tangled covers. Once she was alone in the shower, the dam broke and tears began to fall. She sobbed quietly, letting the water wash the tears down the drain. When she was completely exhausted and had no more strength, she stepped out of the shower and returned to the small cabin bedroom.

Josh sat waiting for her on the edge of their bed. He hugged her close, soothing her hair. "Sometimes I am afraid it will never stop," she quietly confided to her husband.

"You will probably never forget my love, but it will get easier, I promise. But it will take a long time," Josh said trying helplessly to comfort her.

Cherie lay quietly in the still of the night until she was certain that Josh had returned to sleep. Then she got out of bed, taking care not to disturb her sleeping husband. Her sleep was gone for the night. The fear of the nightmare returning would likely keep her from sleeping for many nights to come.

She wrapped herself in a blanket and curled into the window seat in the living room. She sat without making a sound, gazing out into the night and letting her mind wonder. The moon was full and the sky was clear and bright with stars. It had snowed several more inches since they had retired for the night. The snow glistened, smooth and untouched with the moon casting a bluish glow upon it.

Cherie was completely unaware that her mother-in-law stood quietly behind her until she felt a firm hand rest upon her shoulder. Cherie, startled back into reality, looked up to see the older Tolsten woman standing over her. Mary Tolsten was a beautiful woman. Cherie could clearly see where her husband got his good looks and charming personality. Mary stood nearly six inches taller than Cherie, with dark eyes and long thick wavy black hair. Cherie could see the questioning in her mother-in-law's eyes.

"Mind if I join you?" Mary asked as she hugged her bathrobe against her for warmth.

Cherie smiled and nodded, "There's another blanket in that closet. It gets pretty cold in here at night."

Mary wrapped herself in the blanket then climbed in to the window seat, opposite of Cherie. "I heard you crying earlier. Were you having a bad dream?"

"I'm sorry you had to hear that."

"You want to tell me about it?" Mary offered. "Sometimes it helps to talk."

"Josh woke up. He talked to me for a little while. I'm okay now," Cherie said.

For the next few hours Cherie confided almost her entire life story to her mother-in-law. She talked about her own mother and the abuse, and the abuse of the townspeople. She shared in graphic detail the events of her capture and the abuse she endured at the mercy of the Tolsten's former housekeeper. She wasn't certain what had happened, or how Mary had managed to get her to open up and talk so freely, but she had been successful.

In their own rooms, both Josh and Don Tolsten sat and listened as Cherie poured her heart out to her mother-in-law. Josh was grateful for his parent's surprise appearance yesterday afternoon. Maybe his mother was just what Cherie needed. She always had a way of making him feel better when he was a child, and even after he had grown up. He smiled, thinking back to his childhood. Even though he was an only child, his parents were determined that he would not be a 'spoiled little rich kid.' He had many rules and was expected to work, and from the time he was twelve, had to earn anything he wanted over and above the basic necessities. However, sometimes his parents doting could be overwhelming. His mother was always loving and nurturing. How she had managed to be so strict and expect complete obedience to the house rules, and so loving and caring he would probably never understand. But she was. If he felt sad, or scared, or if he had a bad dream, she was always there to love and comfort him.

Mary's heart was breaking for her daughter-in-law. She climbed down from the window seat and walked over to hug Cherie. Having only one child, Mary decided here was the daughter she had always wanted. She knew she loved this young girl almost as much as she loved her own son.

The following morning the two couples enjoyed a long breakfast together. Josh always closed his store for the week of Christmas, so his only obligation was to the ranch. And for that he had enough hired help that he could afford to remain with his wife and parents. Cherie had talked enough with her mother-in-law during the night that she had already developed a level of comfort with her. She felt grateful for the opportunity to know Josh's parents.

Later that day Josh pulled Cherie aside. He had been out to the barn with his father. When he returned, he suddenly had something important to talk with Cherie about. "What is it Josh?"

"Look, hon, I know this is a difficult subject for you, but I need to make a decision. However, since you were the one who was hurt, I would like to make it your decision."

"What is it Josh?" she asked again.

"Stephen has received a progress report on Dean. It seems he is home and is expected to make a full recovery. Now, up until now, Jeff has agreed to stay on at the farm until we knew what was going to happen with Dean. But their contract time has expired."

"So, what are you asking me? Do I have to see them again?" Cherie asked.

"Well, you don't have to. What I was thinking was, well, yes, they did hurt you, but they did the time we expected of them. And believe me, I was not very generous about paying them. But, since they both risked their lives to save you, and I doubt you are going to want anything more to do with that farm, I was considering giving the farm to the two of them."

"Josh that is a wonderful idea! I really do appreciate that they both tried to help me, but I still don't want to have to see or talk to them."

"You won't have to love. I can fly back to Ohio and sign the deed over to them, that is, if they want it, and be back within one or two days. If you don't want to go with me, I can leave you here with Mama, and take my dad with me."

~ CHAPTER 18 ~

BIRTHDAY SURPRISE

April brought completion of the new Tolsten home. A brick ranch home that was certain to be the envy of every homeowner in Montana. Nestled in the hillside of the northern aspect of Tolsten Acres was the center, or core of the house, containing an entrance way that lead into a large formal dining room on the left. Off to the side of the formal dining room was a smaller, more intimate dining room to be used for most family meals. Just on the east side of the small dining room was the kitchen. A kitchen that was every woman's dream: very large and roomey, yet intimate and homey. To the right of the entrance way was a large formal living room, then Josh's den and office on either side. In addition to the center of the house, there were two wings, one on the east side of the house, and one to the west. The two wings came together in the back of the house, forming and enclosed courtyard that one could only enter through the house. The west wing contained Josh and Cherie's private suite – a large bedroom with a sitting room, a small office and an attached bathroom. Down the hall were two private bedroom suites, intended for children the couple hoped to have in the future. The east wing contained the private suite and living area for his parents, four guest suites and Stephen's suite.

At Cherie's request, or rather insistence, there were no provisions made for housekeeping staff to live in the Tolsten home. The couple had yet to hire an additional housekeeper. Betsy, the maid who took care of the cabins two days a week was increased to five days a week. Her schedule was for her to clean the Tolsten home three days a week, and then spend two days a week working in the cabins. She didn't live on the Tolsten acres. Cherie was adamant that she could manage the remainder of the household duties, with her mother-in-law's assistance in the kitchen.

After learning of the tribulations their son and daughter-in-law had been through during the older Tolsten's most recent mission trip, Josh's parents decided they were needed at home. Originally they planned to purchase a small home of their own, but Josh and Cherie insisted they reside with them. "There's more than enough room here," Cherie insisted, "And besides, I like having you around." She meant that with all of her heart. Cherie and Mary Tolsten had developed a genuine bond between the two of them. She felt a comfort she had never known from her own mother, and her life was now fuller than it had ever been.

Josh was grateful. He had always been close to his parents, and unfortunately did not have much opportunity to spend time with them when Leona was alive. In spite if his intense love for her, he was realizing more and more that his marriage to her had not been as good as he had pretended.

Cherie's birthday was also in April. Josh had not been able to celebrate her birthday with her one year ago. Their relationship was still new, and she had neglected to tell him about it. Josh wanted very much to do something extra special for his young bride. Even though Cherie seemed to be slowly getting over the trauma of last fall's events, Josh would carry the guilt through eternity. Every time he looked at his wife's beautiful body, the scars served as a reminder that he had failed to protect her. Fortunately, Cherie's face had healed without any scars, but her chest, where Jeanie had beaten her so brutally, and the lacerations from her fall in the hospital had left significant scars. Josh never did talk with Cherie about them. She seemed either not to notice them, or not bothered. He didn't want to upset her, so he bore the guilt alone.

One rainy spring afternoon, Mary noticed her son's excessive preoccupation. Cherie had gone into town with Don, so Mary took the opportunity to talk with her son. "What is it that troubles you, son?"

"Nothing Mama. I'm just a little frustrated with the rain. I can't do what I needed to do in the barn today," Josh responded, trying to cover up the truth.

Mary and Josh knew each other well. A simple look with folded arms warned Josh he needed to give up the truth to his mother.

"Ok, Mama. I have just been thinking about Cherie. I'll always feel responsible for how badly she was injured. It seems as though I can never do enough to make it up to her."

"Look son," Mary lectured, "You can never undo the past. I don't believe your wife blames you, not even a little for what happened. You must stop blaming yourself and go on with your life."

"I know, I know. But I would like to do something special for her; you know her birthday is the end of this month."

"Well, why not have a party for her. You know a surprise party. I can help you plan it. It'll be fun. I haven't gotten to do a birthday since you were a young boy."

Josh and his mother worked together every day to plan the party for Cherie. Keeping it a surprise was nearly impossible but they managed. After talking with her friends back home, Josh purchased and sent each of them airline tickets. He invited Mongo and Katie and their two girls, and Pastor Mark and family. Sam, to his disappointment, couldn't make the trip, but agreed to manage the diner so Mongo could be free for the trip. He had one last surprise, but it was a lot harder than he had anticipated. He wanted to find Nurse Kerri. It appeared that she had left the hospital after the incident with Cherie.

With all of Josh's connections, it still seemed impossible to locate Kerri. He even took a "business trip," telling Cherie and his parents that there was an emergency at one of the stores in New Mexico. He flew back to Ohio and attempted to locate her. For days he tried. Finally, out of desperation, he revisited the hospital Cherie was treated in less than one year ago. To his good fortune, one of the nurses in the Intensive Care Unit kept in touch with Kerri. Her friend took Josh's name and phone number and agreed to give Kerri the message. It would be Kerri's decision whether or not to contact Josh.

There was nothing left to do but hope and pray. Kerri had been so instrumental in Cherie's recovery. Josh believed with all his heart that her presence at Cherie's surprise birthday party would mean the world to Cherie.

When April 25th arrived, Cherie still had no idea of what lie in store for her. Josh told her he was taking her out to dinner and a movie to celebrate then the couple bid the older Tolsten's goodbye and left the ranch.

As they drove into town, Josh and Cherie reminisced about their first date. Cherie recalled how terrified she was to be alone with Josh, and how he had been the perfect gentleman. The couple talked away until all of a sudden, Josh gasped in surprise.

"What is it Josh?"

"Well, it appears that I have forgotten my wallet. We'll have to go back home to get it. That means we may be late for the movie. I hope you don't mind."

The house was dark when the Tolstens arrived. Cherie opted to wait in the car for Josh, but he gently persuaded her to come in the house with him. "I have no idea where I might have left my wallet. If you will help me to look for it, maybe we can be on our way a little faster. The reservations are in less than one half hour. We need to hurry." Cherie obliged her husband and entered their home with him.

Josh pretended to search the entrance hall, then ask Cherie, "Hon, will you look in the den for me, I think that may have been where I left it.

When she opened the door to the den, she gasped and squealed with delight and shock as all of her friends shouted, SURPRISE!"

Cherie thought she must be dreaming for she saw Mongo and Katie, Pastor Mark and his wife, and Nurse Kerri. With her hands over her mouth, she trembled with this surprise. She looked helplessly at Josh as nurse Kerri rushed over to hug her.

Still trying to recover from the shock, Cherie returned the hug to Kerri then hugged each one of her guests. One last surprise, Don and Mary Tolsten entered from the dining room and asked all of the guests to follow them. In the dining room was more food than Cherie had ever seen in one place.

The group partied and talked for hours, each catching up with the others lives over the past year. Josh sat back and watched his wife, who seemed to be thoroughly enjoying herself. "You did well, Mama, we did well."

When the party was over, Cherie was delighted to find that all of her guests would be staying in the guest rooms for the next couple of days. They made plans to take them all sightseeing in the morning before all of the guests retired. Cherie hugged her husband, "Thank you, Josh. I love you so very much. I really was getting a little homesick. I'm so happy to see everyone."

"You are welcome, Mrs. Tolsten, but I'm not done with you yet. You go and tell Mama and Dad goodnight, then go and get ready for bed. I have one more surprise for you."

"Oh Josh, I don't think I can handle any more surprises tonight. Can't it wait until tomorrow?"

Josh crossed his arms and looked at Cherie, much like his mother did when he would try to argue with her. Cherie nodded in compliance and went to find her in-laws.

Mary and Don were in the kitchen cleaning up the food and dishes from the party. Cherie kissed each one of them and thanked them for a wonderful party. She apologized for not helping to clean up the after mess but Mary told her that was nonsense, "It's your birthday, of course you will have no part in the clean up."

It was over an hour later before Josh finally entered the couple's suite. Cherie sat and quietly watched television, trying to pass the time as she awaited her husband's arrival. *What could it be that he has to give me up here, and what could be taking him so long*, she worried.

Finally she heard Josh's footsteps. She looked up and smiled as he entered the room. Josh, still keeping his bride in suspense, kissed her brow, much like he did on their first date just a little over one year ago. "You look lovely, did you have a nice time tonight?" he asked.

"Yes, I had a wonderful time, thank you," Cherie replied, still wondering what it was he was being so secretive about. But Josh had no mercy. He excused himself to shower and disappeared in the bathroom, leaving Cherie to wait and wait in suspense.

Josh took forever to shower. By the time he re-entered their bedroom suite, Cherie was ready to burst. It was nearly twelve midnight. Josh walked over to Cherie and sat down with her in front of the television set. Making casual conversation, "What's on television?" he asked.

"I don't really know Josh. I'm just watching it while I wait for you. Nothing is really interesting."

Josh smiled inside. He knew he was driving her crazy. But the surprise he had in store for her was worth a little anticipation. Besides, he wanted to wait for the perfect moment.

Finally at exactly one minute until twelve, Josh pulled an envelope out of the pocket of his robe. "I wanted to wait until the perfect moment to give this to you. Today is your birthday, and then after midnight will be the one year anniversary of day you accepted my proposal."

Cherie looked up at her husband, her eyes questioning.

"Impatiently Josh insisted, "Come on, open it, it's midnight!"

Cherie opened the envelope and gasped in surprise, "Oh Josh! How could you, I mean how did you, I mean how, what, I, I just don't know what to say." Her hands trembling violently as she read the contents of the envelope. Suddenly she jumped up from the settee, "What does this mean, does this mean I … is it really true, Josh, I never expected … I didn't think … Josh, is this real?"

Josh reach out and pulled his trembling and stuttering wife into his arms. "Yes, my love, my precious wife, it is true."

"How did you … I mean, I didn't think you even remembered. What do I say? What do I do now?"

"Well, as for what you say, you can start with saying you love me and you won't forget me while you are studying your heart out to become a nurse. And as for what you do now, we will go down to the university and you can assess the program to see if it is to your liking."

"But, this is, or it looks like the tuition is already paid. It has to be, I mean I have to go there to use this, don't I?"

"Actually, no you don't. Yes, this is your tuition, paid in full for the next four years. But, we are not locked in to the university. If you choose to go somewhere else, we can transfer the package."

Cherie collapsed into her husband's arms, "You know I will not sleep now. I'm too excited to sleep."

"Of course I know that Mrs. Tolsten. Why do you think I saved this part for bedtime," he said with a throaty laugh as he carried his wife to bed.

When Stephen joined the Tolsten's and their guests the following morning for breakfast, it appeared as though fireworks were being set. An obvious attraction between Stephen and Kerri was immediately apparent. Stephen was tall, but not as tall as Josh, and even with his muscular build, he was not as attractive as her husband. He was a bit heavier than Josh. With his light brown hair and blue eyes, Cherie had never thought of him as a particularly attractive man, but Kerri could not take her eyes off of him, and the same for Stephen. By the time breakfast was over, Stephen had volunteered to teach Kerri to ride. Kerri decided with little prompting that she would rather ride with Stephen instead of joining the other couples on the sight seeing tour.

In the barn, Kerri was amazed at the skill and knowledge Stephen displayed. She was thrilled to have him teach her about the horses and how to ride. The couple found that they really enjoyed one another's company.

"So how long have you worked for Mr. Tolsten?" she inquired.

"Josh and I have been together since grade school. We separated for a few years while we each pursued different college degrees. But when Josh's grandfather passed away and left the ranch to him, he asked me to come on and work for him."

"What kind of degree did you two pursue?"

"Well, I have a degree in criminal justice. I did work as a police officer for a short time and was in the military for a few years, but I have been with Josh since we were in our early twenties. Since I have been with Josh, I've been in charge of his security, both here and the stores. I'm also second in command here and in charge of the ranch and the stores when Josh is away."

"Wow that sounds like a lot of responsibility. Have you ever married?"

"No, never met anyone that I really wanted to settle down with. This ranch is my life. Most women don't understand that. How about you, have you ever married?"

"No," Kerri confided. "It seems that all of the guys I dated while I was in nursing school were only interested in the fact that I would have a good paying job when I graduated. I just finished school a couple years ago. I wanted to get a handle on my career before I considered anything else."

The two of them talked for hours. Before they knew it, it was almost nightfall. When Stephen realized the late hour, he asked Kerri, "Look, neither of us has had anything to eat since breakfast. How about I take you out to dinner? Just something simple, then we can talk more." It was dark outside, so Stephen walked Kerri back to the house then excused himself to shower and change.

The couple spent the next two days together. Cherie smiled to herself as she watched her friend with Stephen. *I don't think I have ever seen Stephen so happy,* she thought.

Josh, standing beside her at the corral must have heard her thoughts and repeated that exact statement.

~ CHAPTER 19 ~

GRADUATION

THREE YEARS LATER:

Josh and his parents sat in the front row of the auditorium. Josh was beaming with pride as his wife delivered her graduation speech. Cherie had not only graduated earlier than expected, but she graduated at the head of the class. Years of self sacrifice and struggles to survive had served an asset to Cherie, as many of her classmates found it difficult to keep up with the rigid demands of the nursing program.

> ... *Many have compared the nursing program to military boot camp. Perhaps there is a relationship between the two, however boot camp only lasts for a few weeks, not a few years. I believe the demands placed upon us throughout the program merely provide to prepare us for a lifetime of service to others ...*

The crowd roared with applause as Cherie concluded her speech. Josh beamed with pride as he excused himself from his parents and rushed back stage to meet his wife. Three times Josh was stopped by acquaintances while he tried to make his way back stage. Josh tried to be friendly as the other men offered their congratulations on his wife's success, but his heart was with his wife. He had wanted to meet her as she exited the stage, armed with a dozen red roses. He wanted to tell her how proud he was of her. Four years ago, Cherie would have never been able to accept such an award or make a public speech with the poise and confidence that she demonstrated tonight. He had watched her grow from an insecure young lady with virtually no self-confidence to a confident and goal directed young woman, full of love and compassion for him and others.

When he finally escaped the last well-intended patron, he rushed back stage, only to find no trace of his wife. He looked around for her, wondering where she might have gone. *Perhaps the restroom, I'll wait a couple minutes*, he thought. But still, no sign of his wife. He approached a few of her classmates who each stated they hadn't seen her since she delivered her speech on stage. *Maybe she went out front to meet me*, he decided since he had not told her of his intentions. He turned around and headed for the auditorium.

By that time, most of the people had exited the area. There were only a few people standing and chatting in small groups. Josh found his parents outside waiting for him and Cherie. "Mama, Dad, did Cherie come out here? I can't find her."

Mary Tolsten could hear the concern in her son's voice. "No, Josh, we thought you were meeting her backstage. We came out here to wait for the two of you."

"Where's Stephen? Did she leave with Stephen and Kerri?" Josh demanded.

"No, we talked with them just before they left. They left alone. They were going home to set up for Cherie's reception – so everything would be ready when she arrived home."

A sudden chill of doom surrounded Josh. "Oh God, what's happened to her? The last time I had this feeling, my wife nearly died." The concern in Josh's voice had turned to panic.

"Come son, I'll help you look for her," Mary Tolsten, trying to ease her son's concerns, took him by the arm and attempted to direct him back into the auditorium. Before Josh allowed himself to be led back into the school, he turned to his dad and asked him to get security and call the police.

"I know my wife. She would not just disappear. She was too excited about this graduation."

Cherie felt dazed. When she opened her eyes to look around her, the sudden pain in the back of her head brought her to the realization that some one had struck her and rendered her unconscious. A woman who looked to be about thirty years old was pacing over her as Cherie looked around. "Who are you? Where are we?" Cherie asked.

"Shut up you little snit!" the woman shouted.

Cherie tried to stand up but the woman turned abruptly and swung at her with the knife she had been carrying. Recovering her senses, Cherie quickly rolled away from the woman then, with the woman shocked at her maneuver, she managed to stand up. For the first time, Cherie managed to get a look at the woman's face. Terror and dread filled her soul. "Your, y- y- your Jeanie. Th- they told me you were d-d-d-dead."

"I'm not Jeanie you little snit. I'm her sister."

"I didn't know Jeanie had a sister," Cherie said, gasping in surprise.

"Of course you didn't. Jeanie was the only member of my family who even bothered to care for me after they locked me away in that institution. Even she was ashamed to admit she had a sister like me. But at least she came to see me. And now you, you little snit, you took her away from me! How long did you think you would get away with killing my sister! Did you really think I wouldn't come back after you? Well, now you're going to pay!" the woman snorted her, breathing heavy and unstable.

Cherie recognized the same disorganized tangential speech that Jeanie had exhibited after she accosted her. I- I didn't kill her, she nearly killed me!" Cherie snapped. She felt the same dreadful panic she felt with Jeanie.

"If you would have cooperated with her you little snit, she would be alive today. Now I don't want another word from you. We're going to hide out in here until everyone leaves the building, then you are going with me."

Cherie reminded herself of what she learned in the karate classes she had taken in college and managed to regain her composure. She then informed Jeanie's sister, "No, I will not be leaving with you. My husband and family are waiting to help me celebrate my graduation. I'm going out to meet them."

Josh and his mother were standing on the stage when they heard the loud voices. Off to the left of the stage curtain was a small electrical room. Josh attempted to open the door but it was locked. Just then he heard his father and the security guard in the auditorium. "Over here," he motioned to them.

They opened the door just in time to see a woman with a knife lunge at Cherie. Cherie stepped aside before the woman reached her, a maneuver that caused the woman to lose her balance. Infuriated, the woman turned and attempted to swing again, only this time Cherie blocked the swing with her left arm and impacted an upper cut to the woman's jaw with her right. With that, Cherie stepped back, spun around and kicked the woman on the side of her head. The woman dropped to the ground, barely conscious.

Josh rushed to his wife's side while the security guard rushed to handcuff the woman and summons the police. "Cherie!" he gasped. "What happened?"

"I don't really know, Josh. All I know is I finished my speech and I never made it off the stage. I woke up in here a few minutes ago, with a whopping headache."

Josh watched intently as the police officer cuffed the woman then rolled her onto her back. He gasped in shock as he looked directly into Jeanie's face, "You're supposed to be dead!" he exclaimed.

"She said she's Jeanie's sister. Apparently she has been institutionalized for many years. She told me she was furious with me for killing Jeanie."

Josh gave his parents a confused glance. "Mama, all of these years that we've known her, have you ever known of Jeanie having a twin sister?"

Mary confirmed that she no knowledge of Jeanie having s twin sister. "But, I guess insanity runs in that family," she added.

After the woman was removed from the area and Cherie's statement to the police had been completed, Josh could no longer stand the suspense and asked, "How did you, I mean, where did you learn that…" Josh had trouble finding the words to describe his amazement at his wife's actions. A woman who, four years ago could not have inflicted pain upon even the most nuisance of tiny pests had just rendered another woman defenseless.

"Well, Josh, twice in my life I have been rendered totally powerless, first with Dean that night I went out with him, and then to a much greater magnitude, with Jeanie. I promised myself that if I recovered physically, I would never permit myself to be put in that position again."

"So what did you do? How did you learn that?" Josh asked.

"Well, the college offered Tai Kwan Do as an elective. I started taking it when I started my classes."

"Wow, why didn't you tell me?"

"Because, Josh, you told me it was my education and I could manage it the way I saw fit. Besides, I was afraid if I did tell you, you would tell me I couldn't do it. I'm sorry. I hope you're not too angry with me?"

"Well, you're probably right. I would have told you no because I would have been afraid for you to get hurt. But right now, I am just so proud of you, and more than that, I'm thankful you are alright. I was terrified that I was going to lose you again."

Cherie's in-laws hugged her, then Josh interrupted, "Come on, we have some celebrating to do. Let's go home."

EPILOGUE

"What is it, Cherie? For the past couple days you have looked so tired and pale," Mary Tolsten asked.

"I'm not certain, Mama. I'm just so tired all of the time. And there are times when I can't seem to force myself to eat anything."

"So, how far along do you think you are? Have you been to a see you doctor yet?"

"What, I just thought I was putting in too many hours down at work" Cherie stated, confused.

"My darling daughter-in-law, you are about to make me and papa grandparents."

"Oh my, I had never considered, I mean, all these years and no pregnancy. I had all but given up on the idea. What do I tell my husband?"

"Well, first dear girl, let's get you to see your doctor and get it confirmed, and then you tell your husband that he is going to be a daddy."

"But what if he doesn't want children?" Cherie asked nervously. "We only talked about it when we designed the house, but never since."

"Trust me," Mary assured, "Josh will be more ecstatic than I am."

Three days later:

The weather was beautiful as the young couple rode their horses up the side of the mountain. *There is nothing more beautiful than the blue Montana sky on a clear day*, Cherie thought to herself. Josh uplifted the picnic basket and spread the blanket as Cherie dismounted and secured her horse.

"What a beautiful day," Josh exclaimed as the two looked at the beautiful sun over the horizon.

"Yes, and what a beautiful spot for us to picnic. A beautiful spot to tell you that I have gained weight and need to buy some new clothes."

"Of course babe, but why do you think you need to bring me all the way up here to tell me you need new clothes. You can buy whatever you need."

"Yes, but Josh, we are going to need a lot of new things."

All of a sudden the realization of what his young wife was trying to tell him struck and Josh's mouth dropped, "Cherie, what? Are you trying to say what I think you are? Am I? Are we?"

"Yes, Josh, we are, I am and you are! We are going to have a baby!"

Josh picked up his young wife up and swung her around with joy, then kissed her with every ounce of passion within him. All of a sudden he stopped and pulled away from Cherie.

"What is it, Josh?"

"I'm sorry, Cherie. I didn't think to ask you how you feel about becoming a mother. I mean your career and all. I know you're just getting started."

"It's okay, Josh. I was more afraid that you wouldn't be happy. We only spoke of having children when we designed the house. I wasn't sure if you would be ready or if you had changed your mind," her voice trailed off.

"Of course I want children baby. But so much has happened since we've been together. I would spend the rest of my life being happy, just the two of us. I wasn't going to pressure you. I have almost lost you twice; I just want to make you happy."

Cherie's heart ached for the pain her husband had experienced since their marriage, and even before. He must live his life in constant fear of being alone again. Over and over again, Josh had proven that he would sacrifice anything for the sake of his marriage. Now today he admitted he would sacrifice parenthood if it meant making his wife happy. Finally, Cherie found the one gift she could give her husband that money could not buy.

"You know Josh, love changes life, and your love has changed mine. I will always be grateful for you."

Printed in the United States
41543LVS00004B/92

9 781413 721935